All Because of Ava
By: Jessica Terry

All Because of Ava

Jessica Terry

Published by Jessica Terry, 2022.

ALL BECAUSE OF AVA

First edition. December 15, 2022.

ISBN: 979-8986432168

Written by Jessica Terry.

I'm so very thankful for everyone who had anything to do with helping me get this book out, even if it was just an encouraging word of support (like "get your butt in there and finish it.")

My family, church family, friends, and my AWESOME readers and supporters, I appreciate you more than I can say. Thank you for helping me keep this train going.

Content warning: This story contains scenes dealing with or mentioning sexual assault, domestic violence, off-screen death, and miscarriage.

One – Ava

AS SOON AS I SAW HIM, I knew I was in trouble.

I felt something come over me that I had never felt before. As cliché as it sounds, my knees got a little weak and I lost my breath for a moment. And immediately, I wondered if anyone noticed...if *he* noticed.

"It's good to finally meet you," he said to me, extending his large hand. Even his fingers were sexy.

Clearing my throat, I made myself respond as I put my hand in his, feeling the immediate tingles spread over my body. "Yeah...you, too. It's about time, right? I've been hearing about you for months now."

He grinned, showing off deep dimples. Damn. "True. Same here. I feel like we know each other already."

"Right?" I returned his smile, silently willing my body to calm down. Realizing we were still standing there holding hands, I made myself slide mine from his, though the tingling didn't stop; it only intensified. I felt like I was on fire.

My husband of barely six months stood between us, pleased as punch that this introduction was going so well. He put an arm around our shoulders and pulled us into his broad body, squeezing us tightly. Sometimes I don't think he recognized his own strength 'cause I was wincing a little bit.

"I just *knew* you two would hit it off," he boasted, looking back and forth between us. "My two favorite people. And to think both of you were worried about the other not liking you."

I just glanced up at him with a tight smile before daring to look back into trouble's eyes. He was already looking at me. I felt forbidden parts of me wake up and scream.

"Yep, this is going to be great," my husband continued, giving us another squeeze. "I want you two to spend a lot of time together; get to know each other and all that. You're gonna be best friends in no time."

I definitely wasn't looking at this man as a friend. What's worse, I also wasn't looking at him for what he really was: my new stepson.

HIS NAME WAS MARIO. And I loved him already.

I felt like the skank of the century. But that didn't stop me from going right upstairs and pleasuring myself in the bathroom, imagining he was in there with me.

"Ava? You okay in there?"

Biting my lip, I gathered myself before answering. "Yeah, baby, I'm fine. Just...woman stuff." My hand was still between my legs.

"'Nuff said. I'm outta here." Harper, my husband, chuckled. I heard him walk away.

I continued my self-stimulation, doing my best to suppress the moans that wanted to escape from my throat. My body shook as the orgasm hit me, and I hoped the shameful thoughts I was having about my stepson Mario would disappear. But to my surprise (and horror), they didn't budge.

Sighing, I braced my hands on the counter and frowned at myself in the mirror. "You are *so* wrong for this."

I washed my hands and left the bathroom, hoping Mario had left. But when I got to the top of the stairs, I could hear him and Harper laughing about something. Resisting the urge to retreat back to my bedroom, I went to join them after getting something to drink from the kitchen.

"I wanna laugh," I joked, smiling as I took a seat in the armchair near the couch where they were sitting. "What's so funny?"

"Mario was just telling me about some of his exploits when he was overseas," Harper answered.

"I wouldn't call them *exploits*, exactly," Mario amended with a smile. "But there were certainly some interesting experiences. Made a lot of good memories, and got some great content for my site."

"I can imagine," I mused, immediately wondering if any of these international tales involved other women. Reminding myself I shouldn't care about that, I asked, "You're a travel blogger, right?"

"Yeah. I do some travel photography, as well. What is that you're drinking?"

"Chocolate milk with salt."

"For real?"

"Yeah, I love it. Cartoons, too," I admitted, chuckling at his expression. "But getting to travel so much sounds pretty exciting. The only place I've been that's out of the country is Jamaica."

"Oh man, you should try to see more places, if you can. There are some beautiful countries out there."

Why don't you take me? "Well, you know how your dad is." I playfully jerked my head in

Harper's direction.

Mario nudged his father's knee. "Dad, don't tell me you're still afraid of flying."

"I never said I was afraid of flying," Harper quickly refuted. "I just don't need to be going all over the world. There are plenty of places right here in America I haven't even seen. Heck, appreciate your *own* country first."

Mario and I chuckled. Harper could be super-stubborn when he wanted to be. He was also rather proud, which is why he would never outwardly admit to his fear of flying.

"Your wife wants to see the world," Mario persisted. "Take her."

"Nobody's stopping her from seeing anything. She can go with those friends she's always hanging out with. That's who she was with when she went to Jamaica."

"I didn't know you then, Harper," I reminded him amusingly.

"She wants to go with *you*, man," Mario informed him. "Where did y'all go on your honeymoon?"

I scoffed. "*What* honeymoon?"

Mario's eyebrows shot up. "You two didn't have a honeymoon?"

Harper sat forward in his seat, fully prepared to defend himself. "I have every intention of us taking one of those. It's just with work and everything, there hasn't been time yet." He looked at me with those adorable puppy dog eyes of his, pleading for understanding. "I know we had that courthouse wedding when you really wanted something fancier. I wouldn't *not* give you a good honeymoon, too.

You know that, right?"

I smiled at him. He was such a good man. We were so different, but I thought we fit pretty well together. "Yeah, baby, I know that. We're good."

Harper looked a little relieved. I dared to glance at Mario, and he was looking at me again. I couldn't quite read his expression. I would've paid anything to be able to read his mind right then.

Two – Mario

LORD FORGIVE ME.

When my dad told me he'd gotten married to a woman he had only known a few months,

I thought he lost his mind. I was in Singapore at the time, and couldn't make it back for their impromptu wedding. Not that I really wanted to be there, anyway. I thought he was rushing things, big time. But he insisted that she was good for him and he loved her.

Whatever. I had my own things to worry about so I left it alone. Never tried to check out this woman my dad was marrying; didn't know anything about her because I didn't ask. I tried to be sensitive to the fact that Dad was probably lonely; he hadn't been in a serious relationship since Mom died, and that was damn near thirty years ago. I delayed going home because I wasn't in a hurry to meet this woman who was gonna try to be my new mom, but I finally made myself suck it up and go. If Dad needed to get his groove back, hey; I couldn't blame him for that.

But Ava was *not* what I expected.

First of all, she was way younger than I thought she'd be. She was probably early-to-mid thirties, but she could have passed for twenty-five, easily. The short Nia Long-like haircut, freckles, and height that couldn't have been any more than five-foot-five made for a cute package, but she was also mad sexy, in an understated way. As soon as I saw her, my body tensed up deliciously. I felt guilty, but I couldn't help it.

I already knew I was going to have fantasies about this woman, and I was going to enjoy them. But that was as far as it could go. She was my stepmother, for god's sake. Never mind how young or how fine she was. She was off-limits.

Really, I had to wonder what she saw in my dad. Not that he wasn't a good dude, but a husky fifty-two year old truck driver wasn't exactly at the top of a lot of women's wish lists. And he barely went out, so I wondered where he even met her. You would think this would be the kind of detail that a father might tell his grown son, but dad and I didn't have that kind of relationship. We were only semi-close. I loved him, and I believe he loved me, but we never developed that father-son bond that I felt we should've had. There just wasn't a lot we had in common. He always said that was because I got everything from my mom; he was just the sperm donor. Even though he meant it as a joke, it's not far from how I thought of him.

I tried to put my dad and his hot new wife out of my mind as I headed back to my place. To help with that, I made a call to my stand-by.

"What's up, sexy?"

I smiled. "Hey, Mikki."

"You back in town?"

"Yep. Just got back yesterday."

"Good, 'cause I've been missing you. When do I get to see that handsome face?"

"How about now? You got time?"

"Hell yeah."

"We can meet up at Applebee's for drinks and apps and go from there."

"Sounds good. Give me a half hour to pretty up."

"I'm sure that's not necessary. But thirty minutes is cool."

Thankfully the restaurant wasn't that busy. I plunked myself at the bar and ordered a beer, checking my watch. Punctuality wasn't exactly Mikki's strong suit so I knew she'd probably still be a while. I just watched the random game that was on television and checked messages on my phone. Ordered some spinach and artichoke dip. Eventually, I felt warm lips on my cheek.

"Hey sexy," Mikki whispered in my ear.

I smiled, glad to see her. "Hey, yourself. Looking good, as always."

"I have to keep you interested. Wouldn't want your attention starting to wander somewhere else."

Why did that make me think of Ava? "Girl, stop. What do you want to drink?"

"Chardonnay."

I flagged down the bartender to order her drink and slid the menu over to her, in case she wanted some more appetizers. After waiting for her to order grilled chicken wonton tacos and mozzarella sticks, I turned to her.

"So what's been up with you? How's work going?"

"Ugh, it's work. There's nothing all that exciting about teaching a bunch of know-it-all teenagers. Sometimes I wonder what the hell I was thinking, becoming a teacher."

"Being a teacher is an admirable profession. There can never be enough good ones."

"Yeah. It's all right most of the time. But I don't want to talk about that. How was Japan?"

"Very interesting. Best sushi you'll have in your life."

"I never got into sushi. I like my food cooked."

"You should try new things sometime."

"I'm plenty adventurous. Haven't I shown you that?"

"Yeah." It always came back to sex with Mikki. It was like that's what she thought was necessary to keep me and if that was the case, that was pretty sad.

We continued to eat and make small talk, with her rubbing her leg against mine. There were a few instances where her hand made its way to my crotch, which wasn't the most comfortable thing to happen in the middle of a bar.

"Let's save that," I suggested, gently moving her hand away. "I think the TV is giving people enough of a show."

"Wanna come back to my place? Then I can *really* welcome you back."

"Sure, yeah." I motioned to the bartender for the check.

"Good. You didn't sample any *other* Japanese cuisine while you were there, did you? Have a little overseas tryst?"

"No, Mikki. I enjoyed myself but I didn't sleep with anybody. That's not what I was there for."

What I *didn't* say was that I could bang anybody I wanted to, seeing that I was a single man. Mikki and I dated casually but we were not in a relationship.

"Glad to hear it. There's something I wanted to talk to you about, too."

"Yeah? What?"

"Well, I wasn't going to spring it on you now, but since you asked...I'd really like for us to take this to the next level."

I paused the action of pulling my wallet from my back pocket and looked at her. "Take *what* to the next level?"

"Us. I want us to be exclusive."

"Oh." My hands fell to my lap.

Mikki's eyes narrowed. "Is that hesitation I sense?"

"I just don't think we're there yet."

"Why not? We've been dating for four months."

"Even so, Mikki..."

"Wow, Mario. So what the hell have we been doing all this time, then?"

"Getting to know each other. Sleeping together. One of those more than the other."

"What else is it you need to happen to know you want to be with just me?"

While I was trying to think of a nice way to tell her that I thought she was fun but didn't see any kind of future with her, she sucked her teeth and yanked her jacket off the back of her barstool.

"I'm not trying to waste my time," she huffed. "When you figure out what it is you want, give me a call."

I watched her storm out without making any kind of move to stop her. If she was gone that meant we couldn't continue this conversation, so I wasn't mad at it.

True enough, Mikki and I had been dating for a few months. But that didn't automatically mean that I thought we should be exclusive. While I enjoyed her company, I couldn't even say I knew a whole lot about her because every time I tried to start a conversation, she would jump on me and start grinding. I'm not sure if she realized it or not, but to me, that wasn't a very good sign.

Sighing, I paid the bill and left. I might have gotten out of the unwanted conversation about a relationship with Mikki but that also meant I didn't have anything to keep me from thinking about Ava. I already knew my boy Jayden was busy, so there was no point in calling him. It was just me and my raging imagination.

When I pulled up to my condo, I was determined to find something to take my mind off of my sexy stepmother. I still needed to do my last write-up about my Japan trip, or I could watch a good ol' sci-fi movie. Clean out the oven or something equally as mind-numbing.

I was heading towards the building when I heard my name.

"Mario."

Seriously?

I turned, feeling as if I was the butt of some kind of cosmic joke.

"Ava. What brings you by?"

Three - Mario

"I'M SORRY FOR JUST showing up like this," Ava hedged as she followed me into my condo.

"No problem." I closed the door behind her. "Please, have a seat."

"Oh, I'm not gonna be here that long. I'm sure you probably want to get some rest. Harper asked me to bring you the power drill he borrowed."

I hadn't even noticed she was holding anything. I really needed to get it together. "Oh, okay. That could've waited, though; I didn't need it today. And why did he send *you* for this?"

Ava shrugged. "I think he wanted to get me out of the house for a while. I didn't mind."

"Well, I appreciate it, thanks." I took the drill from her and set it on a nearby end table.

"Sure."

"You sure you don't want anything? I'm pretty low on groceries but I have some bottled water, and probably some chips or something."

"It's really okay. I imagine you have stuff you need to do, right?"

"Nothing that can't wait. Plus, you said Dad wanted to get you out of the house. He'd probably be kinda bummed if you came back so quick." I chuckled as if I was joking. Clearly, I didn't want her to leave.

Ava smiled, looking at me thoughtfully. She had yet to make one move towards the door, so I wondered if she really wanted to leave, herself. And if she didn't, if it had more to do with wanting to be around me or *not* wanting to be around Dad. That thought cooled my jets a little. Sexy or not, I still didn't know anything about this woman.

"I guess I can hang for a little bit," she finally conceded.

"Cool." I felt relieved, despite my earlier thoughts. "Have a seat."

She parked it on the couch while I took a seat in my leather recliner. I immediately started playing with the hole in the arm, which had become a mindless habit.

"Super comfy, huh?" Ava asked, nodding towards the chair.

"Is that your nice way of asking why I still have this raggedy thing?"

Blushing, Ava ducked her head briefly before looking back at me with a tentative smile. "Well, it *is* kinda giving me *Frasier* vibes, with the duct tape and everything."

I couldn't help my grin. "You watch *Frasier*?"

"Almost every night! It's one of my favorites."

"Mine, too! My boy Jayden always messes with me about it but I don't care."

"Yeah, Harper doesn't care for it, either. He doesn't even wanna sit in the room with me when I'm watching it."

"Can't say I'm surprised. But yeah, I guess you could say that, about the chair. And I'm about as stubborn as Martin when it comes to getting rid of it. Dad actually tried to buy me another chair a few years ago."

"What happened to it?"

"I gave it away. Dad was upset with me for a minute after that."

"Oh wow. So I guess the chair has some kind of sentimental value?"

I paused without really trying to. The slight frown was automatic. "Something like that."

Ava sensed my change in demeanor and changed the subject. Thankfully.

"You just came back from Japan, right? I think that's what I remember you saying."

"Yeah, Japan."

"How was it? That's on my travel wish list."

"It's beautiful. Of course, my favorite part of any trip is sampling the local cuisine. It's a wonder I'm not as big as a house."

"You seem to keep yourself in pretty good shape," Ava commented, then immediately looked embarrassed. I actually thought it was cute how she was blushing. Must've been one of those I-was-thinking-it-but-didn't-mean-to-say-it-out-loud kind of things. Been there.

"Uh, I just meant that I don't think you have to worry about that, you know," she quickly recovered. "You just, you look like you work out a lot, is all I meant."

Trying to stifle my laughter, I replied, "Yeah, I pretty much keep up my workout routine from when I was playing ball."

"Basketball?"

"No, football."

"Why did you stop playing? Did you get injured or something?"

"Nah, I was drafted in the fifth round by Carolina. Got cut after my rookie contract was up. Bounced around to a couple of different teams but realized my passion for it wasn't there like it used to be. Decided that wasn't really the life I wanted."

"Really? That's not something you usually hear. Playing professional sports is portrayed to be the ultimate dream for most kids."

"For a lot of them, it is. They think if they make it to the pros, all of their problems will be fixed. And going pro is great in a lot of ways but it's not as glamorous as a lot of people think it is. Especially if you're a late draft pick like I was."

"Wasn't that super-popular pretty-boy quarterback with all the rings a late round pick, too?"

My eyebrows shot up. Didn't expect her to know that. "Yeah, he was. And true enough, if you work your ass off and are in a good situation, you can be successful in the league no matter what round you're drafted in. But when it came down to it, I just didn't want it bad enough."

"That's so awesome," Ava gushed, gazing at me with her chin in her hand. "I respect the fact that you walked away from something so many people clamor for because your heart wasn't in it."

"Really? 'Cause a whole bunch of people thought I was an idiot."

"There's nothing idiotic about following your heart."

Our eyes locked for a second, and I felt a warmth spread over me, as if I was drinking hot chocolate on a cold day. I felt a sudden urge to join her on the couch, get closer to her. But I wasn't trying to freak her out, like I was probably doing with all of this staring. Clearing my throat, I dropped my eyes to the hole in my chair.

"Yeah, well," I croaked. "I don't regret it. Though the lady I was seeing at the time certainly did, seeing as how she dumped me after that."

"Good." When I looked at her, she quickly clarified, "Because she apparently wasn't with you for the right reasons, if she would leave you just over that."

I shrugged. "It probably wouldn't have lasted, anyway. I don't have the best track record when it comes to choosing women."

"Why do you say that?"

"It's just the truth. Matter of fact, I just left from someone I've been dating for a little while. She copped an attitude because I didn't jump at her suggestion of us becoming exclusive."

Ava looked intrigued. "You don't want a relationship with her? Or you don't want a relationship with anyone?"

"I definitely want a relationship with someone, but it has to be the right woman. And I'm not sure if Mikki is the right woman. It's really just been four months of sex and small talk."

"Oh okay. Just a causal relationship." Ava leaned against the back of the couch.

"Not by *my* choice. I try to get to know her but she seems more interested in getting physical, so I figured she just wanted to keep it casual, too. This whole let's-be-exclusive thing was totally out of left field."

"You gonna stop seeing her?"

"Don't know. I haven't really had a chance to think about all that yet. If we're not on the same page, there's no point in keeping this going. Especially since I don't really see a future with her, anyway."

Ava nodded as if she understood. What I didn't stop to think about was why I was even telling her all this. It wasn't really like me to tell my business to people I hardly knew. But in under an hour, Ava knew about my relationship status, my aborted football career and my favorite television show. There were people I'd known for years that didn't know all that.

"Well, I don't wanna get all motherly on you, but do you want my advice?"

Motherly, huh? Yeah, right. "Sure."

"I don't know if you want to get married at some point or not, but if you can't see yourself with this woman years from now, don't waste your time. Or hers. Time is just too precious to waste on someone your heart isn't into."

There she goes with the heart stuff again. I figured she was some kind of romantic, one of those people that thought that there was one perfect person out there for everybody. I'm not sure if I believed *that* or not, but I agreed with her on the not wasting time part.

"Thanks for that," I eventually said. I suddenly felt awkward. "You sure you don't want anything to eat? I can order something..."

"Oh. Thanks, but I probably should get going." She glanced at her watch. "I'm sure Harper will be wondering where I am after a while."

"Just text him and let him know we're hanging out. He said he wanted us to get to know each other, right?"

She looked like she was considering my point for a second, but she shook her head. "Right, but...still. It's probably a good idea if I go." She quickly stood, slinging her purse over her shoulder.

I hurried and caught up with her before she got to the door. She put her hand on the knob, but didn't turn it. She was hesitating. I stood behind her, probably closer than I should've been, but I couldn't make myself step back any more than she could seem to make herself turn that doorknob.

"You don't have to run off," I assured her, my voice low. I took notice of the back of her neck, and how sexy her tapered haircut was on her. And she smelled so fresh, like the good soap people reserved for guests. I started to lean closer to her, but stopped myself, my jaw clinching with restraint. "You learned a good bit about me but I didn't get to learn much about you."

Ava looked back at me, her eyes roaming my face before gracing me with that cute smile. "We've got time," she assured me.

Choosing to leave it at that, I gave her a nod as I stepped back. It probably *was* best that she leave.

"True enough. Well, thanks for bringing the drill."
"No problem."
I opened my arms. "Well, come on and give me a hug, Mom."

Ava cut her eyes at me and shook her head. She knew good and well I was being facetious. "Please. We're not even gonna go there."

I grinned innocently. "What?"

"Married to your dad or not, we both know I'm not old enough to be your mother. So just call me Ava."

"Fair enough. So give me a hug...Ava."

Hesitating for a brief second, she stepped into my arms, keeping her body a safe distance from mine. She awkwardly patted me on the back, while I resisted the urge to pull her closer to me. That was just my hormones screaming, though, 'cause the sensible part of me knew that wouldn't be a smart idea.

"See you later, Mario," she finally said, stepping back. She put her hand back on the doorknob.

"Bye, Ava. Get home safe."

With a tight smile, Ava quickly opened the door and left.

Four – Ava

I CHECKED THE CLOCK on the stove before continuing to quickly crank the handle on my spiralizer, turning several plump zucchinis into a mound of curly thin strands. I wanted to have dinner done by the time Harper got home, and I was running behind. It hadn't taken me long to learn that Harper didn't like to wait too long for his food.

I was checking the recipe on the counter when the phone rang. Seeing it was my BFF Trish, I smiled and quickly answered it.

"Hey, girl."

"What's up, newlywed? What you doing?"

"Making that dish you told me about the other day."

"Which one? With the spicy peanut sauce?"

"Yeah."

"You're gonna love it. Even my picky-ass kids gobbled it up."

"Yeah? And what about Leroy?" I asked with a chuckle, referring to Trish's husband.

"He tried to act funny at first but he eventually ate his. He liked it all right."

"Well, it's good that he's at least open to trying stuff."

"Yeah, that's one thing I can say about my man. He has an open mind. About most things, at least."

"Well, I hope Harper has one when he sees I made this. I know he likes spicy food."

"Let me know how he likes it. I'm headed to the gym before I gotta go pick up the kids. It's gonna be a pizza night over here later on."

"So you're going to the gym and then eating pizza?" I asked amusingly while I minced some garlic.

"For all you know, I could be planning on having cheese-less veggie pizza with gluten-free crust."

"Uh-huh. But we both know I know you better than that."

"Yeah, you're right. I'm not even gonna try to front. I don't do pizza without meat. But hey, the gym is just to maintain this sexy size sixteen I got going on. I'm not trying to lose weight."

"I know. Hell, if I had your boobs, I wouldn't be trying to lose them, either."

"We'll see if you're singing that same tune some years down the line when they're either setting my back on fire or hanging to my knees. But I'll cross that bridge when I get to it. For now I'm thoroughly enjoying my triple D's."

"And so is Leroy, I bet."

"Oh, you know it!"

I laughed. Trish was too much. "What's Vera up to? I tried to call her earlier but it went straight to voicemail."

"She's probably still crying over getting dumped. You know it's her life's mission to get married and have babies and she can't hear anything but that biological clock tickin' away."

"What? I didn't know she got dumped. I wonder why she didn't call me."

"She was probably embarrassed. You know she was going on and on about how this one was *the one*, like she doesn't think that about every dude she likes. Only reason *I* know about it is 'cause I dragged it out of her. But she'll be all right. I went by and checked on her."

"I'll try to get over there tomorrow. She doesn't have to be embarrassed around me; I've known her since eighth grade. And anyway, we've all been dumped at one point or another."

"Yeah, but we didn't look at every man as a potential husband like she does. I tried to tell her men can smell desperation like that. I wish she'd just chill and let things happen naturally but she feels like her time is running out or something."

"Wow."

"Especially now that you're married to Harper, *and* after knowing him only a few months. Vera is feeling very fifth-wheel-ish."

"I know I got married quickly, but it had nothing to do with being desperate."

"Girl, you don't have to tell me. But you know Vera. She's thinking there's something wrong with her, since she's the last one of us to get hitched. And trying to convince her how ridiculous that is is pointless. So I just make sure I'm there to hold her hand and bring her chocolate-covered pretzels."

"I have her back, too. And I'm sure she'll find the right man for her."

"I sure hope so. She's a great woman, just a little over-eager. Well anyway, let me get on to this gym. I'll talk to you later. Let me know how Harper likes that dish."

"Will do."

I hung up the phone and continued cooking. It bothered me to hear about my friend Vera being so upset, and even more so that she felt she couldn't talk to me about it. When I had told her and Trish that I was marrying Harper, she wasn't over-the-moon about it but I figured it was just concern about me marrying someone I hadn't known that long. It didn't occur to me that it could be anything else, like jealousy. Of course I knew how badly Vera wanted to get married; she'd been talking about that ever since high school. I guess it made sense that she would feel some kind of way about being the last one in our group to find someone.

When I heard the front door open, I made myself push Vera's relationship issues out of my mind. I just wanted to enjoy the evening with my husband. He'd been on the road and I hadn't seen him in a few days. Being the wife of a truck driver was going to take some getting used to, but Harper loved what he did for a living so I never griped about how much time he had to spend away from me. At least, not where he could hear it.

"Ava!" Harper yelled.

"I'm in the kitchen, sweetie. I'll be in there in a second."

"Okay. Whatever you're making smells good."

I grinned, encouraged. Quickly washing my hands, I rushed out to the living room, where Harper had already kicked his shoes off and was flicking through the channels on the television with the remote. He smiled when he saw me.

"Hey babe," he greeted, dropping the remote onto the couch. He pulled me into a hug, lifting me off the ground.

I hugged him back, my wince from his super-tight hug fading into a smile as I pulled back to look at him. Taking his round face in my hands, I planted a deep welcome-home kiss on him.

"I missed you," I whispered between kisses.

"Mmm, I missed you, too," he mumbled back. His hand gripped my butt.

We kissed for several more moments before he finally lowered me back to the ground, apparently reaching his limit. I wasn't quite done, and slid my hands up his chest.

"You wanna go upstairs for a minute?" I asked, eyeing those thick lips of his I loved so much. My lust was blatant but I didn't care. I reached between us and caressed his crotch, thrilled at how hard he already was.

He licked his lips, clearly enjoying what I was doing. "After we eat..."

"The food isn't going anywhere. I want you *now*. Come on, baby, it's been over a week. Just sit on the couch and I'll ride you."

"You know I don't like it on the couch. I promise, I'll make it up to you later. In the bed." He reluctantly grabbed my hand, stopping my caressing. "Let's eat; I'm starving. I haven't had anything but a sausage and egg biscuit and that was hours ago."

"Fine." Pouting, I turned and sulked back to the kitchen. I was frustrated that Harper didn't indulge me in the quickie I wanted. Sex didn't just have to be in the bedroom at the end of the day, like he seemed to think.

Harper washed his hands before meeting me in the kitchen, taking a seat at the round glass table. When I set his plate in front of him, he looked at it with a frown.

"What's this?"

"Spicy sesame noodles with-"

"These *ain't* noodles." He picked up a long strand of zucchini with his fingers.

"They're zucchini noodles, Harper. Just as good as the regular ones."

"I beg to differ. And what kind of meat is this, here?"

I hesitated, knowing he wouldn't like the answer. "It's crispy tofu."

"Tofu?" Harper frowned as if I said they were horse testicles. "You know I don't eat that mess."

"Have you ever even had it, Harper?"

"I don't need to have it to know I don't want any. Since when did you become a vegetarian?"

"I'm not a vegetarian; you know that. I was just trying something new. Trish told me about it. She made it for her family and they loved it, and they love meat more than you do."

"Well, good for them. But I'll pass." He pushed his plate away. "And this isn't even hot!"

"It's not supposed to be."

"Why would I want some cold food?"

Trying my best to keep my rising frustration at bay, I persisted, "You said yourself it smelled good. And you love spicy food."

"Yeah, but I thought it was chicken wings or something. Can you make some of those?"

"We don't have any chicken wings, Harper."

"That's fine. I'll just order some, then." He actually pulled out his phone.

"Seriously? You're just gonna order some freakin' takeout right in my face after I've been rushing to make sure you had a home-cooked meal ready when you got back?

"Babe, come on. I appreciate it, but I can't help that I like what I like."

"How do you know you don't like something you've never tried? Can you tell me that?"

"Ava..."

"How about at least trying it out of consideration for me? I try stuff *you* like. You think I was excited about eating cornbread crumbled up in some buttermilk? But I tried it just because you wanted me to. I guess you can't do the same for me."

"Why are you getting so upset about this? It's nothing personal, babe, come on."

Turning away from him in my chair, I crossed my arms in a huff. "I'm upset because you're being stubborn."

"Stubborn? I'm fifty-two years old."

I looked at him. "So?"

"So I'm too old to be trying new stuff."

My face screwed into an incredulous frown. "What kind of ridiculous mess is that? You being fifty-two doesn't have anything to do with anything. Like I said, you're just being stubborn."

"And like *I* said, I like what I like."

He actually had an attitude with *me* now. I was too through.

"Whatever. Order all the wings in Atlanta, I don't care." I began eating my own dinner, the fact that my zucchini pasta had wilted considerably since we got engaged in this stupid conversation only adding to my frustration. I tried my best to forget Harper was even there as I ate my food, but couldn't help sucking my teeth when the jackass proceeded to order twenty wings and fries. He could've at least left the room to do that.

When I was done eating, I put my plate in the sink, and packed up the leftovers, including Harper's uneaten portion. At least I wouldn't have to worry about what to have for lunch the next day. I left the dirty dishes in the sink and headed upstairs, leaving Harper at the table with his Postmates-delivered meal.

Trying to calm down, I took a quick shower, slathering myself with Dove soap. I could hear Harper in the bedroom, which meant he most likely didn't clean up the kitchen. Shaking my head, I just took my time smoothing on my body oil.

Harper was taking his shirt off when I finally emerged from the bathroom. He stood and watched me as I walked, naked, over to the dresser to get my nightgown. I guess he was expecting me to say something, but I still wasn't trying to pay him any attention. Finally, he sighed and went to the bathroom to take his own shower.

I got into bed and wished I could make myself fall asleep immediately, but I was too wound up. Worry started to creep in. Marriage was supposed to be about two people coming together, compromising when necessary, thinking of each other. But I was starting to wonder if Harper was capable of that. I knew he was a good man, but was he too set in his ways to ever make any concessions for me? I could gladly make compromises for him, and I had. But I couldn't say the same about him, and I hated to think that it would always be that way.

When Harper came out of the bathroom a little while later, I quickly turned away from him. He got into bed, and before too long I felt his hand on my hip.

"Babe?"

I started to ignore him, but I eventually sighed. "What?"

"I'll clean up the kitchen in the morning."

"Whatever."

"You still mad at me?"

"Does it matter?"

"Of course it matters, babe."

"I sure can't tell."

"Are you really this pissed at me 'cause I wouldn't eat some tofu?"

I rolled my eyes. "This is not about the damn tofu, Harper. It's bigger than that. Everything is always about what *you* like and don't like. What *you* want to do and don't want to do. And I apparently just have to deal with it."

"It's not like that."

"Yes, it is."

"Well, I don't mean for it to be like that. I absolutely care about what you want. I'm not a selfish man; you don't know that by now?" He gently turned me onto my back and leaned over me. Tracing his finger down my cheek, his eyes roamed my face. "I know I can be a pain to deal with. But I'd never do anything to intentionally hurt you. I care about you way too much for that, Ava."

Despite myself, I felt my anger start to dissipate a little bit. I knew Harper was a little stubborn during our brief courtship, so what did I expect? For him to change overnight? Like I said, he was a good man. And if this was the worst thing that was wrong with him, I couldn't complain too much. Besides, maybe over time, he'd learn to bend on some things a little bit.

I pulled his face down to mine, and he eagerly kissed me, glad that I was no longer giving him the cold shoulder. He didn't like for me to be upset with him, and I didn't like *being* upset with him. I didn't get married so I could be at odds with my husband, though of course I knew it would happen every now and then.

"Hey," he said after a few moments. "I'm going to be going back on the road in a couple of days. It'll be for about a week. Big job."

"Already, Harper? You just got back from another long trip."

"This is how I make my money, babe. You knew I was a truck driver when you met me."

"Yeah, but I didn't think it meant that you were going to be gone for such long stretches of time. When we were dating, the trips were only for a day or two."

"I started taking on longer jobs after we got married. More money."

I frowned. "Why would you do something like that without talking to me first?"

He shrugged. "Didn't think I needed to. You're mad 'cause I want to make more money to take care of you?"

"I didn't marry you for you to take care of me, Harper. I appreciate you wanting to do that, but I have my own career. I've been taking care of myself for years before I met you. What's important to me is us spending time together. We don't get enough of that."

"I know, babe. It's not gonna be like this forever."

"Well, while it is, what am I supposed to do?"

"Hang out with your girls. Or Mario."

My eyes widened. "Mario? Why would you suggest that I hang out with Mario?"

"Because y'all are family now, and I want y'all to be close."

The thought of getting close to Mario felt wrong while I was in bed with my husband. I had managed to put that man out of my mind for the past couple of days, but at the mention of his name, all those forbidden feelings that I experienced when we met came rushing back.

"I'm sure he doesn't want to hang out with me," I managed to say.

"Nah, don't think like that. My boy might take a while to open up to you but once he does, you've got a friend for life."

"Right."

"Seriously, call him up when I'm gone and have him over for dinner or something. Go to a movie; he loves movies. I just don't want you sitting around the house by yourself when you don't have to."

We needed to change the subject. Now.

"I'll figure all that out when I need to." I took his hand and placed it on my breast while rubbing my leg against his. "Right now, I just want to focus on *us*. Can we do that?"

Smiling, he rolled his big body on top of mine, and I tried to adjust to all the weight. Harper weighed almost three hundred pounds, which was a lot on my little self.

"Let me get on top," I breathed, out of both desire and necessity.

"In a minute," he grunted, grinding on me. He was already naked, because that's how he always went to bed. His hands tore at my nightgown.

After several more moments, I gently pushed at his shoulders. "Ease up so I can take this off."

Thankfully, he crawled back onto his knees, and I tried not to make my breath of relief too obvious as I lifted my nightgown over my head. He bit his lip, eyeing me as I got naked for him, and yanked me down by my legs as soon as my nightgown hit the floor. Before he could climb on top of me again, though, I threw my arms around his neck and sucked on his ear, which I knew was his weak spot. I managed to nudge him onto his back, and I climbed on top, smiling naughtily at him.

"I'm glad we made up, baby," I purred at him.

He moaned, his fingers pressing into my hips. "Me too."

I started to wind my hips, but stopped myself and got a condom out of the nightstand before I lost my head completely. Harper just silently eyed me as I did so, apparently forgetting that step, too. We might've been married, but we weren't at the point where children were a consideration yet. I wasn't even a hundred percent sure of Harper's stance on that, but I knew it would be a while before I was ready for motherhood.

Putting all of that out of my mind, I covered him and slid down onto his thick shaft. He immediately started to moan louder as I moved on him. He was so responsive, and I loved it. My pent-up sexual frustration made me move faster sooner than I wanted to, and his hands grabbed my breasts, urging me towards orgasm. But I wasn't ready to reach the mountaintop just yet.

"You know what would be fun?" I asked as I slowed my hips to a leisurely wind.

"What?"

"Let's do it against the wall."

"Why?"

"Just to do something different. We've never done that before."

"You don't like it like this?"

"Yes, baby, I love it. But it's fun to try different things every now and then, right?"

He shook his head and started teasing my nipples. "Let's just keep it like this. I'm close..."

Why did I expect anything different? Hadn't we already established that Harper was stubborn? Maybe because I had literally *just* griped about how everything was all about him that I thought that he would oblige me what I wanted for once. I guess I thought the sex I was putting on him would have him too pleased to say no.

Just like that, my fire was diminished. But Harper didn't notice. He flipped me over and started pumping into me like he had a battery in his back, his sweat dripping onto my face like rain from the sky. He sweated a lot, which was another reason I liked to avoid missionary. But of course, that was his favorite position.

"Ahhh yeah," he grunted, biting his lip. His eyes were closed and his head was thrown back, and I had a feeling that he was in his own world by then. He either didn't notice or care that I wasn't moving or saying anything.

Before too long, he was banging me so hard that I had to brace my hand against the headboard to keep my head from hitting it. I knew it would be any second now.

"I'm comin', baby," he panted, still not looking at me. His sweat dropped into my eye, and I just kept them closed after wiping them with the bed sheet. It's not like he would notice. "I'm coming!"

He yelled out a string of obscenities at the top of his lungs, releasing everything he had into the condom before gently pulling out of me and collapsing. I rolled out of the way before all of that weight fell on me, but again, he didn't notice. He had gotten his. Not two minutes later, he was snoring, his big body taking up most of the bed.

I turned away and curled into a ball, not even caring about finishing the pleasure for myself. All I could do was lay there and wonder if it was always gonna be like this.

Five - Ava

AFTER BEING IN THE house all day working on some web copy for one of my copywriting clients, I pushed away from my desk with a languid stretch. I rubbed my slightly aching neck while I turned my phone back on. There were a couple of texts from Vera, and I quickly called her back.

"Hey, Ava!"

My eyebrows shot up, surprised she sounded so cheerful. It usually took her a while to get over it when one of her relationships ended. "Hey, girl. I'm sorry it took so long to get back to you."

"Were you writing?"

"Yeah."

"Yeah, I figured. I know you usually turn your phone off when you're working."

"If I don't, I won't get anything done. What are you up to?"

"Getting ready for Trish to come over. We're just gonna have some peach cobbler and Moscato and sit around gabbing about everything. If you're done working, you should come over. Even if you're not done, still come over. Finish it later."

I chuckled. "I've been at it for hours so I'm done. I need to get out of this house, especially now that Harper is gone again."

"Aww. Well you definitely need to come over, then. Hurry up."

"Okay, let me take a quick shower then I'll be on my way. Can I bring anything?"

"Nope. Just come on."

After hanging up with Vera, I took a brief shower, moisturized, threw on a cute little blue shorts romper and some flip-flops, and headed out the door. The thought of an evening with my girls rejuvenated me after being in front of my computer all day. And while being alone didn't bother me most of the time, this was an evening where I really wanted some company.

Trish had beaten me over to Vera's, and they were laughing about something when I walked in. Trish was leaning against the counter with a glass in her hand while Vera dished up the cobbler.

"Ladies!" I sang, sauntering in to the kitchen.

"Hey!" they chorused, both grinning. They were just as happy to see me as I was to see them.

"What y'all in here giggling about?"

"Trish was telling me about the little talent show her kids put on for her and Leroy last night," Vera informed, sliding a bowl full of her homemade peach cobbler over to me. She'd hooked me up with a lot of crust, knowing how much I loved that. "She said they were worse than those *American Idol* auditions."

"Yeah, girl, my babies are tone deaf like a mug." Trish shook her head. "It took everything me and Leroy had not to laugh out loud 'cause they really thought they were killin' it."

"I bet it was cute, though." I stepped into the living room to kick off my flip-flops before picking up the glass of

Moscato I had just poured for myself. "How come y'all didn't film it?"

"I didn't even think about it, really. By the time I thought about grabbing my phone, they were about done. I'm sure there'll be another show, though. They've been working on some new dance moves."

"Now see, that's what I want. To have some kids that want to put on little shows for me and their dad." Vera smiled wistfully. "You're so lucky, Trish."

"Look, don't get me wrong, being married with kids is a blessing, but it can also be a lot to deal with at times," Trish replied. "I love my man and I love my babies, but lord knows they can grate my nerves sometimes. If I didn't have y'all to talk to and hang out with, I'd probably lose my mind."

"That's a problem I'd love to have."

Trish eyed her before shaking her head and taking another swig from her glass. "Be careful what you wish for, is all I'm gonna say."

"It can't be that bad."

"No, it's not *bad*. I wouldn't trade my family for anything. But marriage only works if you find the right person. And it takes working together every day to make things go. It doesn't just *happen*."

Vera looked at me. "What about you, Ava? Do you think you married the right person?"

I stuck a huge forkful of cobbler into my mouth and took my time chewing it, wondering how I was going to answer that.

"I mean, I *want* to say yes," I finally answered, swallowing. "But honestly, I'm starting to wonder about some things."

Trish looked at me, surprised. "Like what? Y'all having issues already?"

"Not really *issues*, just some things that concern me."

"Such as?"

I weighed how much I should reveal. These were my girls, but there were some things in a marriage that I felt should remain between a man and wife. Call me old-fashioned.

"I just wonder if we're on the same page with some things, you know? There are times when he just won't bend on even the smallest things 'cause he's so set in his ways. And there are some things I don't know where he stands on, like religion. Or kids! He has a grown son; I'm not sure if he wants to have any more kids or not."

"Girl...isn't this the kind of stuff you talk about *before* you get married?"

"Yes, it is. I'm the first to admit that we did some things ass-backwards. But Harper is such a good man, and I guess maybe he came along at a time when...I just really needed somebody. We hit it off. Always had a good time when we hung out..."

"So because of that, you got married?"

"I know it doesn't make sense. Sometimes I can't believe it myself." I gazed down at my small wedding ring.

"Are you saying you're unhappy?" Vera eyed me.

"Not really unhappy; just a little wary. I mean, what if he *does* want kids? I honestly don't know if I ever want to be a mother. Certainly not any time soon, if I do."

"You don't want kids? How could you not want to be a mother?"

"Believe me, it is *not* for everybody," Trish jumped in. "I think its good that she's being honest about that, because too many women are out here just having babies that they don't want. Then they dump them off on a relative while they go do their thing, or mistreat or abuse the child because they resent them for messing their life up. So yeah, if you know you don't *really* want to be a mother, don't."

"Don't get me wrong, y'all; I love kids. But y'all know the relationship I had with my parents before they died; we weren't very close. I don't know if I could give a child the kind of love I never had myself."

As we migrated into the living room with our desserts and alcohol, Vera had a thoughtful look on her face.

"So...what kind of relationship does Harper have with his son? What was his name, again?"

"Mario. And they seem cool with each other, but so far I can't see a lot that they have in common. I mean, they don't look alike, have the same mannerisms, anything. I'd never think they were father and son by just hanging around them."

"Maybe he just takes after his mother."

"Ooh, you don't think that Mario's mama had an affair or something before she died, and she just passed him off as Harper's son, do you?" Trish actually looked excited about this suggestion. "That would be something else!"

"Cool your jets, girl, it's nothing like that." I chuckled.

"It could be. You don't know."

"So tell me about this Mario," Vera said to me excitedly, tucking her feet under her on her tan overstuffed couch. "Is he single?"

"Yeah..."

"How old is he?"

"Early thirties, I think. I don't know exactly."

"And no kids, right?"

"Damn girl, you want Ava to hook you up with Mario or something?" Trish asked, amused. She refilled her glass.

Vera looked a little sheepish. "Well, if he's not seeing anybody..."

"Are you serious? You don't know anything about the man; what he looks like, anything. And you're asking for a hook-up?"

"Well, I figured if he was a jerk, Ava would have said so by now."

"Vera, look, he's really cool and everything, but I can't say I know a whole lot about him. We've only really talked once." I sipped my wine, feeling nervous suddenly.

"Talk me up. Tell him how good a cook I am. Does he like peach cobbler? Tell him how good my peach cobbler is. I mean, you're about to be on your second bowl now."

"Vera, you're drifting, girl," Trish warned.

"I'm just saying; what could it hurt?"

I took a long sip from my glass while Vera looked at me expectantly and Trish eyed me. There was no reason why I shouldn't at least introduce Mario to Vera; they were both single, attractive adults. I didn't even know if Mario would be interested in Vera or not but if I was honest with myself, I didn't want to find out.

"Trying to keep him for yourself or something, Ava?" Trish joked, nudging me with her bare foot. "You sure are taking a long time to answer."

"Please," I made myself scoff. "I am a happily married woman."

"That's not what you were saying a minute ago."

"I never said I was unhappy. Just that I had concerns."

"Maybe because you up and married a man you barely knew?"

"Trish, you know as well as I do that time doesn't mean much of anything. There are couples that have been together for years and years that split up, saying they grew apart or they felt like they didn't know their spouse anymore."

"Okay, you have a point."

"So, there's a good chance that Mario and I could work," Vera chimed back in. "You should give him my number, Ava. Show him one of my social media profiles. He can add me on Facebook if he wants; I'll accept. Is his last name Downing, too?"

"Yes, Vera."

"Okay, Mario Downing; I'll be on the lookout for it. But my Instagram has better pictures. Tell him I don't mind DMs."

Vera was officially in thirsty mode and when she got like this, there was little we could say to pull her out of it. I eventually gave her a weak agreement that I would mention her to Mario, and she was too excited to notice that my heart wasn't in it.

Trish did, though. And as soon as we were both back at our respective homes later that night, she called me on it.

"Okay, out with it, missy."

"What? I just got home."

"You know good and well what I'm talking about, Ava. What was up with all the hesitation when Vera was asking you to set her up with Mario?"

"Oh, that."

"Yeah, *that*."

"I don't know. I'm just not sure if they'd be a good match."

"How do you know they wouldn't? Unless you've been holding out on me, you can't know Mario any better than you know Harper. They might actually hit it off."

I was so glad Trish couldn't see the automatic frown that occurred all on its own when she said that. "I've spent a little bit of time with Mario. Harper asked me to take something to his apartment and we sat and talked for a little bit. From what I know of him, he's a good guy. But still..."

"Are you attracted to him?"

My mouth opened, but nothing came out.

"Ava?"

"A little bit. But it doesn't mean anything," I quickly added. "I think my head is just all clouded from the stuff with Harper. I don't have all my bearings."

"So you're saying if you didn't have those concerns about Harper and you were *truly* happy in your marriage to him, you wouldn't hesitate to hook Mario up with Vera?"

"Right. Yeah."

"Why don't I believe you?"

"Because you love drama. You know you do."

"Yeah, on TV. Not between my friends. And I'm telling you, if you set up Mario and Vera and they hit it off while you're feeling like this, it's just not gonna end well. You're gonna be resenting them, probably resenting Harper, hell, maybe even resenting me for not trying to talk you out of it..."

"That's not gonna happen."

"It *could* happen. All I'm saying is, if you're feeling some kind of way about Mario, be honest about it. If not to Vera or Harper, or me, at least with yourself."

I chewed on my lip while I considered her advice. Maybe she had a point. But whatever I felt about Mario, I had no right to feel it. So if my best friend really wanted me to introduce them, I wasn't going to say no to that just because of my wayward hormones. I'd just deal with it if they hit it off.

"I get what you're saying," I finally conceded. "But Mario is a good guy and Vera deserves a good guy. And I need to be putting my energy towards improving things between me and my husband. So..."

"So...you're gonna introduce them."

"Yeah. I'm gonna introduce them."

"Okay, girl," Trish replied with a sigh. "I sure hope you know what you're doing."

So did I.

Six - Mario

"SO YOU GO ON THE ROAD for a week, then come over here? How come you're not home with your new wife?"

Dad just looked away and shrugged. "I told you I'd help you mount your new TV. Ava's been acting like she's mad at me, anyway."

"Why, what did you do?"

"Who said I did anything? It doesn't have to automatically be my fault."

"So she's mad at you for no reason, then?"

Dad started to answer, then waved me off. "I didn't come over here to talk about this. What room do you want this TV in? And how big is it?"

"It's a 55-inch. I'm gonna put it in here in the bedroom." I led the way, then pointed to the wall in my room that I wanted my new splurge on.

"Why in here and not in the living room?"

"I like to relax at the end of the day and watch movies in bed. Plus, the one in here is older."

"Hmm." Dad started rummaging through his toolbox. "Ava likes to do that."

I stood there watching him, my arms folded. "What?"

"Lay in the bed and watch movies. It kinda gets on my nerves."

"Why would that get on your nerves? What's wrong with it?"

"I think the bedroom is for sleeping. I tell her if she wants to watch movies or whatever, to go back downstairs."

"Yeah. Sounds about right."

He looked at me. "Why do you say that?"

"You've never liked movies. I used to try to get you to take me back in the day and you never did."

"Yes I did. Once."

"Something like going to the movies together shouldn't be a once-in-a-lifetime experience, Dad. Especially when we lived in the same house and everything."

"Well, I don't know what to tell you. I've just never been into movies like that."

"Hmm." I didn't bother saying how it would've been nice if he had put my wants ahead of his every now and then. The one time he did take me to the movies, he acted like he was doing me this huge favor. He refused to buy any snacks from the concession stand, and he fussed all through the movie. After that, I really didn't *want* him to take me again.

"What do you need me to do?" I asked after several quiet moments.

"Nothing. I got it."

"You sure?"

"Yeah. I'll work faster by myself. You can start taking the TV out of the box, though."

I started to unpack the television, already looking forward to enjoying football games and movies on the bigger screen. Usually I was pretty frugal and didn't make a lot of big purchases that weren't absolutely necessary, but when I saw this one on sale for damn near half off, I couldn't resist.

"So what's been going on with you? You seeing anybody?" he asked me.

"Kinda. I've been dating this girl Mikki for a little while, but that might be over."

Dad glanced at me. "Why?"

"She wants to be exclusive and I'm not really feeling that."

"How come? And you've never said anything about this Mikki before now."

I shrugged. "It's nothing serious so I never thought to bring her up."

Truth be told, I wasn't usually in the habit of telling Dad about my lady friends. It was only if I was really serious about them, and that had only been two women. When I thought about it, I realized Dad didn't know about most of the experiences I've had with women. I frowned slightly at the realization.

"What's the matter?"

I was so caught up in my thoughts that his question jarred me a little. "Hmm? What?"

"What you frowning for?"

"Was I? Oh, probably just thinking about something with this Mikki situation."

"Well, what's wrong with her? Why don't you want to be exclusive?"

I leaned the television against the bed and started picking up the packing cardboard and styrofoam. "I'm not feeling her like that. She's cool, but it's more physical than anything else. I can't say I even know her all that well."

"That doesn't mean you can't, though. If she's good enough to date, she's good enough to be in a relationship with. You can always learn to love her."

"Sounds a lot like settling, Dad."

"It's not settling. It's adapting. I'm sure if she was a bad person you wouldn't be messing with her at all."

"Okay, but still. If I'm gonna be in a relationship with somebody, a *serious* relationship, it's gonna be somebody I really want to be with; somebody I just can't get enough of. And I like Mikki, but that's not her."

"I'm just saying. Don't be so picky about it. Relationships can't be all about trying to find the perfect person."

What kind of philosophy was that? To hear Dad tell it, I shouldn't have any kind of standards for who I'm with whatsoever.

"So are you trying to say that you're not all that into Ava; you just married her for the hell of it? That would explain why you got married so fast, I guess; saw a good woman and figured you'd lock her down first and get to know her later."

"It wasn't even like that. I fell for her hard. First time I saw her, I was imagining putting a ring on her finger."

"And did she fall for you just as fast?"

"Probably not." Dad pulled out his tape measure and started measuring the wall.

I frowned. "And you married her anyway?"

"Hell yeah. Ava was too good a catch to let her get away just because she wasn't feeling me the way I was feeling her."

What the hell? "Why did she marry *you*, then?"

"She says I'm a cutie pie," Dad winked at me. "She likes how big I am. And I treat her well, too."

"That's it?"

"That's enough for me. I'll earn whatever love I don't have yet. I just want to take care of her; make it so she doesn't have to worry about anything."

"Uh-huh." I folded my arms again. "And what is she doing for *you*? What do you get out of this...arrangement?"

"I get to have Ava as my wife." He paused, smiling. "That's all I need."

Dad was standing there looking lovestruck, but I was starting to wonder about my new stepmother. Did she even love my dad or was she just with him so she could be a kept woman? I didn't know what she did for a living, if anything. Older men and younger women wasn't a new thing at all, but I would have never put Ava and my dad together. What did they even have in common? I knew good and well she didn't just marry him because he was *a cutie pie*.

"Dad," I tried to choose my words carefully, "How much do you even really know about this woman?"

"I know enough. It's not like we don't talk, Mario. She's not a stranger."

"But y'all aren't even in love, from what it sounds like. At least, *she's* not. Why not just date her until her feelings are as deep as yours? What was the rush?"

"I already told you. I wanted her to be my wife. I've been by myself since your mama died. She's the first one that even made me think about getting re-married. Figured that had to mean something."

I really didn't get this mindset of his. He marries a woman he hardly knows because he's smitten, and just hopes she'll eventually be as into him as he's into her? What kind of woman would marry a man she didn't love if she didn't have some kind of ulterior motive? Dad wasn't rich, but he did pretty well for himself. The life insurance from Mama's death set him up pretty well, and he'd been driving trucks for years and made pretty good money. Maybe Ava figured that if she got with my dad, she could just lounge around with her girls drinking wine and ordering stuff online.

"As long as you're happy, I guess," I finally mumbled.

"Oh, I am."

Dad might have been satisfied with Ava, but now I had some questions. I didn't care how fine she was, I wasn't about to sit around and let her take advantage of my dad.

Well, since Dad didn't think it was necessary to get the rundown on his new wife, I guess I'd just have to do it for him.

Seven - Mario

DAD ENDED UP HAVING to go out on another job the next day at the last minute, so I figured that was the perfect opportunity for me to confront Ava about her intentions with him.

After calling to make sure she was home, I asked if I could stop by, and she quickly said yes. I tried to tell myself not to be too confrontational, but the more I thought about her using my father, the less interested I was in trying to be cordial. It was time for this woman to explain herself.

"Hey!" she greeted when I arrived, looking all happy to see me.

"Hey." I stepped inside and closed the door.

She had enough sense to tell I wasn't in the mood for pleasantries. "What's going on?"

"I need to know some things, Ava."

She looked confused. "About what?"

"About why the hell you married my dad."

Her confused expression morphed into an offended one. "Excuse me?"

"You heard me, Ava. Look, you seem like a nice woman. But I find it very strange that you just up and married him after only knowing him for a minute."

After glaring at me for a few moments, Ava slowly turned and headed for the living room. I was right on her heels, ready to hear what she was going to come back with.

"How the hell is this any of your business?" she finally asked after taking a seat on the couch.

"Because that's my father and I'm concerned about him, and he's so lovestruck that he apparently isn't thinking straight. You have to know this doesn't make much sense. Dad is in his fifties and I'd be surprised if you're even thirty-"

"I'm thirty-*four*." She folded her arms.

"Okay, fine, but still. Just from what I've seen and heard, you have next to nothing in common. He's on the road more than he's home, a lot of the time. What, did you figure you could just marry him and have him foot the bill while you got to enjoy having his house to yourself while he worked?"

"Wow, well you just have me all figured out, huh?"

"I'm asking you."

"No, you're accusing me of being some kind of gold digger."

"I certainly don't hear you denying any of this."

"For your damn information, Mario, I have my own career. I've been a freelance copywriter for years and do just fine for myself. I don't need Harper's money."

I perked up upon hearing that she was in the same field as I was, but reminded myself to keep my game face on. "Do you even know anything *about* my dad? More importantly, do you love him? Because from what I heard from him yesterday, it seems like he is just satisfied loving you and hoping he'll eventually get some of that back. That's not fair to him."

"I don't know what it is Harper told you or what you think you know, but for the record, yes I love him. Did we move super fast? Yes. Do I know *everything* there is to know about him? No. But so what? I can learn all that in time."

"You can learn all that in time." I shook my head. "I'd be surprised if you even talk to each other. You can't spend that much time together since he's always on the road. What the hell kind of marriage is this?"

"The kind that's between me and Harper." Ava stood, facing me. "I get that he's your dad and you're concerned about him, Mario, but that's really all you need to know. Harper and I are just fine. And whatever issues we *do* have, we will deal with them *on our own*. And you really don't have to worry about it."

"Doesn't matter how many times you say that, Ava, I'm still gonna worry about it. Some woman shows up out of the blue and marries my dad, you better believe I'm gonna worry about it."

"Well, that's your business. But I'm telling you that this marriage is *not*. So, with that being said..." She started walking towards the door.

"We're not done, Ava."

"Yes, we are, Mario."

"If you're not in love with the man you married, at least be woman enough to admit it. 'Cause I'd be willing to bet my car that you love gummy bears more than you love Dad."

"Well, it's a good thing I don't want your car, because I'd win that bet. I hate gummy bears." Ava opened the front door and looked at me pointedly.

I stayed where I was, twisting my lips defiantly. "Again, who said I was done?"

"I don't really care if you're done or not. You need to leave, Mario."

"And if I don't? What, are you gonna call the cops on me? Make it seem like I broke in or something and you feared for your life so they can beat me down while you stand and watch? Maybe you'll even film it on Facebook Live or something so all your people can see how you put another Black man in check."

I was tripping and I knew it, and that's exactly how she was looking at me. "You *really* don't know me, and clearly don't think much of me if you think I'd even conceive of some nonsense like that. Like I said, I understand you looking out for your dad. But the way you came at me was jacked up. So until you can learn how to have Harper's back while still respecting me, I don't want to see you. Now please leave."

There were some more things I wanted to say, but I finally stomped towards the door. I couldn't resist a parting shot as I passed her, though.

"It's not like it's your house, anyway," I muttered.

I know she heard me. But she just sucked her teeth and slammed the door, barely waiting for me to get across the threshold before she did.

I was steaming. That didn't go as planned at all. I really hadn't intended to be so combative and confrontational, but I couldn't help myself. When it all came down to it, though, I still felt I was justified. Ava could've been some kind of con artist or somebody who liked to prey on vulnerable men, getting them to trust and fall for them so she could swoop in and take everything they had. What kind of son would I be if I just sat back and didn't say anything while my dad got played like a chump?

Knowing I wouldn't be able to concentrate on anything if I went home, I texted my boy Jayden and asked him to meet me to get a drink. I needed to clear my head, and cool off. I couldn't remember the last time I was so keyed up.

Jayden was already at Taco Mac when I got there, nursing a beer as he sat stretched out in a booth with his back against the wall. I knew I was gonna need something stronger than that and asked the first waitress I saw for some tequila.

"That wasn't our waitress," Jayden informed me, clearly amused, as I sat down across from him.

"Whatever. She can tell whoever is."

"So what's wrong with you?"

"I'm pissed off, that's what's wrong with me."

"About what?"

"This woman my dad up and married," I spat. "We don't know anything about her."

"You mean *you* don't know anything about her?"

"I bet Dad doesn't know much more than I do. They only knew each other four measly months before deciding to get married."

"That happens, man."

"It doesn't happen with Dad. He's not impulsive like that."

"Clearly he is."

"You know she watches cartoons? And drinks chocolate milk with salt in it?"

"Hell, that sounds good. I might try that, myself."

"This mess is crazy," I shook my head as the server set my drink in front of me. I was too in my thoughts to even thank her. "He hardly knows this woman but goes and marries her and moves her into his house?"

"You want them to live separately?" Jayden was clearly getting a kick out of this.

"Nothing about this is funny. He's got this chick up in his space and she could be some kind of international spy or thief."

"International. And she decided to come to Atlanta to hook up with a truck driver."

"That's not impossible."

"Have you been watching *The Fast and the Furious* or something?"

"Man, I'm serious! It just doesn't make sense. He's acting like he's never had a woman before and I bet she's not even in love with him."

"You don't know that, though."

"But I bet I'm right."

"Okay, so what if you are? They're both grown. Maybe they hit it off and really like each other."

"Who gets married 'cause they *like* each other? What kind of crap is that?"

"Folks get married for all kinds of reasons nowadays, man, you know that. Sometimes it's nothing more than two people who are tired of being by themselves and want companionship. Sometimes it *is* all about money, but they both know that and don't try to make it about something else."

"Well, she tried to say she loves him."

He frowned at me. "Please don't tell me you confronted her about this."

"Hell yeah! Went right over and asked her to her face why she married my dad."

"And?"

"She basically told me it's none of my business."

"She's not wrong." Jayden sipped his beer.

I glared at him. "What?"

"You're buggin' right now. And I get it; that's your pops. But the man is what, in his fifties? And I'm figuring she's an adult, right?"

"She's significantly younger. But yeah."

"Okay, then. They're both grown. And maybe they aren't head-over-heels for each other, but as long as they're both cool with how things are between them, then that's what it is."

"That's what it is, huh? I bet you wouldn't be so cavalier about it if it was *your* dad."

"I'm not being cavalier at all. But what I'm mainly curious about is the fact that you're so incensed over it all of a sudden. It's not like you just found out about them getting married today; your dad told you about it weeks ago. And hadn't you met her already?"

I took a big gulp of my drink. "Yeah."

"And you were apparently cool with her then. I don't get why you're so pissed about it now."

"Maybe between now and then I've thought about it some more."

"Maybe. But I know you well enough to know there's more to it than that." He eyed me. "What's going on?"

This is where I would admit to how attracted I was to Ava when I first saw her. If I was going to confide in anybody about that, it would be Jayden. But I wasn't trying to admit I had the hots for my stepmother to anyone, I don't care if he was a priest sitting behind a screen.

"I guess after talking to Dad the other day and hearing how things came about, it got me wondering about her, is all," I finally grunted.

"Man, look...I understand being concerned. But I know your pops. He's not an idiot. I think he can handle choosing his wife."

"I just don't get the urgency. Why couldn't they just date? What did they have to rush and get married for?"

"Who knows? But doesn't the fact that he felt compelled to do that so many years after losing his first wife say something about how special a woman this lady must be? What was her name again?"

I rolled my eyes, partially because he kind of had a point. "Ava."

"Ava. How 'bout spending some time with her and getting to know her instead of being all suspicious? 'Cause you're not gonna do anything but make them not want to be around you if you're going to keep questioning them and pointing fingers."

I wished I had gone to drink with somebody else. Jayden was making too much sense.

"Fine," I huffed as I sat back in my seat. "I'll chill out."

"Good. And while you're chilling out, maybe you need to ask yourself why you *really* got this upset, because you don't usually get this riled up about anything. We didn't name you M. Chill for nothing."

"I still say that's a stupid-ass nickname."

"Whatever. You answered to it."

I sighed. "What's your point, man?"

"Are you jealous that your dad got married before you did?"

"What? No!"

"Are you sure? You can admit it; it's understandable."

"I am not jealous. Getting female attention has never been an issue for me."

"Yeah, but there's a difference between getting female attention and finding the woman you want to marry."

"I'm not looking for that. If I happen to meet her, great, but I'm not looking."

"Well, *something* is going on. Maybe you just don't want to tell me, but I know it's more to it than you wanting to protect your dad's virtue, whether you admit it or not."

Eying my fingers as they pushed my glass around, I considered Jayden's words. Maybe I had concocted all of this anger so I would have an excuse to go see Ava, even if it was just to confront her. Maybe part of me actually wanted to get her to admit that she *didn't* really love my dad so I could be there to offer a sympathetic ear and comforting arms. Maybe I just wanted to test her a little bit.

Or maybe I wanted her and the fact that my dad was the obstacle preventing me from acting on it was eating at me more than I realized.

Regardless, I knew I had to clean up the mess I made. Ava didn't deserve to be attacked by me like that. I started to call her and apologize, but I'd confronted her to her face so I needed to apologize to her face. And anyway, I was pretty sure she wouldn't answer the phone if I called.

So after I left Jayden, I headed back over to see Ava. I had made an ass of myself, and needed to make it right. Of course, she was in no hurry to see me again, though.

"What do you want, Mario?" she asked from behind the closed door.

"May I come in, please?"

"I think you've said quite enough. Or did you think of some more stuff to accuse me of?"

"I'm not here to accuse you of anything. I just want to apologize."

She was quiet for a moment. "Really?"

"Yes, really."

"Well, go ahead."

"I'd rather not do it through the door. I'm not gonna take up too much of your time; I just wanna say my piece and apologize for acting like an ass and then I'll be on my way."

I heard her sigh, but she finally opened the door. She peered at me for a second before turning and heading to the living room. I stepped inside and closed the door behind me, looking around as if I expected her to have changed the decor since I was there a couple of hours before. When I stepped into the living room, she was perched on the arm of the couch, tapping her bare foot on the floor. The red polish against the light carpet made me notice how cute her toes were. Then, of course, I had to look at her legs. They were kinda shiny, like she had rubbed them with some kind of oil. It kinda made me wonder if the rest of her was-

"Mario?"

Oh, damn. I cleared my throat. "My bad. Yeah, um, Ava...I had no right to come at you like I did earlier. For whatever reason, I got all these ideas in my head and I let my imagination get away from me. I'm usually not like that, I swear."

She eyed me skeptically.

"You've gotta understand; Mama died so long ago and it's just been me and Dad since then. He hasn't even talked about *wanting* to get married before he ran off with you. He's dated over the years, but it never went anywhere. So you come along and I just naturally wonder..."

Ava held up a hand. "Mario...I get it. Some of the things you said were really hurtful, but I understand you were just looking out for Harper. It's not like I've never let my emotions drive me to do something stupid."

I slid my hands into my pockets. "So you forgive me?"

She folded her arms. "I don't know..."

"For real?"

"I might get where you were coming from with everything you said but that doesn't mean I'm gonna just forget about it."

"Ava, come on..."

"If I came at you like you came at me, would you be so quick to forgive *me*?"

I hesitated, knowing I probably wouldn't be. "Okay, you got me with that. But I really want us to be on good terms. And I don't wanna leave here knowing you're still upset with me."

She eyed me.

Taking a tiny step towards her, I eyed her right back. "What is it I have to do to get you to forgive me, Ava?"

Her tight facial expression melted and I heard her draw in a tiny breath. I could see her chest start to heave a little bit.

"What are you *willing* to do?" she asked in a low voice, looking at me from under her lashes.

Damn if my body didn't react to that. "Try me and see."

Her eyes roamed up and down my body for a moment before she must have caught herself, because she shook her head, startled. Blinking, she looked away and rubbed the back of her neck.

"We should probably, um..."

Somehow I was closer to her without even remembering moving my feet. "Yes?"

"You don't have to worry about us being at odds. I forgive you."

The amount of relief I felt was surprising. "Good."

There were a few awkward moments where we just looked everywhere but at each other. Finally, she cleared her throat and stood up. "You want something to drink? A snack, maybe?"

I started to accept, but `thought better of it. "Nah, I said I'd apologize and get out of your hair, so I should get going."

Ava opened her mouth to say something, then apparently changed her mind. She just slowly eased past me – hesitating just a little bit as she did - and headed towards the door, her thumbs hooked into the back pockets of her shorts. I couldn't help but notice how nice her shape was. She was a small woman, but still had enough shapeliness to her where she couldn't be considered skinny. I never cared for skinny women.

She stopped right before she got to the door, but didn't turn around. Didn't move to open the door, either. Her breaths were deep, like she was working up the nerve for something. When she finally turned, she gasped when she realized how close to her I was. She looked up at me.

"What's wrong?" I asked, my voice low.

"I'm not sure..." she whispered. The fear in her eyes was evident. But she wasn't scared of me. She was scared of the affect I had on her. I knew because she was having the same one on me.

Being this close to her, smelling her, practically feeling the heat radiating from her body, was causing my heart to thump like max bass in a car. I tried to get my feet to step around her and get the hell out of there, but I was stuck in that spot. She was looking at me and I was looking at her.

"I should go," I eventually muttered.

"Yeah. You should."

She turned to put her hand on the knob, and barely opened the door before slamming it shut. As soon as she turned back around, my lips were on hers. She grabbed my face, almost as if she'd been expecting it. And clearly wanting it.

I wrapped her up in my arms, holding her close to me as we kissed deeply. Her arms slid around my neck. We were both moaning, panting, gasping...too caught up in the moment to worry how incredibly wrong it was. And it *was* wrong, no doubt. But it also felt more right than anything I'd ever done.

"We should stop," she panted, leaning her head back as I licked her neck. "Oh my god, Mario..."

"I know." I planted several slow, wet kisses on her lips. My hands were all over her. "I know."

Her mouth was saying one thing, but her hands were holding me closer to her, gripping my clothes like she was holding on for dear life.

"This is *so* wrong..."

"It is. It really is."

"We shouldn't..."

"No, we shouldn't."

Our kisses never stopped. Our hands on each other never stopped. Even though we both knew we had no business doing what we were doing, at the time, it just didn't matter. I wasn't thinking about Dad at all. All that mattered to me right then was Ava.

So when she held me closer and begged me not to stop, I gladly obliged.

Eight - Ava

I DON'T KNOW WHY I was bothering trying to get any work done. It wasn't happening.

Maybe I was the slut of the week for making out with Mario like I did, who was my stepson whether I liked to think of him like that or not. And I *did* feel guilty about it.

But the bigger part of me loved it so much, I was hoping for a repeat.

He was so different from Harper. His kisses, the way he touched me, how he took his time...I don't even know how long we stood there all wrapped up together. Harper only did so much kissing until he got tired of it; Mario seemed like he could kiss me forever.

If I was honest with myself, I loved every second of it. As wrong as I knew it was, I simply hadn't wanted to stop. Thank goodness that we had the willpower to not take it any further than we did, because God knows I wanted to.

Hell, I *still* want to.

Damn. Not even married seven months and already fucking up.

I ran my hands down my face. I wanted to just forget about my weak moment with Mario, because that's what I considered it to be. My concerns about Harper were clouding my brain so much that I did something I *never* would have done otherwise. I had never cheated in any of my relationships; I'd rather just leave first. But did what happened with Mario mean I wanted to leave Harper?

I didn't think so. Things might not have been perfect between us, but they weren't *that* bad. Leaving him certainly hadn't entered my mind before, despite how frustrated I had been lately. This just meant I would have to put even more effort towards improving things in our marriage; my kiss with Mario was just a minor slip-up. Nothing more.

And it would *not* happen again.

WITH SOME MAJOR EFFORT, I managed to push my thoughts of Mario aside and get some work done. I was working on an email series for a client and it was due in the next couple of days. I had already made several errors I didn't usually make because my head was all jacked up.

"Get it together, girl!" I admonished myself as I corrected yet another misspelled word.

Deciding I needed a break, I slipped on my sneakers and headed outside, locking the door behind me. Taking a walk around the neighborhood usually did the trick when I couldn't concentrate. Then again, the *reason* I couldn't concentrate this time was certainly a first, so I could only hope that worked this time. I put my earbuds in and listened to an audiobook as I walked, keeping the volume low enough so I was still aware of my surroundings.

As I walked, I thought about calling Harper. Maybe hearing his voice would snatch my head from out of the clouds. I usually didn't bother him when he was on the road; I always just waited for him to call me when he could. But, desperate times...

Stopping my walk, I dialed his number and waited, chewing my lip as I anxiously shifted my weight. I waved to one of my passing neighbors as I waited, then groaned in frustration when the call went to voicemail. I immediately called back, and that's when I heard Harper's voice, though he didn't sound very welcoming.

"Can't talk now, Ava," he said, his voice rushed and bothered. "I told you I'd call you when I could."

"I know, but..." Sighing, I figured there was no point. He clearly wouldn't care that I just needed to talk to him; something would have to be on fire to justify bothering him on the road. "Forget it. Sorry I bothered you."

"All right, bye." He hung up. No question as to what might be wrong, no concern about why I would call when I normally wouldn't. Just that I didn't wait for him to call me like he preferred. I should've known.

A little dejected, I walked for a little longer before heading back to the house. When I got there, I groaned loudly, wondering how much more frustrating this day was going to get. The familiar Cadillac that was in my driveway made me want to run in the other direction.

"There's my hot daughter-in-law," Everette, Harper's dad, emerged from his car with his arms open, a big smile on his face.

I stopped several feet away from him, a hand on my hip. My skin already felt like it was starting to itch.

"Hello."

"That's all you have for me? *Hello*?"

"Not sure what you'd like for me to say. Harper isn't here, if that's what brings you by."

"I figured. That boy is always driving up and down the road. I tell ya, if I had a fine little lady in my house, I'd make sure I was at home as much as possible."

Since I was apparently supposed to be flattered by this, I passed him a tight smile as I moved towards the house, giving him a wide berth. His arms were still open and waiting for a hug, but that wasn't happening. I didn't want his hands on me.

To my chagrin, Everette followed me into the house. I was hoping that he would leave since Harper wasn't here, but no such luck. And despite how much he creeped me out, I couldn't bring myself to be rude to him. He *was* my father-in-law, after all. Plus, I'm sure it would upset Harper, if he found out about it.

"Is there something you need, Everette?" I asked as politely as I could manage.

He winked at me as he strolled around the living room like he'd never been there before, his hands the pockets of his white linen suit. He wore a lot of those, I noticed.

"Just visiting," he replied with a shrug. "Was over this way so I thought I'd swing by."

"I see. Do you want some water or something?"

"I'm all right."

Thank god. "Well, I don't want to be rude, but I need to get back to work..."

He smiled at me, his gold tooth gleaming. "You can't spare a few minutes to kick it with me?"

Hell no. "I really can't. I'm up against a deadline."

"Hmm. Well, I can respect that." His eyes roamed up and down my frame, and I felt the sudden urge to shower. "You're looking good, by the way."

"Thanks."

"You work out?"

"Sometimes."

"I can tell. Those are some of the prettiest legs in creation."

"Thank you..."

"Yeah, you good and *tight*."

In what world was it okay to say this kind of stuff to your daughter-in-law? What the hell was I supposed to say to this?

"I'll be sure to let Harper know you stopped by whenever he calls, Everette," I finally dismissed, moving towards the door.

"Yeah, I know how he is about folks calling him on the road. With his stubborn ass."

Well, that's one thing we agreed on.

"I'll just talk to him later on," Everette announced as he passed by me. I took a subtle step back as he did so, in case he wanted to reach out and touch. I already knew he liked to be a little too affectionate.

"All right, then."

"See you soon, pretty lady." He winked at me, tipped his white fedora, and left. I shuddered as I closed the door behind him, making sure it was good and locked.

The only good thing about Everette stopping by was that it took my mind off of what happened with Mario. Now I needed to take my mind off Everette. Going back to my computer, I dove into my work, managing to forget about everything else.

HARPER CALLED BACK a few hours later, when he stopped to fill up and get something to eat. I was lounging in bed watching *Brown Sugar*, taking advantage of being able to do so in the bedroom. Harper always acted like this was some kind of cardinal sin.

"What's up, babe?" he asked.

"Nothing much. Just watching a movie."

"No, I mean why did you call?"

"That was hours ago, Harper. I said to forget about it."

"I figured it must have been pretty important for you to call me in the middle of the day."

"It was to me. But you were acting like I was bothering you so I just dealt with it on my own."

"I'm sorry, but you know how I am about that."

"Of course. Not only do I have to deal with you being gone most of the time, I have to wait for permission to call you while you are. I totally get it."

"Why are you getting an attitude?"

"Because apparently my being your wife means nothing if it interferes with your work. What if I just missed you and wanted to hear your voice? What about that?"

"Ava, I'm not trying to fuss with you. I'm too tired for that."

"Yeah," I grunted. "I'm tired, too."

"What?"

"Nothing. Well, it's a good thing you called, anyway, because there is something I wanted to talk to you about."

"What is it?"

"Your dad came by here earlier. He really makes me uncomfortable, Harper."

"What did he come by for?"

"I don't know. Apparently nothing. Did you hear the part about him making me uncomfortable?"

"You just have to get used to him, babe. My dad is cool."

"Yeah, well, as *cool* as he may be, I really don't like how he flirts with me all the time. Some of the comments he makes are downright inappropriate."

"He's always been a flirt. I wouldn't sweat it."

I frowned. "So no matter how much it bothers me, you're just gonna act like it's no big deal, huh?"

"I mean, don't take this the wrong way, but it kinda isn't. Dad is harmless. He's not gonna do anything to you, if that's what you're worried about."

"Wow." I really couldn't believe this. He was totally dismissing my feelings. "Nice to know that my concerns mean nothing to you."

"Come on, babe. You know that's not it."

"That's exactly it. And I don't have anything else to say to you right now. I'm going back to my movie. So be safe or whatever."

"Ava, come on-"

"Bye." I hung up, tossing the phone across the bed. In that moment, I couldn't stand my husband.

I bet Mario wouldn't just disregard my feelings like that.

The thought came all on its own. I had managed to put Mario out of my mind for the better part of the day, but just like that, he was back. Maybe it was because of the frustrating conversation with Harper I'd just had. If that was the reason, I was in for some trouble because I was sure that wasn't going to be the last time Harper got on my nerves. I couldn't start fantasizing about my stepson every time I had a fight with my husband.

My phone chimed with an incoming text message, and I started to ignore it, figuring it was Harper trying to sweet-talk me. But then I remembered that Harper wasn't too big on texting, so I leaned over and grabbed my phone, already grateful for the distraction. I didn't count on it being from who I needed to be distracted *from*.

I'm going out of town for a little while. Just wanted to let you know.

Mario

While I was trying to convince myself that this was a good thing, the phone chimed again.

Part of the reason is because I haven't been able to get you out of my mind.

Delete this message.

Mario

Despite myself, I was grinning. It was comforting to know that our kiss was conflicting him so much so that he needed to get out of town. I didn't like the thought of him being gone, but I also didn't trust myself with him there. So his leaving for a while was just what we both needed. I could only pray that I would be over this infatuation with him by the time he got back.

And honestly, I loved hearing that he was thinking about me as much as I was thinking about him. It let me know I wasn't in this by myself.

Nine – Ava

"HOW COULD HE DO THIS to me? After that awesome kiss we had, I was *sure* he was feeling the connection I felt!"

I put my arm around my crying friend, trying to come up with a comforting platitude I hadn't already used.

"I'm sorry, sweetie," I soothed, smoothing some of her wayward honey brown hair. I remembered when she started dying it that shade a few years earlier, because some guy told her it would look good on her. The color lasted longer than he did. "He just wasn't the right one for you."

"Then who *is*? I'm so sick of falling flat on my face over and over!"

"I know..."

"All I want is to love somebody and for them to love me back. Why is that so hard??"

"Vera, your right man is out there for you, sweetie. I know it. It's just taking him a little longer to show up. Maybe this is meant to be a test of your patience."

"I've been *more* than patient! Ava, I am *thirty-five* years old! I don't want to be in my fifties trying to have kids! My eggs are gonna be dried up before I make it to a third date with somebody, at this rate!"

"Don't say that, Vera. Don't even think like that."

"That's easy for you to say, Ava. You've got somebody. Trish has somebody. *I'm* the one that keeps being left high and dry."

"Maybe you're trying too hard. How about taking your mind off of finding a husband and focus on the other things in your life? You have a great career; you used to talk about being a dermatologist back in the day and now you're one of the top ones in the city. That's something to be proud of."

"I love my career, but dermatology doesn't keep me warm at night or knock me up."

"I'm just saying, Vera. You know the thing they say about finding stuff when you stop looking. Just date to enjoy it and not to find a husband."

"Then what's the point? One thing leads to the other."

"But that takes time. You have to be patient and let these things evolve naturally."

She glared at me. "Are you really talking to me about *taking my time* when you got married after only knowing Harper for four months?"

I knew she was hurting, so I chose not to take her snippy comment personally. "Harper and I are something of an anomaly, I know..."

"So why did it happen for you but it can't happen for me?"

"I didn't say it *can't*. I'm just saying you need to relax and let it happen how it's gonna happen, however that's gonna be."

"Well, I'm sorry that I can't be more patient, especially since *nothing* is happening." She wiped her eyes with the tissues I'd given her. "What about Mario? Did you mention me to him yet? I haven't heard from him."

"Oh...no, I haven't really had a chance to."

"You have his phone number, right?"

"Yeah, but it's not like we're best friends, Vera. I don't exactly feel comfortable hitting him up out of the blue and trying to tell him who he should date."

"You're talking up your best friend. And you said he was a good guy."

"From what I know of him, yes. But keep in mind, I haven't known him long at all."

"Still. Just work it into the conversation. It shouldn't be that awkward. It's common for mothers to try to set up their sons."

Grimacing, I briefly closed my eyes. "I'm *not* his mother, Vera."

"Well, stepmother. Whatever. Can you just do it?"

"All right, all right." I continued to rub her back, chewing my lip nervously. "Oh, wait..."

She looked at me. "What?"

"I *do* remember hearing recently that he was seeing somebody." It wasn't a lie. Mario told me that himself the day I stopped by his place, even though he also said he didn't see a future with her. I already knew I wasn't going to mention that part. "I *just* remembered that."

"Damn it. It figures," Vera muttered, looking absolutely dejected. I felt like the worst friend ever. "Well, is it serious? If it's not, there's still hope for me."

I hated hearing her sound so desperate. Vera had too much going for herself to be so utterly consumed with getting a man. I understood wanting someone to share your life with, but damn. This was literally *all* she seemed to think about. We couldn't have a conversation without her relationship woes coming up.

"All right, Vera," I sighed, literally feeling myself running out of energy for this conversation. "Fine. I will bring you up to Mario. I can't promise anything else."

"Thank you, Ava!" She threw her arms around me, as if I had guaranteed Mario would be putting a ring on her finger tomorrow. "Just be sure to mention my cooking. Men love that."

It would have been cruel of me to say that if that was all it took, she would have a man by now. So I didn't say it.

"All right. I'll be sure to let him know that you're a great cook. Now come on, let's go shopping or something. Take our mind off of men for a while."

"Ehh, I shouldn't," Vera said, checking her watch. "I have some things I need to do."

"Please don't tell me it's going home to take some updated pictures for your dating profiles."

"Why do I need to do that? You're introducing me to Mario. Hey, how about if I ended up being your step-daughter-in-law? How crazy would that be?"

Lord. "Yeah, girl, crazy is the perfect word for that."

After Vera left, I started gathering all the dirty laundry, figuring I could get that out of the way while I figured out what I wanted for dinner. Since Harper wasn't there, I could have whatever I wanted without worrying about his limited tastes. It's sad how much that thought excited me.

The guilt for misleading Vera inched back over me as I went about my housework. While I hadn't exactly lied to her, I did imply that Mario might not be available when I knew that wasn't true. I knew I was wrong for that, but I simply did not want to set Vera up with Mario.

But I also knew there was no good reason I could give for not doing so. I was married, and to Mario's dad, no less. Who Mario dated wasn't supposed to matter to me.

I had to wonder just how enamored I would be with Mario if things were going better between me and Harper. If our marriage had me walking on air, would I even have given Mario a second look? That question poked at me over and over, and it got increasingly annoying because I knew I had no real way of knowing the answer. Of course I'd *like* to say no, but what if the magnetism Mario and I shared was just that strong that it would've been there regardless?

Shaking my head, I hurriedly threw the clothes into the washing machine and rushed to my computer. I felt the need for some kind of grand gesture; something big that I could do to prove, if only to myself, that I was as committed to Harper as I was supposed to be.

Since we still had yet to go on a honeymoon, I figured it was time to take a trip together, hoping that if I gave him enough notice, he wouldn't try to use work as an excuse not to go. Knowing he had no interest in traveling internationally, I booked a nice trip to Knoxville, Tennessee. I figured it was perfect, since it was out of state but still relatively close. When I started looking around for things we could do there together, prickles of excitement began to pop up all over me. A romantic getaway was just what we needed.

Harper was due home the next day, and I couldn't wait to surprise him with this trip. We hadn't talked that much since our argument about him dismissing my feelings about Everette, and I wanted us to move past that. I was never really one to hold grudges. And after my rather unpleasant childhood, I needed a house with peace in it. I wasn't interested in any more negativity and turmoil.

By the time Harper got home the next day, I was ready for him. The house was clean and smelling like Pine-Sol, as he liked. I was wearing his Atlanta Falcons jersey, which went past my knees, and nothing else. And there was a hearty rib dinner from his favorite barbecue place waiting for him in the microwave. I prayed all this was enough to butter him up about the trip.

He looked a little timid when he came into the house, which I had to admit was kind of cute. Ever since I met him, I always thought he had the most adorable baby face. It was one of the things that endeared me to him. Such a cutie pie.

"Hey," he cautiously greeted, eying me.

"Hey." I smiled.

"How are you? Still mad at me?"

I walked over to him and raised my arms for a hug, which he quickly gave me, lifting me off the ground and squeezing me like a stress ball, as usual.

"I don't want to think about what happened the other day," I finally replied, pulling back to look at him. "I'm glad you're home."

"Me, too. I missed you. And you're looking tasty in my jersey."

"I'm glad you like it." I slid back to my feet and took his hand, leading him to the couch.

"You cleaned the house? It smells really good in here."

"I sure did."

"What's the occasion?"

He acted like I never cleaned the house before. "No occasion. Just because."

I didn't want to stress that my using the Pine-Sol and wearing the jersey were done just because he liked them, because I didn't want it to seem like I was throwing it in his face or using it as some kind of bargaining chip to get my way. I didn't need an ulterior motive to do things for my husband, but I'd be lying if I said that wasn't the case this time, at least in part.

"Well, I damn sure appreciate it."

"Good." I grinned at him. "I have dinner waiting for you, too. But before you do anything else, I have a surprise for you."

"Yeah? What?"

"I booked us a trip. To Tennessee."

His expression faltered a bit. "What?"

"I think we should finally go on our honeymoon. I booked it for a couple of months from now, so you have plenty of time to square things away with work. We need this, sweetie."

Harper fidgeted in his seat. "And you want to have our honeymoon in Tennessee?"

"It's not at the top of my wish list, but I know you wouldn't agree to go overseas anywhere, and Tennessee is still relatively close. What's more important to me is us being there together. That's all that really matters, at the end of the day."

"Yeah. True."

"It's gonna be great. And since Tennessee is so close, it won't be a long flight at all."

His head snapped to me so hard I was afraid he hurt himself. "Flight?"

"Yeah...how else did you think we were gonna get there?"

"I thought we were gonna drive."

"I don't want to drive. Why spend all that time in the car when a flight only takes about an hour?"

"Still. Driving is what I do. It soothes me."

"Well, it doesn't soothe me. I want to go ahead and get there so we can start our honeymoon as quickly as possible. And you promised me we would take one, Harper."

"I know..."

"I've already done all the work. All you have to do is get on the plane."

Pursing his lips, he looked at me with resolve. "All right. You're right, our honeymoon is overdue. And I want to make you happy." He grabbed my hand. "We can go."

Grinning, I clapped my hands excitedly before jumping into his lap with a squeal, throwing my arms around him and smothering his face with kisses. He chuckled, holding me tightly as I kissed all over him. I couldn't remember the last time I was so excited.

And that excitement had me sliding down to my knees on the floor, looking at him naughtily. He smirked back at me.

"Whatcha doin'?"

"Whatcha think?"

I tugged at the waistband of his pants, and he lifted slightly so I could yank them down. Licking up and down the inside of his thighs, I caressed him through his boxers, part of me expecting him to pump the brakes for some reason. When he didn't, and he just leaned his head back and enjoyed what I was doing, I licked my lips in anticipation. I was about to give him the head of his life.

Finally, I pulled his boxers down and stroked his dick a few times before sliding my mouth over it. He shuddered immediately.

"Ahhhh," he groaned.

He wasn't long but he was thick, so my mouth was full of him. I started playing with his balls with one hand while I began bobbing my head up and down, slobbing him up real good while I caught a smooth rhythm. Before I could *really* get going, though, he suddenly grabbed my head so hard it's a wonder I didn't bite his junk off.

"I'm coming!"

Already??

In seconds, he was exploding into my mouth. He maintained his hold on my head as he convulsed for several moments after that, coming down off of his (rather premature) high. It was only when he calmed down and his breathing slowed that he let me go, and smiled down at me.

"You are the *best*, babe," he breathlessly praised.

Before I could even suggest another round, he was snoring.

I was just there, on my knees, looking at him with narrowed eyes, hoping he was going to spring up any second so we could keep going. But nope. He was out cold, snoring with his mouth open and his pants and boxers down around his ankles.

With an incredulous shake of my head, I got up to go find some aspirin for the headache I suddenly had.

A few hours later, I was doing some work when Harper wandered in, finally awake from his post-fellatio nap.

"Babe, thanks for dinner. Those ribs were banging."

"You're welcome."

"You working?"

"Yeah."

"Well, I'm glad I won't be going back on the road for a little while. Seems like I've spent more time in that truck than here with you lately."

"You have. But if anything, I'd rather you get any other jobs out of the way before we go to Tennessee. I know I can work from anywhere but I don't plan on even taking my computer when we go. I want it to be all about us."

Harper looked at the ground. "About that, Ava..."

I looked up at him. "What?"

"I've had a change of heart about us flying there. If we're gonna go, we need to drive."

Frowning, I saved my work and closed my laptop. I tried hard to calm myself. "Why?"

"Because I don't want to fly. Tennessee isn't that far. We can drive and still have plenty of time to do whatever we're gonna do there."

"What changed in the last few hours? You already agreed to fly there, Harper. It's one freakin' hour. You can't even do that for me?"

"I'm *going* on the trip for you, ain't I? Damn, I don't wanna be up in the air, I don't care if it's for five minutes. What part of that can't you understand?"

Reeling at his sudden change of attitude, I tried to decide which part of his temper tantrum I was going to address first.

Standing, I crossed my arms as I slowly made my way around the desk. "Well, excuse me, but I make a *lot* of concessions for you. Way more than you do for me. And I'm a little tired of always having to forget what I want just so you can have your way."

"It ain't about me having my way. I just need you to respect my wishes on this."

"Oh, like you ever respect mine? You don't give a damn about *my* wishes, Harper; as usual, I'm supposed to just go along with your way like a good little wife and shut up. Just so you know, I'm tired of that."

"Ava..."

"Oh, and I *thought* that you wanted to go on our honeymoon as much as I did. I didn't realize you were doing me some fucking favor."

"Oh, you cussin' at me now? Since when do you talk like that?"

"When I'm as pissed off as I am right now, Harper, I'll say whatever. Not to mention, I am a grown-ass woman, so I can talk however I want to."

"You're trippin'," Harper accused, holding up his hands. "If you're gonna act like this, we don't need to talk. Let's just wait 'til you calm down to have this conversation."

"This is not a conversation, this is an argument. And if you think letting me cool off is going to make me change my mind and give in to keep the peace like it usually does, you are sadly mistaken. Don't try to act like this is all on me."

"You're the one fussing. All I said was I didn't want to fly. I really don't see what the big deal is."

"You never see what the big deal is, Harper. That's what you always say; *I don't see what the big deal is*. Well, whether you see it or not, it's a *big* deal. It's about the bigger picture, which you don't seem to get. And you're old enough to where you *should* be able to get it. If you can't, then I don't know what to say about you."

He reeled. "What does *that* mean?"

"That means I'm not trying to be your relationship tutor. You're not an idiot. Figure it out." I stomped towards the door.

He grabbed my arm. "Are you really acting like this right now?"

"Are *you*?" I yanked my arm from his grasp.

He shook his head. "I'm so surprised at you, Ava."

I wanted to hit him. Kick him. *Something*. "Likewise. Kiss my ass, Harper."

I left him standing there. After quickly changing out of his humongous-ass jersey, I grabbed my keys and called Vera. It was time for me to cry on *her* shoulder now.

"Hey, girl, I need to come over," I blurted as soon as she answered. The angry tears that had formed were already giving way to the sad ones. "And I hope to high heaven you have some wine."

HARPER AND I DIDN'T speak for several days after that night. I didn't have anything to say to him, and I could tell that he wanted to break our silence a couple of times but I shot him a look that clearly told him not to try it. I hated the silent treatment, but I was more tired of bending over backwards for Harper and getting nothing in return.

I started to cancel the honeymoon altogether, but I couldn't bring myself to do it. Despite my anger, I still hoped that we could work things out before it was time for the trip. I knew Harper had an aversion to flying, which is exactly why I chose a place so close; the flight would be super-short. Flying freaked out a lot of people, and I wasn't trying to be insensitive to that, but damn. Just like he didn't want to fly, I didn't want to spend hours cooped up in a car. I mean, meet me halfway, here.

When Harper was out of the house one evening, I tried to get some work done, but my concentration was shot. Thankfully the deadline for that particular project was a few weeks out, so I promised myself I'd buckle down the next day and went to the living room to watch a movie, opting not to go to our bedroom in case Harper came back and tried to join me (after requesting I turn the movie off, of course).

I munched on some celery and hummus while I watched *Brown Sugar* for the tenth time, then started to watch *Black Panther* when Trish called. While we both bitched about our husbands, I wandered upstairs and into the guest room, not wanting to see any of his things. That's how mad I still was.

"I swear, girl, sometimes I wonder if he'll ever get what I'm talking about," I whined, crouching on the full-sized bed. "I mean, tell me the truth; am I being unreasonable, here?"

"I don't think you are. But when they have their heels dug in on something, it doesn't matter *what* we say or how much sense it makes when we say it. They want what they want."

"How in the world do you put up with that?"

"Girl, over the years, Leroy and I have learned to work through this kind of stuff. He might act stubborn in the moment, but after a while, he'll think about it and realize he was being unreasonable. So I usually just leave him alone until he does, which doesn't take long, thankfully."

"Hmph. A damn month could go by and Harper wouldn't change his mind about anything," I grunted. "I'm just supposed to bend to his will."

"Don't do it this time. Show him you mean business and stick to your guns. Men are like kids sometimes; if they see they can get away with stuff, they'll keep doing it, wrong or not."

Flopping onto my side, I traced the design on the bedspread with my finger. "Trish, honestly...sometimes I feel like I'm living with a stranger. I thought I felt such a connection to Harper when we met but now...I'm wondering if I was wrong."

"You're just going through a rough patch right now. You've only been married a few months. And I know you think I'm gonna tease you about marrying him so quick, but I'm not. Sometimes, people click right off the bat, and it doesn't take months or years to know you want to be with them. You two just have to find your rhythm together, that's all."

"You really think that?"

"You know I wouldn't say it if I didn't."

"Well, I hope you're right." I pushed myself up and slid off the bed. Stepping into the almost-empty closet, I flipped the light on and glanced at the couple of boxes that were in there. "'Cause this is *not* the kind of marriage I signed up for."

"Just don't do anything you're gonna regret later," Trish warned. "I know you're pissed at him, and you should be, but he's still your husband. You married him for a reason. Try to remember that."

"I will." Sighing, I smoothed my hair back, only feeling slightly better. "Thanks for listening, girl."

"You know I got you."

We ended the call, and I curiously looked at the boxes again. I almost never came into the guest room, so it was my first time noticing they were in there. Reaching up, I managed to inch the box off the shelf with my fingertips, pushing it forward from underneath through the slots in the shelving. I had to be on my tiptoes the whole time. Sometimes I really hated being short.

The box wasn't heavy at all, and I peeked inside, seeing it was mostly papers. Kneeling down, I eased the box open and began rifling through it. I wasn't trying to be nosey, but it wasn't like Harper was trying to hide them, since they were right there in the closet. I was just curious as to what they were, that's all; I figured they were probably things like Harper's birth certificate and other old health records, maybe some old tax papers. Stuff like that.

What I *wasn't* expecting to find was an old newspaper article detailing the time Harper had been arrested for sexual assault.

Ten - Mario

NEW ORLEANS WAS ONE of my favorite cities, and a place I frequented when I just wanted to get away for a few days. Usually the lively atmosphere, awesome food, and the pretty women were enough to distract me from whatever I needed to get away from, but no such luck this time.

Ava was still dominating my thoughts like LeBron dominated the NBA. And neither seemed like they were letting up any time soon.

The scene of our kiss replayed in my mind like the replay button was stuck, and I didn't want to fix it. I can't even say what came over me; when I went back to her house, it was for the sole purpose of apologizing for the unfounded accusations I'd made about her and her intentions with my dad. But when I got close to her, it was like something pushed me to kiss her. And once I got going, I didn't want to stop.

I didn't even feel that guilty. As jacked up as that sounds, the fact that I kissed my father's wife, my stepmother (who was younger than me), in his house, didn't fill me with remorse. Whenever I thought about it, I smiled like a teenager who'd just gotten some for the first time. No doubt I wanted to do it again. One taste of Ava just wasn't enough.

But the little bit of good sense I had left reminded me that I wasn't supposed to want to do that. Regardless of how good it felt—how *amazing* it felt—I needed to cool my jets. Whatever connection I felt with Ava, I'd just have to do my best to ignore. She was married to my father. Nothing could happen between us; nothing that would last, anyway. It's not like she was going to leave him for me. How messy would *that* be?

And speaking of Dad, I was wondering if I should tell him what happened. Ava and I had agreed after we finally pried ourselves off of each other that day that what happened couldn't happen again, and would stay between us. No sense in hurting Dad over a one-time slip.

But now the tiny voice of consciousness was knawing at me to let him know. Dad and I might not have been best buds, but we didn't keep secrets from each other. Maybe he would understand; hell, I *had* been drinking tequila that day. I could've lost my head. And who knows if Ava had anything to drink, herself. We could blame it all on the alcohol. I'd heard a few stories about Dad from back in the day; he wasn't exactly a boy scout.

Flopping backwards onto my hotel bed, I stared at the ceiling, my hand on my chest. Getting out of town wasn't doing me any good if all I was gonna do was agonize over Ava the same way I did when I was at home.

Jumping off the bed, I took a quick shower, got dressed, and headed out. I didn't even know where I was going; I just knew I needed to get around some noise so I could drown my thoughts out for a while. My hotel was just a couple of blocks from the French Quarter and less than a mile from Bourbon Street, so I headed to Olde Nola Cookery to satisfy my seafood craving. No surprise that it was rather full, but I wasn't in a hurry.

I felt someone looking at me, and sure enough, I saw two ladies giving me the eye when I glanced up from my phone. They smiled flirtatiously, and I acknowledged them both with a nod before turning my eyes away. Not a minute later, one of them came over to me.

"Hi."

I looked at her, giving her another nod. "Hey."

"You're not from here, are you?"

"Nah. Just visiting."

"Let me guess...Alabama?"

Chuckling, I corrected her. "Georgia."

"Ah, I was close." She snapped her fingers playfully, grinning. "I'm Zora."

I took her offered hand. "Nice to meet you. Mario."

"You can come join me and my girl, if you want," she offered. "Then you won't have to wait so long."

"That's cool of you. I'm not in any real hurry, though."

"Well, how about you join us anyway, since I worked up the nerve to come over here and talk to you?" she persisted, still smiling.

I had to admit I kinda liked her vibe. She was definitely a cutie, with her bushy hair, dewy maple brown skin, and titties that might as well have been on a shelf. Sitting with her and her equally cute friend wouldn't be the worst thing in the world.

"Well, since you put it like that..." I tucked my phone into my pocket. "Lead the way."

We snaked our way over to where her friend stood, sheathed in a cool yellow sundress and sandals, her braids wound into a bun on top of her head. She was looking at me anxiously.

"Celine, this is Mario," Zora introduced us. "Mario is from Georgia, as you'll hear as soon as he says something."

"You're not making fun of me, are you?" I asked her playfully, taking Celine's offered hand in both of mine.

"Not at all. I think that southern twang is sexy."

"So do I," Celine added. She was eying me like a hot beignet.

"Well, that's good to know. You ladies getting your seafood fix, too, huh?"

"I am. Zora here just wants dessert."

"I can't help it. The Kentucky Bourbon Pecan Pie was in my dream last night."

"Sounds tasty." I tried not to look at her chest.

We all made small talk for a couple of minutes before we were shown to our table, at which point Zora looked at her watch and sucked her teeth.

"Awww *damn*!" she exclaimed dramatically. "Look at the time...I've gotta get outta here and get to that appointment. See how time sneaks up on you? I didn't even realize how late it was." She threw up her hands dramatically, looking back and forth between us. "Looks like I'll have to leave you two here alone."

"Zora!" Celine shrieked, putting her hands on her hips in a fake huff. "I wish you had checked your calendar before! You're completely leaving me hanging, here!"

"I'm sorry, girl. Guess I'll have to get that pecan pie another day. I'm sure Mario wouldn't mind keeping you company, though, right?" She smiled at me expectantly.

Celine looked at me sheepishly, and I tried to hide my laugh. I hope they didn't think I was falling for this.

"Yeah, I'll keep her company," I replied, barely hiding my amusement. "It was nice meeting you, Zora. I hope you arrive safely to your *appointment.*"

"Thanks, Mario. Call me later, girl," she winked at Celine before leaving, not being able to hide her giggles.

Celine smiled at me as we took our seats. "It's cool that you were able to hang out for a while. I hate eating alone."

"Well, with your girl's timely appointment and all..."

A smile tugged at her lips. "Didn't buy that, huh?"

"Let's just say Tyler Perry won't be knocking on your doors any time soon."

"Well, hey," she shrugged. "Subtlety isn't my strong suit."

"I see."

"How long are you in town for?"

"Maybe another day or two."

After we placed our orders, Celine crossed her legs and eyed me from under her false lashes. "You have family here or something?"

"Nah. Just love the city. You from here?"

"Moved here when I was a kid so might as well say so."

"If I was gonna relocate, it would certainly be at the top of the list."

"You should consider it. In the meantime, though, we should hang out while you're here, if you have time. I'm off work for a couple of days. And I have a feeling Zora is gonna be busy."

"Yeah, I'm sure she is," I chuckled, not committing to anything.

We continued to do a lite version of the getting-to-know-you game while we waited for our food.

Celine was laying the flirtation on pretty thick, and while I appreciated it, I was only mildly interested. I wouldn't be in town that much longer and wasn't sure when I'd be back, so I didn't see the point of trying to start anything. The long distance thing wasn't my bag.

More than a couple of times as we ate, my mind strayed to Ava. I damn sure wasn't trying to, but I found myself mentally comparing everything about Celine to Ava, from her hair down to her toes, which I have to admit, were *not* as cute as Ava's were. Ava had those kind of toes where you could just drizzle some caramel on those bad boys and-

"Mario?"

Damn. "Yeah?"

"Where were you? Seemed like you were deep in thought for a second."

"My bad. Was just thinking about something I needed to do back home."

"Oh." She looked like she was working up the nerve to ask her next question. "Well, what are you doing after you leave here?"

"Not sure yet."

I didn't bother asking why she asked. I knew why she asked.

"Would you like to do something? We can go to a movie or just...chill together."

Chill together, huh? "Intriguing offer..."

"I could just come to your hotel room," she boldly blurted. "I live a little ways away and I imagine your hotel is probably nearby."

"Yeah, it's not far from here."

"So?" She sat forward in her seat, eying me. Her intentions were clear. Lust radiated from her like heat bouncing off the asphalt. I felt her foot brush my leg under the table.

I pondered her invitation, looking right back at her. It's not like I wasn't tempted. Celine was very attractive; sexy, even. But it was clear what she wanted, and while I was no stick-in-the-mud, I didn't just sleep with random women.

Besides, she wasn't who I wanted.

The server brought the check, and I paid the bill while she waited patiently for my answer. When I finished with that, I told her as gently as I could, "Part of me is right there with you, but I'm gonna have to go back alone. A hot woman in my hotel room is most likely just gonna end up one way, if we're both real about it."

Disappointment flitted across her face, but she tried to recover. "What's so wrong with that?"

"Stuff like that should only go down if both people are all into it, and I wouldn't be. Honestly, I can't get down with one woman while I have feelings for another."

Looking mildly surprised, she sat back in her seat. I thought she might get angry or offended, but she looked okay with it.

"I guess it's my fault for not asking up front if there's someone else in the picture," she finally mused.

"Don't sweat it. This was an impromptu thing."

"Truth be told, I've never even propositioned anyone like that. This was all Zora's influence. She's already texted me three times asking how it's going."

I couldn't help but laugh. "Well, hopefully you won't dog me too much whenever you talk to her."

"Not at all. I actually appreciate the honesty. And on some level, I'm glad you turned me down instead of just getting yours and then acting like I don't exist. I'm too familiar with that."

"Not my style, sweetheart."

"I'm appreciate it." She smiled at me as she grabbed her purse that was hanging on the back of her chair. "Thanks for lunch."

"No problem. Thanks for inviting me to sit with you. This was much more pleasant than eating alone."

Grinning, she stood and we walked out of the restaurant together. "Are all of you Atlanta guys this smooth?"

"Am I smooth? I guess I'm just born with it."

Laughing, she leaned in for a hug, which I obliged. She smelled like maple.

"I won't bother asking if you want to keep in touch, but just in case, my last name is Carmichael if you want to add me on Facebook or something."

"Good to know."

"It was nice meeting you, Mario."

"You too, Celine. Take care."

We went our separate ways, and just like that, I knew it was time for me to go home. Getting propositioned by another woman just made me want to get back to what I'd come here running from.

WHEN I GOT BACK TO Georgia, I started to head home but instead, I changed course and went to Dad and Ava's. I wanted to let them know I was back in town. Yeah, I could've just called. Yeah, it was a weak excuse to see Ava. But that's the one I went with.

The last thing I expected was to see Ava bursting through the front door in tears, duffel bag in hand.

"Whoa, whoa!" I caught her when she stumbled during her sprint to her car. Her tears were blinding her. "What's going on? What's wrong?"

"I have to get out of here," she sobbed, reaching for her door handle.

I gently caught her hand. "You are in *no* condition to drive. What in the world happened? Where's Dad?"

"He's in the house. I can't be around him right now."

I frowned. "He didn't do anything to you, did he?"

"Please don't make me talk about this, Mario." She sniffed and wiped her eyes with the back of her hand. "I can't...I'm just so upset and I can't even think straight right now..."

"Okay, okay," I said gently, taking her into my arms. "You don't have to tell me anything you don't want to. But I'm not comfortable with you getting behind the wheel when you're this upset."

"I *have* to get away from here, Mario!"

"Fine, then I'll take you back to my place. You can calm down, get yourself together. Stay as long as you need to. I promise I won't press you for any details you don't wanna give. But please, for my peace of mind, just get in my car, Ava."

She looked up at me, her eyes disturbingly red, nose running, and hiccupping so much I was afraid it would start to hurt. Seeming too tired to protest, she wordlessly got in my car, closed the door, and put her face in her hands.

I was worried, curious, and trying to tell myself not to jump to any conclusions either way. She could've had a legitimate reason for running away from Dad, or she could've been overreacting to something. I didn't know what was up, and I tried to remember that as I called out to Ava that I'd be right back and headed into the house. To be honest, though, I was already a little pissed off.

Seeing Ava in tears like that did something to me.

I stormed into the house, determined to get some answers. "Dad!"

"What?"

Following his voice, I went into the kitchen, where he was finishing a bowl of cereal. He didn't seem all that concerned that his wife was so distraught that she couldn't even be around him.

"What's going on with you and Ava?" I demanded.

He sucked his teeth. "She got all bent out of shape over something small. Welcome back, by the way."

"Yeah, thanks. Um, not trying to get all up in y'all's business or anything, but-"

"She found out about my arrest."

I blinked. "*What* arrest?"

"For sexual assault."

He said that like it was no big deal at all. As casually as he would tell me that he was getting extra sausage on his pizza.

It took me a moment to gather myself. Hell, this was the first I was hearing of this, too.

"Excuse me?"

Dad went to rinse his bowl in the sink. "I was seventeen. This white girl had been sniffing behind me because she wanted to be able to say she was with a football player, and I finally went ahead and took her out since she was basically putting it out there on a silver platter. We went out, then she snuck me back to her house, in the basement. We started fooling around, and the girl liked it rough and asked me to...*not* be gentle. Their maid caught us while I was tossing her around and ran and told her parents. It didn't help that my hands were around the girl's throat when we got caught; apparently, that turned her on. They flipped out, called the police, and..." He shrugged.

"So...what came of it?"

"They ended up dropping the charges when the girl threatened to expose some family drama if they didn't. The mom was some kind of city official or something up for re-election and didn't want that stuff out. So they paid me five hundred bucks under the table to stay away from their daughter and I went on about my business."

"How come you never said anything about this before now?"

"I was seventeen. I don't think about stuff I did when I was seventeen. It was ages ago. And it's not exactly something I want to broadcast."

"So how did Ava find out about it, then?"

"She was going through some boxes upstairs and saw an old newspaper article. It was kind of a big deal back then but after they dropped the charges, thankfully the hoopla around me died down after a little while. Thank God there was no social media back then."

He was looking different to me. Just hearing this story, dropped charges or not, made me see him in a new light, and it wasn't a great one. Sure, it was many years ago. But getting arrested for sexual assault isn't exactly something you *forget*. And I was tripping over the fact that I had never heard anything about this before now. What else didn't I know about my father?

"Wow," I marveled, perching on one of the barstools in front of the island. "I don't even know what to say about this right now..."

"There's nothing to say. It's over and done with."

"Why is Ava so upset?"

"Because I never told her about it. I tried to tell her that I hadn't thought anything about that arrest since I met her, but she wasn't trying to hear that. She freaked out and started screaming about how she never knows what to expect with me, and how it's like she doesn't even know me, and started accusing me of keeping secrets and all this. Then she threw some clothes in a bag and said she can't be in a house with somebody she doesn't know."

"And you didn't try to stop her?"

"What was I supposed to do? Grab her and tie her to the chair?"

"You don't seem to care about her feelings at all, Dad. You've got this whole blasé thing going on right now and it's kinda throwing me off."

"How am I supposed to be acting?"

"You could be a little more concerned about your wife. Hell, *I* seem more upset than you do."

"Maybe you should be the one to talk some sense into her, then." Dad got a beer out of the refrigerator and tipped it towards me. "You want one?"

"Nah. What do you mean, I should talk some sense into her? I actually think it's perfectly understandable that she's as upset as she is. It must have been some jolt finding that out about you, regardless of how many years ago it was. I'd bet anything she's wondering what other major stuff about you she doesn't know."

Just like I am, I added silently.

"I don't know every little thing about *her*, either," Dad defended. "We haven't been together long enough to know all that."

"Dad, I know y'all haven't been married that long, but it's certainly been long enough for you to tell her the major stuff. People can tell their life stories in one night."

He sighed. "It's not like I was keeping it from her on purpose. Like I said, I never think about it. I try to put unpleasant memories out of my mind completely."

"Is that why we never talk about Mama?"

His head snapped to me. It was a kind of unspoken thing between us that the subject of my mother stayed a buried one. Whenever I asked about her back in the day, he'd tell me the least amount possible before changing the subject. It was clearly an uncomfortable topic for him, and while I wanted to respect that, she *was* my mother. I didn't get to know her because she passed when I was barely out of Superman underwear. I didn't know nearly as much about my mother as I should have.

"I've told you plenty about her," Dad muttered, the beer bottle against his lips.

"I'm sure there's plenty I *don't* know," I countered. "I don't even know where her side of the family is. Don't I have some cousins, grandparents, aunts, uncles, *something*?"

"Look, every time you ask me this, I tell you the same thing: she wasn't close to her family. They don't even live down here; they're all on the other side of the country, whichever ones of them there are left. I doubt she even told them about you, herself."

"Well, that's nice. That's nice to know."

"It's nothing you should take personal. She loved you more than anything. Ever since I met her, she wanted to have a kid. When you came along, she was over the moon. But anyway, I need to focus on Ava right now, and I already know she's not going to be talking to me any time soon. So if you can calm her down and get her to see some reason, I'd appreciate it, son."

I hesitated. Not because I didn't want to help (Ava), but because I couldn't see myself pleading my Dad's case right then. If I were in Ava's shoes, I'd be upset, too.

"Please?" Dad persisted, pulling me out of my thoughts.

Sighing, I shook my head. This was the last thing I was expecting to deal with when I came over here.

"Fine, Dad," I finally said. "I'll talk to her. But whether she forgives you for this or not is totally her decision. I can't make her forgive you and I'm not gonna try to."

"What? Why not?"

"Because like I said, Dad, I see why she's upset. All I can do is try to get her to talk to you so you can explain yourself. If that happens, you can't be acting like you are right now, like this is nothing. Doing that just totally dismisses her feelings."

"Yeah, she's been saying I do that a lot lately," he mused. "Every other day, it's something else."

"See there, that? You can't do that."

"Do what?"

"Turn this on her. It's not on her."

"I'm not trying to do that."

"But that's what you're doing."

"Look, I feel like I just don't know what I'm doing anymore," Dad suddenly confessed, plunking his beer onto the counter and rubbing a hand down the back of his neck. "It's been a long time since I've been married. I think I was better at it the first time."

"Yeah, well, you're gonna have to figure out how to fix things *this* time," I eyed him. "Ava deserves to know who it is she's sharing her life with."

"Fine. I'll work on that. But in the meantime, can you please go take care of her? Just make sure she doesn't do anything crazy."

"I can't promise anything, Dad." I hunched my shoulders. "But I'll see what I can do."

"Thanks, son."

Without another word, I got up and headed back outside. Ava was still in my car, her head leaned against the window, eyes closed. I thought maybe she had dozed off, but when I got in the car, her eyes opened.

"Please don't try to tell me to go back in there," she pleaded.

I started the car. "I'm not."

"You really don't have to take me to your house. I can call Trish or Vera."

"Why do that when I'm right here?"

"I just don't want to put you in the middle of all this. That's your dad..."

"Don't worry about that," I assured her, pulling out of the driveway. "I don't even have to say anything about it. My main concern is getting you to where you can calm down and get your head together."

Ava just nodded, looking down at her hands in her lap.

I didn't say anything else as we headed to my place. It still made me uncomfortable seeing her so upset, and I couldn't help but be a little miffed at Dad. I mean, for real; what kind of reaction did he expect her to have, finding out something like that about her new husband by accident? Sure, it was thirty-five years ago and the charges were dropped, but still. Even if she was overreacting, he could've been more sensitive to her feelings about it. I'm sure that played as big a part in how upset she was as finding out what he did.

When we got to my place, Ava took a seat on the couch, declining my offer for something to drink. She just rested her elbow on the arm of the couch, her head in her hand, looking emotionally spent.

Knowing she didn't want to talk, I grabbed my laptop and worked on a piece about my latest trip to New Orleans. Even though I had mostly gone there to get away from my budding feelings for Ava, that didn't mean I couldn't benefit from it.

After a while, Ava sat forward, dropping her head between her knees, her fingers snaking through her short hair.

"You all right?" I asked, concerned.

"My head is killing me," she softly informed me.

"I can get you some Advil or Motrin."

"Advil would be great, thanks."

I got up to get her the Advil and a bottle of water, and she popped two of them and chugged most of the water before releasing a long sigh. After making sure she was good, I went back to my work.

"Did he tell you what happened?" she muttered after a while.

My eyes stayed on the computer screen. "Yeah."

"Do you think I'm overreacting?"

"Not for me to say."

"I'm asking you."

"I can see why you'd be upset, finding out something like that."

"But did I blow it out of proportion?"

"I wasn't in there when y'all discussed all this, Ava. No real way I can know that. Is your reaction *all* about finding out about his arrest?"

"Not *all*. It was jarring to find out, but I also understand it was a long time ago. What pissed me off was his dismissive attitude. Not only did he think this wasn't even something I needed to know about at all, but he gave me the bare minimum on details, and brushed me off when I tried talking to him about it some more."

That was Dad, all right.

"The fact that I was concerned about it didn't matter at all; he didn't think it was worth discussing, so I was just supposed to drop it. This kind of thing has happened so many times, and I just snapped."

"So...this has been a habit with y'all?"

"Yes! It's always about what Harper wants and doesn't want. He doesn't seem to know a damn thing about compromise, or empathy. Even when I tried explaining why I was so upset, he just brushed it off." She sniffled as fresh tears brimmed in her eyes. "If it's like this now, I have no reason to believe it's going to change any time soon, if ever."

"People can change, though," I defended, even though I didn't have any more confidence in Dad doing so than Ava did. If Dad didn't think anything was wrong with him – and he didn't – he wouldn't see any reason to change anything.

"I know people *can*. But Harper *won't*. And I can't live like this forever. I *won't* live like this forever."

I looked at her. "What are you saying?"

Ava looked me right in the eye. "I'm saying I'm starting to wonder if marrying Harper was a mistake."

Wow. I hadn't expected that.

"Are you serious?"

"I'm dead serious."

"Ava, come on..." I felt the need to at least *try* to defend Dad. "Dad has his flaws but he never means any harm to anyone. He's not upsetting you for the hell of it."

"Mario. If he kept *this* from me, how many *other* surprises are there? Am I *always* gonna have to fight to learn the details of him, or to get him to try something new, or convince him to do something just because it might make me happy? He doesn't seem to care about that at all. I swear, he didn't seem like this when we were dating. If I'd had *any* idea..."

She buried her face in her hands again. I closed my laptop and moved it to the end table before scooting closer to her, sliding an arm around her shoulders. She immediately fell against me, crying into my chest. I instinctively put my other arm around her, holding her close. Hearing her cry caused a pang in my gut that I didn't like.

"I wish I could promise you that he'll get it together," I eventually said, "But I can't. Dad is stubborn, I'll be the first to admit it. As old as he is, he hasn't been in many relationships at all. He and my mom weren't married all that long before she died. It might just take some time and patience to get him to see how a marriage is supposed to work."

"What if I don't want to be patient? What if I want someone who knows already?"

She lifted her head, and our eyes locked. I suddenly felt warm all over.

"You deserve to have what you want," I practically whispered.

Her hand landed on my chest. "I think so, too."

As if choreographed, we came together. I swear I hadn't planned on kissing her. But in that moment, I couldn't help it.

Her tongue felt like silk against mine. Every time she sighed or moaned, assumedly in pleasure, it sent a jolt all the way through me. I knew we should stop; this wasn't why I brought her over here. Dad asked me to talk to her, not slob her down. But every time I started to pull away, she held me closer. It didn't take long for me to stop trying, because I didn't want to stop, anyway.

Our kisses started getting deeper and more intense. All pretense was gone. We both wanted this, and we were both succumbing to the temptation. Her small hand came up to grab my face, and I possessively returned the favor. I was kissing her like she was my woman, and loving it.

She climbed onto my lap, wrapping her arms around my neck as mine slid around her waist. There was no grinding, no fondling. I was absolutely aroused, but I was more enjoying feeling and exploring her. Getting acquainted with her kisses and her sounds and the feel of her, savoring every second of what we were allowing to happen. I was in no rush to take it any further, and she didn't seem to be, either.

"You feel *so* amazing," she breathed, tilting her head as I helped myself to her neck.

"Mmm, so do you."

She squirmed a little as my hands roamed over her back, occasionally dipping close to her ass, and I could hear her whimpering faintly. Her tears were still flowing, though I expected now for a different reason.

Pulling back slightly, she took my face in her hands, her eyes roaming mine intensely.

"What are we doing?" Her voice was full of anguish.

I bit my lip, shaking my head slightly. "I wish I knew."

"This...doesn't feel as wrong as it should."

"I'm right there with you. You've taken a hold of me, Ava. As much as I wanna fight it..."

"Oh, Mario..."

We came together again, our kiss more powerful and intense than before. I couldn't hold her close enough. She smelled so good, she felt so good...and she was bringing me to realizations that I knew I wasn't ready to face. All I was sure of was that I never felt with another woman what I was feeling with Ava right then.

A knock at the door made us both stop in our tracks. She looked at me, slight fear in her eyes, and I rubbed her back reassuringly.

"Who is that?" she whispered in a panic, starting to move off of my lap.

"Ava, chill." I held her tighter to keep her in place. "I'm not even expecting anybody and it's not like just anyone can come up here."

"What if it's Harper??"

"Dad never comes by unannounced. It's probably my boy Jayden."

She peered at me. "Does he know about...*this*?"

"He knows about *you*. Not about *this*."

When she pursed her lips at my response, I wondered what was going through her mind. I didn't have time to think about it, though, because the knocking resumed, louder this time.

"Lemme go see who it is," I grunted, patting her hip. "Stay right here."

"You don't want me to go to the back or something?"

"I do not. Because whoever this is, I'm planning on getting rid of."

She still looked wary as she raked her fingers through her short hair and fanned her slightly-flushed face.

Running a hand down my own face and chest, I went and checked the peephole on the door, cursing under my breath when I saw who was on the other side.

"Great," I muttered.

"Who is it?"

Sighing as I put in a pre-prayer for no drama to pop off, I looked over at her. "Mikki."

Eleven – Ava

I TOLD MYSELF NOT TO freak out.

Mikki wasn't Mario's girlfriend, but that didn't mean she wouldn't feel some kind of way about showing up at his place and seeing me there. She didn't know me, and I'm sure she wouldn't buy that I was Mario's stepmother, even though I was. Hell, Mario was older than me!

Would she be able to tell that we had *just* been making out?

As soon as she entered the apartment, she tried to hug Mario, and he wasn't nearly as enthusiastic about it as she was. I started to doubt listening to Mario as far as staying right there in the living room, because I had a feeling Mikki wasn't going to leave as quickly as he wanted her to.

"Why haven't you called me?" she purred to him, nuzzling his neck. "I've been missing you."

"You remember the last conversation we had," Mario reminded her, easing back slightly. "You told me *not* to call you until I figured out what I wanted, remember?"

It was then that she saw me. She frowned, looking back and forth between me and Mario. I could almost feel the instant attitude from across the room.

"So I guess *this* is what you want, huh?" she asked him, glaring at me.

"Don't start, Mikki."

"Don't start, what? If you were messing with somebody else, you could've just told me that instead of stringing me along all this time."

"Ain't nobody stringing you along. For your information, this is my stepmother."

Mikki scoffed, just like I thought she would. I probably would have too, really. I was *just* thirty-four years old but could pass for younger, and Mario was a grown man. Most people *wouldn't* immediately believe I was his stepmother.

"Oh please. You can't think of anything better than that?"

"It's not a lie, Mikki. She married my dad when I was out of the country."

"I don't believe that."

"Well, whatever. I'm not gonna put a whole lot of effort into trying to convince you. You can go on and roll 'cause I'm not in the mood for an interrogation."

Clearly not expecting that response, Mikki's strong stance faltered. "For real?"

"Yes, for real. And it shouldn't matter *who* she is since I'm a single man and can have whoever I want up in here. And you have a lot of nerve trying to get an attitude about it, anyway, since you stomped off that day at Applebee's and haven't contacted me since."

"But...you were acting all hesitant so I left you alone for a while so you would know what you'd be missing!"

"Yeah, good plan. I don't have time for games, Mikki."

While they went back and forth, I pulled out my phone and requested an Uber. I was low-key grateful for the distraction, because what Mario and I were doing...it needed to stop. I didn't *want* it to, but it needed to. Because this man was doing something to me that I wasn't ready for.

Opting to wait outside for my ride, I stood and headed for the door. I didn't want or need to hear any more of Mario and Mikki's drama.

"Where are you going?" Mario asked me, stopping his conversation with Mikki mid-sentence, which she did *not* appreciate.

"I've called an Uber so I can head over to Trish's. You two should be alone."

"You don't have to leave." His voice was adamant.

"No, you two should talk and work things out. I'm just in the way. It's totally fine, Mario." I looked at Mikki, ignoring the stink eye she was giving me. "Nice to meet you, Mikki."

Her eyes dropped to my wedding ring, then swept me up and down. I could tell she was still skeptical, but she wasn't about to get further into Mario's doghouse than she already was.

"Yeah," she huffed. "You too."

Without another word, I walked out, careful not to look at Mario although I could feel his eyes on me. I was anxious to get out of there. I had enough of my own mess to worry about without dealing with Mikki, too.

My heart was racing as I texted Trish to let her know I was about to head over there. I guess I should have guessed that something would happen between me and Mario if we were alone long enough. I swear to *God*, that was the furthest thing from my mind when I went over there. My fight with Harper was the only thing I was thinking about. Mario happened to come along at the right time and get me away from it, which I appreciated, because I had been close to throwing something heavy right at Harper's head. But now, Harper had been pushed to the backburner and Mario was at the forefront of my mind.

I remembered that my bag was still in Mario's car, but I wasn't about to go back in there to ask Mario to get it. I'd just have to get it later, but I still had no intention of going back home any time soon. I still didn't want to be around Harper.

"Girl, what in the world is going on?" Trish asked when I finally made it to her house. She had a glass of wine ready for me.

"I don't even know where to start." I plopped onto the couch. Noticing the quiet house, I looked around. "Where's Leroy and the kids?"

"The kids are at my mama's. Leroy's at work."

"Oh, okay."

"So what's up? Why did you have to take an Uber over here? Where's your car?"

"At home." I took a long swig of wine. "I had a fight with Harper and ran out."

Trish sat up, concerned. "It was that bad?"

"Yes. That bad."

"What happened?"

I didn't have the energy to go into all of the details of what started the fight, so I went into the realization the fight left me with. "I'm wondering if marrying Harper was a mistake. I'm seriously, seriously questioning my decision to be with that man."

Trish gasped. "What??"

After going ahead and giving her a quick rundown of how this latest disagreement kicked off, I sighed and leaned my head back. "Girl, I just don't think Harper is going to change. And I refuse to be miserable forever if I don't have to be."

"Wow, I had no idea it was like *that*," Trish marveled, sinking back down into her seat.

"It is, but there's something happening that's even worse than that."

"What?"

How could I say this right? "I think...I think I might be falling for Mario."

Trish jumped out of her seat, arms flailing. "*What?!*"

"I know, it's crazy! But I'm feeling things for him I'm not supposed to feel; things I don't even feel for Harper. And that honestly freaks me out."

"Has anything gone down between you two? Have you-"

"No, we haven't slept together." I took another sip and looked at her sheepishly, too ashamed to admit what we *had* done. "Not that I haven't thought about it...a few times even when I was in bed with Harper, which just feels too wrong for words."

"Oh, so you've been holding out on me, huh?"

"Well, it's not exactly something I'm proud of. And it's certainly not anything I planned. Picturing Mario's face when Harper is making love to me? Fantasizing about my husband's son while I'm masturbating in the bathroom so Harper won't hear me? It's happened too many times to count. It's like I can't stop myself."

"Damn, he's got you messed up like *that*?"

"Like *that*. But then I keep telling myself, hey, me and Harper are having all of these issues; my head is just jacked up right now...it doesn't mean anything. I *really* tried to re-focus on Harper and do my part to make things better between us. But the more we butt heads, and the more I learn about him, the more I think that it just isn't going to work. And that's whether Mario is in the picture or not."

"You sure about that? If Mario wasn't a factor, would you be so quick to give up on Harper?"

"I wouldn't say I'm *quick* to do anything; it's not like I told him I want a divorce. But I'm the first to acknowledge we got married before really learning about each other. And sometimes, that can still turn out great. But I'm not seeing that happening with Harper."

"Maybe it will, though. Maybe something or someone will make him wake up and see what it is that's starting to drive you away."

I shook my head vigorously. "No. He's way too stubborn."

"People change when they want to."

"But why would he change when he doesn't think he's doing anything wrong? I'm telling you, Trish, I'm really afraid this is how it's going to be forever."

"Ava," Trish sat down next to me, her eyes boring right into mine, "Do you want me to tell you that it's okay for you to leave your husband?"

"I honestly don't know what I want," I confessed with a sigh. I drained the rest of my glass. "I just know that today was the most upset I've been in a *long* time. Harper pissed me off so much that I packed a bag and left."

Trish looked around. "I don't see a bag. Didn't you come straight here?"

"Ahh..."

"*Ahhh...?*"

"I'm actually coming from Mario's."

"What the hell??"

"I hadn't planned on going there. I didn't even know he was coming to the house, but he showed up right when I was leaving and convinced me to get in his car, since he said I was too upset to drive. And he was probably right; I was hysterical. Crying my eyes out, all that."

"Well, I have to say I'm glad he did that. If you were in that condition, you didn't need to be behind the wheel."

"Right. So I'm sure Harper asked him to get me to come to my senses when Mario went inside to see what was going on. Then we went back to Mario's place. We were just talking, then I started venting about Harper, then we had a *moment*."

"A moment?"

"Girl, you know; when your eyes lock and everything else around you just kinda fades away...you just become lost in it."

"Oh yeah, I've had several of those."

"That's what happened between me and Mario. Girl, I just...something came over me. It was wrong but it felt so *right*."

"You got a picture of this dude or something? He must be hotter than chicken grease."

"It's not even about that, though," I protested. "I mean, I'm not gonna front; Mario is super sexy. But when we were together just now, it wasn't about lust or anything freaky. It was about our connection. I felt a strong, genuine connection with this man, Trish. And I don't think it was because I was emotional about Harper or confused, or anything else. I think it's just *Mario*."

"Well, girl...if you feel that strongly about Mario, you need to do something about it."

"What am I supposed to do about it?"

"Be honest with Harper."

"As mad as I am at him right now, I'm not sure I can tell him I might be falling for his son," I replied. The thought alone pained me. "I *do* still love him."

"Sometimes, love isn't enough. You said yourself you were miserable. Look, at least take the time to figure out what it is you really want. If that means staying away from Mario so you can keep your head together, then do that. But there's no harm in admitting you jumped the gun with marrying Harper if that's what you sincerely feel, and if you can honestly say you tried to make things work. Think about yourself first on this."

She had a point. But that didn't make any of this easier.

"Ugh, why does everything have to be so difficult?" I whined, falling against her arm, which encircled me.

"It's just designed that way, girl. But we appreciate it more when we finally do get what we want."

"Ugh."

"So you think you might love Mario, huh?" she asked after a few quiet moments, rubbing my arm comfortingly.

"I don't know. Maybe I do. Or I'm at least starting to."

"Hey; you can't help who you fall in love with."

"And it's just great timing, since I still have to introduce him to Vera."

"What? You're still gonna do that after this?"

"What else can I do? I already promised her. And you know she'll grill me to death if I try to back out of it. I can't very well tell her the real reason. And please, don't tell her about anything I've told you."

"Now you know me better than that. I'm loud but I'm not a blabbermouth."

"I appreciate it. Vera just wouldn't understand this. She might try to say I'm being greedy or something, nabbing two men when she can't even get one."

"I still say introducing them is a bad idea. If they hit it off, you'll be even more miserable than you are now."

"I'll just have to risk it."

"Do you think Mario would even be interested in Vera?"

"I can't see them together. But you never know, I guess."

"You never told me why it was you left Mario's and came here."

"Oh, some woman he was dating showed up. The one he wasn't interested in a relationship with."

"Did she trip, seeing you there?"

"She started to, but Mario checked her. She understandably didn't believe I'm his stepmother."

"I probably wouldn't have, either. You look just barely out of puberty."

"Shut up!" I laughed, pushing her shoulder. My cell phone rang and I groaned when I saw it was Harper.

"You gonna answer it?" Trish asked when she saw his name on my phone screen.

I looked at her with an arched brow as I wordlessly declined the call, but he called right back. I sat and watched the phone ring through two more calls before I finally answered on the fourth one.

"What, Harper?"

"Babe! Where are you?"

"Why?"

"Because I called over to Mario's and he said you left. I was gonna come pick you up; we need to work this out."

"I don't think you're really ready to work anything out. You just don't want me to be mad at you."

"You know I hate when you're mad at me."

"Well, maybe if you took me more seriously, I wouldn't be."

"Ava," he sounded so earnest and sincere that I couldn't help but soften just a little bit. "Please let me bring you home so we can deal with this stuff."

I sighed. "Whatever. But you don't need to come get me; I'll just get an Uber home."

"You don't need to do that. I want to come get you."

Glancing at Trish, I finally relented. "Fine, Harper. I'm at Trish's."

"Just text me the address."

Ending the call, I looked at Trish pointedly, shaking my head. "*Girl*."

"I know, girl."

Twelve - Ava

I AGREED TO LET HARPER pick me up, but that didn't mean I had anything to say to him still.

"So you're still mad at me, I guess," the big genius surmised.

I looked at him only so he could see me roll my eyes, then I went back to looking out the window.

"Come on, Ava. I want us to get past this."

"Does that mean you're going to start taking some ownership and try to see my side on things?"

"I mean, yeah..."

"Does that mean you're going to start compromising and not being so set in your ways about everything?"

"If I have to, yeah."

My head whipped around so hard I actually hurt myself a little bit. "If you have to? How 'bout doing it just because you *should*?"

"Isn't that the same thing?"

"You're playing with me. Please tell me you're playing with me."

"What?"

"You *cannot* be this clueless, Harper. Someone actually has to tell you that compromise and empathy and consideration are vital parts of a marriage?"

"I'm not stupid, Ava."

"If I thought you were stupid, all of this would be irrelevant because I wouldn't be here. But damn, weren't you married before?"

He shifted uncomfortably. "Yeah. But that was a long time ago."

"Doesn't matter. It still applies now."

I could tell that he didn't like the direction the conversation had taken. As soon as I mentioned his previous marriage, his whole demeanor changed. Of course, this piqued my curiosity.

"Tell me about your first wife," I suggested, turning my body towards his.

"Oh, uh..." He wouldn't look at me. "There's really not much to tell. We were just kids, practically."

"Okay, but what was she like? What made you want to marry her? Were you two happy?"

He hesitated a few times before finally saying, "Can we talk about something else?"

I threw up my hands. "See? You're doing it again!"

"Doing what again?"

"Getting all tight-lipped about stuff. It's the same thing you did about the arrest. What is the big damn secret? Why can't you tell me about your first wife??"

"It's not a *secret*, it's just...just an uncomfortable subject."

I took a pause and gathered myself. "I don't want to be insensitive to that. I really don't. But it does concern me that you're so hesitant to tell me about some of the most important aspects of your life. This was your first love and the mother of your child. And so many years have passed...I just can't imagine why it's still *so* uncomfortable."

His hands were gripping the steering wheel so hard that I thought he was gonna catch a cramp. He still wouldn't look at me.

We arrived at our house, but neither of us moved to get out of the truck. He looked deep in thought and I was trying to be patient, hoping he would finally tell me something significant.

"Let's take a road trip," is what he finally said.

I blinked. "What?"

"A road trip. Anywhere you wanna go. That'll be a fun thing for us to do."

"So you're just gonna act like we were done with our conversation? And I still want us to use those plane tickets, anyway."

He sighed, rubbing his eyes. "You still have those?"

"Why wouldn't I still have them?"

"I just, I thought we had resolved this already."

I sucked my teeth. "Look Harper, if you're still gonna act the same way as before, I'll get out of this truck right now and make my way back to Trish's. I told you, I'm tired of this. *I'm* in this marriage, too."

He looked at me quickly, as if he feared I would jump out of the truck right then. He knew I'd do it. I wasn't trying to give him an ultimatum or anything, but I wasn't going to keep doing the same thing over and over with him. Nor was I trying to keep having the same damn conversation.

"Please don't leave, Ava," he pleaded, grabbing my arm.

"Well, I need to hear something, then. And you're hurting me."

"Oh, I'm sorry," he quickly apologized, releasing his hold. He rubbed the spot with his meaty hand. "I'm so sorry. I didn't mean to."

"I know," I assured, softening only slightly at the remorseful look in his adorable eyes. "But for real, if things don't start to change soon, Harper, I might have to re-think some things about you and me."

His eyes widened. "You wanna leave me?"

"*Want* to? No. Will I if I continue to be unhappy? Please believe it. I love you, Harper, but I'm not gonna be miserable."

Reeling, he rubbed his hands down his face. It was the first time I'd ever threatened to leave him, and I think he was finally starting to realize that I meant business and wasn't just saying stuff for the hell of it. Really, I hadn't even planned on saying that, because I was still going back and forth about it within myself, but maybe that's what he needed to hear in order to take me and my concerns seriously.

"Look, what if you take one of your girls to Tennessee with you, and when you come back, we can go to counseling or something?"

Lord, this man... "*That's* your solution?"

"I'm compromising. You can still go on your trip and I'm showing that I'm willing to work on our marriage by doing the counseling thing."

"The trip to Tennessee is supposed to be a honeymoon, Harper. I don't want to go with one of my girlfriends."

"Okay, what about Mario, then? You know he loves to travel. And he'd be a lot more fun-"

"Are you *seriously* suggesting that I go on what I *just* said was a honeymoon trip with your *son* instead of you?"

"I figured you and Mario had become good friends by now. It's not like it's anything romantic; you don't *have* to call it a honeymoon. Just call it a mother-son bonding trip."

Oh, if Harper only knew. The last thing I needed was to do any more *bonding* with Mario.

"We can take our honeymoon another time," Harper continued. "Yeah, that sounds like a good compromise to me."

"No, it does not."

"Ava, can you...just meet me halfway on this, please?"

"Meet you halfway? Why should I? You won't tell me any real reason why you're so dead-set against anything I suggest. I'm the last person you should be keeping secrets from, Harper. And if you won't open up to *me*, why should I believe you'd say anything once we got in front of a counselor?" I put my hand on the door handle. "You know what? I'm sick of this-"

"Ava!" he yelled as I opened the door, reaching over to grab my arm again, harder than before.

Shrieking in pain, I snatched my arm away. "Damn, Harper! Stop grabbing on me!"

"I'm sorry, but please don't leave me!"

"We're not getting anywhere, Harper. I can see I'm just wasting my time." I moved to get out of the truck.

"My wife died on a plane."

My eyes snapped to him, mouth hanging open in shock. He looked at me pleadingly.

Easing myself back into the truck, I closed the door. "What?"

"That's why I'm so freaked out about getting on a plane," Harper confessed. He grabbed the steering wheel, needing to do something with his hands. "She was in a crash on a flight back from visiting out west. One of her childhood friends had died, and she went to the funeral. On the way home, her plane went down. Some kind of mechanical error or something."

He looked near tears, and most of my anger went out the window. His aversion to planes made so much sense now.

But why couldn't he have just told me that from the beginning?

Leaning over, I hugged him best I could with the console between us. "Oh baby, I am so, so sorry."

He wrapped an arm around me, and I chose not to comment on how tight his squeeze was. I just held him, letting him get his emotions out on my shoulder.

"Harper, you don't have to keep these kinds of things from me," I informed him, caressing the back of his bald head. "You can always talk to me, even if it's about something difficult. We can work through it together. If I'd known this before, I never would have gotten those plane tickets. I promise not to say anything else about them."

"No," Harper quickly refuted. He pulled back slightly to look in my face. "I want to do this for you. It's time I...dealt with this fear of mine."

"You don't have to do that. I totally get it."

"No, babe, I *need* to do it. I can't live in fear forever. Honestly, nobody has ever really made me face this before...it's a hard subject to talk about 'cause it really messed me up at the time, and I never dealt with it. So I actually feel a little better having told you about this."

I looked at him. "Are you sure?"

He nodded, determined. "Yeah." His fingers stroked my side. "I'm sure. You've been real patient with me, and I don't want you to think I don't care about what you want. And I definitely don't want you leaving me. So I can make the effort for you."

Grinning at him, I leaned in and kissed his thick lips, my hand on the side of face. "I'm so proud of you for wanting to do that."

"I'm *gonna* do it," he proclaimed. "You're important to me, Ava."

"Thanks, baby. I needed to hear that."

He kissed me, hard. Grabbing the back of my head, he jammed his tongue as deep into my mouth as it could go, sliding his seat back before lifting me over the console and onto his lap. His hands squeezed my butt before clawing at my shirt, panting and moaning against my lips, his arousal building by the second.

"I've got to have you, babe," he grunted. "I've got to have you *now*."

Literally tearing my shirt off, he yanked my bra aside and dove for my breasts. His sudden aggression had thrown me off, but it was also kind of a turn-on. I braced a hand against the ceiling while Harper sucked hard on my nipples, grinding increasingly harder on his lap, the pain and pleasure of what he was doing distorting my face to almost a grotesque degree. It would've been much easier to pause and go into the house where we had more room, but there was something so hot about getting it in in the truck. I didn't think Harper had this kind of thing in him.

"Get these off," he ordered, tugging on the waistband of my jeans.

I moved off of him long enough for both of us to get our pants either off or pulled down far enough, and hopped back onto his lap.

"Do you have a condom?" I asked breathlessly.

"No, but it's cool. I'll be careful," he promised, lifting his hips.

I hesitated for just a second before sliding down onto his hardness, silently telling myself to get out of dodge when he started to get excited. Pretty soon, though, I wasn't thinking about anything else but the pleasure I was feeling as I rode Harper in the front seat of his truck, bouncing on him and screaming repeated obscenities, both of us good and sweaty within minutes. Cars cruised by our house and people strolled by, no doubt noticing the slightly rocking truck with the foggy windows, but neither of us cared. I just rode the hell out of my husband, sweat stinging my eyes, hoping that that his revelation about his fears and initiation of this impromptu driveway romp meant that things were going to start getting better between us.

And I also tried to forget that I was kissing on his son in this same position just a few hours earlier.

I WAS HUMMING AS I cleaned up the kitchen when there was a knock on the door. Harper and I had just finished dinner, and I was still pretty light on my feet after our romp in the truck a few days earlier. Things seemed to be improving between us; Harper was being more considerate and I was trying not to take things so personally. I knew it would take effort on *both* of our parts in order for our relationship to improve.

"Babe, can you get that?" Harper called from upstairs.

Quickly hanging up the dish towel I'd been using, I hurried to the door as our unexpected visitor knocked again.

"Who is it?"

"It's Everette, baby."

I wondered if he could hear the groan that automatically came out. He was one of the last people I wanted to see.

Resisting the urge to go insist Harper come get the door so I could retreat, I hesitantly let my father-in-law in.

"Everette," I greeted, my smile tight and forced. "Come in."

He tipped his hat to me as he entered the house, his gold tooth gleaming as he flashed a creepy smile at me. He turned to face me as I closed the door behind him.

"It's good to see ya," he declared, arms open.

"That's nice of you to say." I deftly sidestepped him, the tight smile still straining my face. "I'll go get Harper."

"No hug again, huh?" Everette chuckled, dropping his arms as he followed me into the living room. "That's all right. One day."

Ignoring him, I went to the bottom of the stairs. "Harper! Your dad is here!"

Harper immediately rushed from the bedroom, grinning like I said one of the Atlanta Falcons cheerleaders had come to see him.

"Pops!" he exclaimed, practically running down the stairs.

"There's my boy," Everette greeted, opening his arms, which Harper gladly ran into. They hugged tightly, clearly glad to see one another. I watched them with mixed feelings. Harper certainly never got this excited to see *me*. Or Mario.

"Have a seat, Pops," Harper instructed after their hug ended. "Did you eat? We just finished eating some spaghetti but there's leftovers."

"Nah, I'm fine. I'm gonna have dinner with a lady friend in a little while. You got any beer, though?"

"Yes sir! Ava, you mind getting us some beers?"

Choosing not to make a big deal out of it, I wordlessly padded towards the kitchen. I grabbed two bottles from the refrigerator and handed one to each of them before turning to go upstairs.

"Babe, where you going?" Harper asked, grabbing my arm.

"Just figured I'd leave you two alone."

"You don't have to do that. Come on and sit down."

"I have some work I need to do."

"It can't wait a few minutes? You and Pops need to spend some time together. That work isn't going anywhere." He practically yanked me down to the couch.

"Yeah, baby, I'm not gonna be here all that long. Just swinging by while my boy isn't on the road."

"Well, we're glad you did," Harper replied.

We are? Since when did he speak for me?

"So who is this lady friend you're going out with?" Harper asked Everette, popping the top from his beer with his big hand before doing the same for Everette's. I winced at the action. "I didn't know you were seeing anybody."

"Oh, you know me; I don't broadcast everything. She's just somebody I met at the grocery store."

"Is it serious?"

"Not on my part, it ain't. Can't speak for her."

I wanted to roll my eyes *so* bad.

"So she's just another notch on the belt, huh?"

"I wouldn't call it that but I guess. She's a nice lady and we have a good time together. That's all I'm looking for right now."

"When are you gonna settle down, Pops?"

"Maybe when I meet somebody as fine as that wife you got next to you." Everette winked at me, taking a long swig of his beer.

I frowned slightly and glanced at Harper, but he didn't seem bothered by this statement at all. In fact, he looked flattered by it.

"Yeah, she *is* a good lookin' little thing, isn't she?" Harper concurred, proudly clamping a hand on my thigh.

Thing??

I told myself to calm down. I'm sure Harper didn't mean anything by that.

They continued to talk amongst themselves about various things for a while as I just sat there, wishing I could be anywhere else. I didn't know why Harper insisted I stay down there with them if they weren't going to include me in their conversation. Everette talked about his upcoming retirement, Harper told stories about his road trips, and I sat there reading the latest issue of *Ebony*.

"You did good with this one, boy," Everette nodded approvingly, leering at me. "I don't blame you for snatching her up. Marry her now, get to know her later."

Harper laughed, like that was funny.

"Yep, nothing like a younger woman."

"I'm *really* looking forward to getting to know you better," Everette said to me, actually licking his lips. "We're gonna be real close, baby."

Disgusted, I again looked at Harper. No reaction to his father's blatantly inappropriate statement.

Well, I was done holding my tongue. If Harper wasn't going to defend me, then I would certainly defend myself. I put down my magazine and looked Everette right in the eye.

"With all due respect, Everette, it makes me very uncomfortable when you say things like that."

Harper's head whipped around, looking at me like I'd just cussed his dad out or something. "Ava!"

"What? It does." I looked back to Everette. "You tend to make these inappropriate comments and do a little too much flirting, and I'm just telling you, respectfully, that I don't like it."

"Oh my god!" Harper put his hands on his head, aghast. And he had the nerve to call *me* dramatic.

"Calm down, son," Everette ordered, his voice even. He looked at me. "I apologize if I've made you uncomfortable. That wasn't my intent."

Choosing to believe him, I nodded. "Thank you."

Everette drained the rest of his beer. "I'd better be going," he announced, slapping his thighs before standing up.

"What? You don't have to leave," Harper exclaimed. "Is it because of what Ava just said?"

He actually shot an accusatory glance my way. Like *I* was the one that ruined this visit. I hadn't wanted to be down there in the first place.

"She didn't say anything wrong. If she feels uncomfortable in her own house, she has every right to say so. I've got some running around to do before I go meet Paula."

I was surprised, and mildly appreciative, that Everette was defending me. He might have been creepy but he was still way more mature than his son was. Harper was still shooting daggers at me like I'd committed the ultimate betrayal.

Shoot, this was nothing compared to my *real* transgression. It made me wonder just how Harper would react if he were to ever find out about me and Mario. I had yet to see him really angry. It seemed to take a good bit to get him ticked off, because he didn't really like confrontation or discord. That didn't seem to be the case now, though, because he seemed pretty miffed at me.

"You have a good evening, Ava," Everette said, tipping his fedora.

"You too, Everette."

"I'll walk you to the door, Pops," Harper offered, plunking his bottle down and standing. He shot another frown at me as the two of them left the room.

Shaking my head, I started to go upstairs. But I stayed right where I was, because I was sure Harper would just follow me up there.

Sure enough, he stormed back into the living room once Everette was gone, eyes blazing.

"How could you disrespect my father like that?"

"I did nothing of the sort, Harper. I was completely respectful when I told him how I felt about those comments he made. If anything, *I'm* the one that should be upset that you don't seem to care about your dad flirting with your wife right in your face."

"I told you he doesn't mean anything by that. He flirts with everybody. Why couldn't you just let it go?"

"Why are you so upset? *He* didn't take any offense to it."

"I'm upset because you always want to stir up some mess. Things have been going good between us and now you want to go and start this."

I couldn't believe I was hearing this. "I didn't *start* anything; he did. And you're the one making it into a big thing."

"I think you just like drama," he muttered. "If it ain't one thing, it's something else."

I started to respond to that, but instead just held up a hand, taking a breath. He was being irrational, and I wasn't about to stick around and listen to any more of this. Without a word, I turned to head upstairs.

"We're not done, Ava!" Harper yelled. "Get back here!"

Stopping, I cocked my head to the side, *sure* this man didn't just holler at me like that. I had been trying to avoid a fight but now all bets were off.

"I don't know who the *hell* you think you're talking to," I began, turning and stalking back towards him. "But my daddy is in the ground. And I don't care how in your feelings you are right now, you will *not* yell at me like that. You're my husband, *not* my father."

"Well, then you need to *respect* me as your husband, then, and not walk away from me when we're talking about something!"

"We're not talking, we're arguing, *again*. And we're arguing because you have the damn balls to blame *me* for standing up for myself when I was being disrespected. I don't care if it's your dad or the president, I don't deserve that!"

"Look, you're tripping right now," Harper held up his hands, as if I was the one trying to keep this stupid argument going and not him. "You need to know that I'm very close to my dad and I don't take well to anybody disrespecting him. And when I tell you his flirting is no big deal and you make an issue out of it anyway, that ticks me off."

"You *ass*hole! Are you seriously standing here in my face and telling me that just because *you* don't consider your dad flirting and making creepy comments a big deal, I should just disregard how *I* feel about it? Are you telling me that you care more about your dad's feelings than mine? What if some player from the Falcons came and felt me up, would that be okay, too? Or is your dad the only one with a free pass on objectifying me?"

"He wasn't *objectifying* you-"

"*You* don't get to make that call, Harper!" I exclaimed, pointing a finger at him. "*You* don't get to tell me when I can and cannot feel disrespected. *You* don't get to tell me what to say and when to say it. *You* don't get to decide what bothers me and what doesn't. And *you* don't get to scold me when I stand up for myself! How *dare* you!"

I'm sure my face was flaming red, because I was practically screaming. I didn't like getting this angry, but Harper's disrespect right then was way worse than Everette's; he accepted what I said and apologized. He even defended me. Harper just wanted to play the blame game, and with *me*, not the person that actually deserved it.

"You need to calm down," Harper said, taking a step back. "Doing all this screaming and hollerin' and I'm just trying to talk to you."

Angry tears stung my eyes. I really couldn't believe him.

"How 'bout this," I began, clamping my hands together as I tried to compose myself. "Let's not talk *at all*. Because right now, you are the last person I want to be around, and I really can't stand the sight of you. So just leave me alone."

I stomped upstairs, part of me wanting to just leave the house altogether.

Thirteen – Mario

I WAS PUTTING IN SOME work on my blog, smiling to myself on how well it was doing.

When I started *Moves with Mario* about eight years earlier, it was really just something to do in my spare time. But when I decided to walk away from football, I started taking it more seriously. I knew I didn't want to go work for anyone else. After a while, I built my following up to the thousands, and now it was knocking on half a million. Yeah, being a former pro baller helped as far as recognition, but that only got folks in the door; good content kept them there. Between sponsorships and affiliate marketing, on my blog and my social media, I was doing just fine for myself. Not to mention I still had the bulk of my football money because I had the sense to live below my means, and I invested well.

Dad thought I was nuts for thinking I could make any money from just writing about the places I traveled to. We actually had an argument about it. Really, he hadn't been thrilled about it when I "gave up" on football; he thought I was wasting a God-given opportunity. I think he was just salty because he never even got close to going pro, and he was living his football dreams through me. He liked being able to say he had a son in the league, and I just messed all that up.

He actually tried to act like I had done *him* wrong, some kind of way.

Oh well. I didn't say anything when he married a woman he barely knew.

And speaking of unpleasant encounters, Mikki had come by that morning, cloaked in nothing but a trench coat and heels. I didn't think people really did that.

"What are you doing here, Mikki?" I had greeted her, not even trying to hide my frustration. "And what's up with all these unannounced visits? Your phone broke?"

"I wanted to surprise you." She stood there with a seductive smile, her hands on her hips.

"I'm working, Mikki."

"You can take a break, can't you?" Opening her coat, she proudly revealed her nakedness, giving me a little wiggle of her hips. "I've missed you."

"Booty calls usually happen at night."

"This isn't a booty call. This is me trying to get back in good with you."

"And coming over here naked is the only way you can think of to do that?"

"Mario," she replied, exasperated that I hadn't jumped her bones already. "Can I please come in?"

"I don't have time to argue with you."

"Believe me, arguing is the *last* thing I want to do with you."

Even though I knew better, I stepped aside to let her in. By the time I had turned around from closing the door, she had dropped the coat and was pressing herself against me like a sticker on a wall.

"Mmm, you have no idea how much I've missed you, baby," she whispered, kissing my lips. She wrapped her arms around my neck and stuck her tongue in my mouth, rubbing her bare thigh against my hip. "You ready to make up?"

"Mikki..."

"Shhh, don't talk," she briefly pressed a finger to my lips before moving my hands to her ass. "Let's just enjoy each other right now."

She started licking my neck, and I'd be lying if I said that didn't feel amazing. If I couldn't give Mikki props for anything else, her sexual skills were on point. It's just too bad that's *all* she was coming with.

Her lips slid back up to mine, and despite myself, I started kissing her back. My head was telling me this wouldn't be worth the trouble, but my body that hadn't had sex in several weeks wasn't caring about that.

I started slowly walking her backwards towards the couch, now as turned on as she was. My hands slid across her chocolate skin, palming both sides of her ass and squeezing. All my common sense had temporarily left the building.

She hastily lifted my t-shirt over my head, tossing it aside. Her hand was aggressively stroking me through my pants, and I bit my lip at how good it felt.

"Can I have this?" she whispered as she tongue-kissed my jawbone, giving me a little squeeze. Right then, I would've given her my car.

I just nodded, and she wasted no time reminding me of her below-the-belt skills. She yanked my sweatpants to my ankles and took me into her mouth with an eager moan, enjoying it as much as I was. And hell yeah, I was enjoying it. There wasn't any part of me that wanted to stop her right then, and I didn't try to come up with one. The sight of her squatting in nothing but stilettos while she sucked my dick had made hash of my good sense.

Before too long, we were sexing on the couch. Both naked, both into it, both not caring about my neighbors hearing our noise. And we were loud. When I got a mental flash of me and Ava in that very spot kissing, it only spurned me on even more. I started banging Mikki like a man possessed.

"Oh *yes*! *Shit!*" she screamed, loving my energy. "Yes, Mario! Don't stop! *Please* don't stop!"

I just grunted, holding her hips as I got her from behind, my sweat dripping onto her back. Closing my eyes, I started imagining she was Ava through no effort of my own. Picturing Ava and knowing she wasn't there, and that I most likely would never be with her like this, only frustrated me. And I took it out on Mikki, to her delight.

"Ooh, you-really-did-miss-me-huh?" she managed to ask, her words matching my thrusts. She didn't care that I didn't respond, because she was too busy screaming how good it felt. My neighbors must have been at work or something 'cause I was sure someone would have knocked on my door by then if they weren't.

Finally, we collapsed to the floor. She rested her head on my chest, her leg thrown across me, and raked her nails across my sweaty abs.

"That was amazing, baby," she gushed, smoothing her wild hair from her face. "You've never put it on me like *that* before."

I shrugged a shoulder, not sure what I was supposed to say to that. "Guess I was motivated."

"By the thought of us getting back together?"

This is the conversation that I knew I was going to have to face if I gave in to Mikki's advances, but I let my little head overtake my big one. I was just too horny to care at the time. But now, I was already regretting losing my head like that.

"Look, Mikki-"

"No, let me say this," she interrupted, putting a finger to my lips again. "I'm so sorry for how I tripped out the last time I came over here. I shouldn't have acted like that. You were right; I was the one who walked out with an attitude in the restaurant that day. You've always been straight up with me and I should have believed you when you said that woman was your stepmother, no matter how young she looks."

I sighed, rubbing my eyes. "Yeah, she does look young. She's younger than I am, actually. But I wasn't lying about who she is."

"I know. My girls think I'm being a fool for believing you, but I know you have no reason to lie. Like you said, we aren't together, and you can do what you want. But I hope what we just did means that you've changed your mind about just wanting *me*. 'Cause I still just want you."

Aw, hell. This is what happens when I lose my damn mind.

I had to be honest with her. I hadn't changed my mind about anything and she needed to know that.

Already feeling like shit, I sat up on my elbows and tried to think of the best way to say what needed to be said.

"Mikki...this is gonna make me look really foul but I have to be straight up. I actually haven't changed my mind about us. I like you, but I still don't think we're that compatible.

The only thing we really have in common is what we just did. A real relationship can't be *just* about sex."

Her eyes widening slightly, she sat up. I couldn't tell if she was gonna cry or cuss me out.

"So you've just been wasting my time these past few months?" she finally asked.

"Nobody's been trying to waste your time, Mikki. Don't try to act like this was ever anything deep. I bet you couldn't name ten real things about me, other than whatever you might see online. I know I couldn't do that about you, because we don't talk. Whenever I tried, you always steered it back to this, so I figured you just wanted to keep it casual."

"Even if I did in the beginning, I've changed my mind."

"Well, I haven't. And I can't force myself to feel something just because you've decided that you feel it."

"Wow, Mario." She shook her head and tried to cover her breasts with her arm. Fine time to try to be modest. "I have to admit, I kinda feel used right now."

I sucked my teeth. "Don't try that. You're the one who came over here naked and unexpected. I admit I had a weak moment, but you could have just as easily come over here fully clothed and with the intent to talk about us, if that's what you really wanted to do. But you made the mistake of trying to use sex as a ticket to what you want, and that might work with some dudes but it doesn't work with me."

She glared at me. "You calling me a hoe?"

"Is that what I said? I didn't call you anything; I'm just saying what happened."

"If you knew you didn't want me like that, you shouldn't have sexed me like you just did."

Sighing, I shook my head. "Fine, Mikki. Make me out to be the bad guy if you want. Hopefully one day you'll see what I'm talking about. But don't bring a hungry man a meal then gets mad when he eats it."

Her chest heaving in anger, Mikki hopped up off the floor and yanked her trench coat back on.

"You won't have to worry about me bringing any more *meals* over here," she declared, stuffing her feet back into her black shiny heels. "I get the message, loud and clear. Just don't come running back when you realize what you threw away."

"I'll try to control myself."

Frowning at my obvious sarcasm, she stormed out, slamming the door behind her.

And that was that. I made a mental note to have her taken off the approved guest list downstairs in case she changed her mind and decided to try to make another random visit.

Knowing that I was done with Mikki was a relief. We weren't going anywhere. But I had to admit, getting with her would have been a lot easier than pining for a woman I couldn't have.

LATER ON THAT EVENING, after I ran a few errands, I met up with Jayden to watch the fight. Of course he laughed at me when I told him about what went down with Mikki that morning. He never saw us lasting that long, anyway. But the conversation took a different turn when I decided to finally tell him who I really wanted.

"*What?*" He almost spit out his drink. "What did you just say??"

"I said that I have feelings for Ava."

"Ava as in your *stepmother*, Ava?"

"Yes, man."

"Since when??"

"If I'm honest, since I met her. Since that first time I laid eyes on her, I haven't been able to get her out of my head."

"I know you said she was younger, but I thought you meant like in her forties or something."

"Nah. She's a couple years younger than me."

"Damn. I didn't know your dad liked 'em *that* young. So I guess she's fine as hell, then, huh?"

"It's not even about her looks, though. I mean, yeah, she's hot, but so was Mikki. There's more to it than that. Ava and I just...connected. And I can't say that about any other woman."

"So is that why you got so pissed off about them getting married?"

"I was genuinely curious about her intentions, but I can admit that most of it was fueled by my attraction to her. I guess I just wanted something to be mad at her about. It's a lot easier to be petty than deal with wanting someone I'm not supposed to."

"Wow." Jayden looked at me in wonderment. "You seriously like her like *that*?"

"Seriously."

"Does she know?"

"I mean, I haven't said anything to her about it. But..." I debated if I wanted to tell him about kissing Ava or not.

He eyed me expectantly. "But what?" His eyebrows shot up. "Did you make a move on her?"

"It was more like we just...came together. Both times we kissed-"

"*Both* times??"

"Okay, we kissed a couple of times. But neither time was planned on my part, and I'm willing to bet it wasn't on hers, either. It just *happened*. We both wanted it. It was like some cosmic force drawing us together."

"A cosmic force? Really?"

"I know it sounds corny but I'm serious. And I could be wrong, but I think she's feeling me, too."

"Okay, so say she is. Y'all can't do nothing about it; she's married. To your *pops*."

"I'm aware of that. It's not like I *want* to want her. But I can't help it."

"Do you think Mr. Downing has any idea about y'all?"

"No. Dad can be kind of oblivious about stuff. In fact, he's been suggesting me and Ava spend time together, saying he wants us to be close."

"Well. He got his wish."

"You're hilarious."

"Well he did, didn't he?"

"I'm not proud of any of this. Regardless of how I feel about Ava, I know I'm in the wrong for ever touching her. But at the same time, I'm hoping I get to do it again. I just lose my head when I'm around her, and not in the bad way like I did this morning with Mikki. It's like nothing else matters but Ava when I'm around her."

"Bruh..." Jayden shook his head. "You sound like you're in love with her."

Maybe I was. But I wasn't ready to admit it. "I don't know."

"And I guess just staying away from her isn't an option?"

"I don't see how. Dad will just get suspicious if I start acting like I don't want to be around her. That'll open up a whole other can of worms 'cause he'll start asking a bunch of questions."

"So what are you gonna do, then? Why don't you and Ava talk about it?"

"I don't know if talking to Ava about it would do any good. It's not like I'm gonna ask her to leave Dad for me. But I *have* been thinking about talking to Dad about it."

"What? You're gonna tell your dad that you have the hots for his wife? And that you've kissed her?"

"I didn't say I'd tell him every little thing. Just the part about my having feelings for her."

"And how do you think he'd respond to that?"

"I think he'd appreciate my honesty. And the fact that I was coming to him man-to-man."

"You've kissed her already, Mario."

"He doesn't need to know that."

He shook his head again. "I don't know, man. I just can't see any man being *that* understanding. You know *you* wouldn't be, if the roles were reversed."

"True, but Dad isn't like me. We don't have much in common at all."

"You must take after your mom, then."

"I guess. That's what I always figured. I can't even say I really remember her since she died when I was so young. But I must take after her 'cause Dad and I are like night and day."

"Still, I don't know about telling him how you feel about Ava. I just don't see what good it would do. Unless you're hoping he'll step aside and let you have her."

"That would be ridiculous, to hope that. I just want to be straight up."

"If you wanted that, you would have said something to him *before* you slobbed his wife down."

"Whatever." I waved him off as I sipped my beer, even though he had a point.

My cell phone buzzed on the table, and my chest tightened when I saw it was Ava.

"Speak of the devil," Jayden quipped when he saw her name.

Rolling my eyes at him, I answered the call. "Hello?"

"Hey, Mario. You busy?"

"Not really. Just with my boy watching the fight. What's up?"

"I wanted to see if you could come to dinner at the house this weekend."

"I'm sure I can. What's the occasion?"

"Actually, there's someone I want you to meet."

I paused, my eyes widening slightly. Jayden stopped his motion of reaching for more nachos, noticing the apparent shock on my face. He looked at me expectantly, mouthing "What?" as if I could answer him right then.

Clearing my throat, I tried to check myself. "Oh really? Who?"

"Her name is Vera. She's one of my best friends; known her since we were kids. She's a sweetheart. I think you two would hit it off."

"You do, huh?" I croaked. Jayden arched a curious brow at me.

"You okay?" Ava asked. "You sound different."

"I'm cool. But um, yeah, I'll be there. What day this weekend?"

"Sunday. Seven o'clock."

"See you then. Bye, Ava." I hung up without waiting for her to say anything else. My head was swimming a little bit.

"What's wrong?" Jayden pestered. "You're frowning."

I hadn't even realized that, but I didn't try to fix it. "Ava wants to set me up with one of her girls."

"Whoa," Jayden whistled. "This just gets more and more interesting. I thought she was feeling you like you're feeling her?"

Shrugging, I pushed my cell phone around with my fingers. "Guess I was wrong."

"Don't even sweat that, man. Maybe her girl will make you forget all about Ava. This might be just what y'all need. Try to think of it as a good thing."

That wasn't happening.

I felt sick to my stomach. Had I been wrong about the vibe I thought Ava and I shared? How could she just pass me off to one of her friends if she really had feelings for me like I thought she did? But maybe I misread her. So we kissed a couple of times. Just because it was amazing for me doesn't necessarily mean it was the same for her. Maybe she wanted me to date her friend to get me out of her hair.

Well, fine. If that's what she wanted, that's what she was gonna get. By the time Sunday rolled around, I'd have my head together and ready to meet this friend of hers. And in the meantime, I'd just have to do my best to get over Ava.

'Cause I wasn't trying to make a fool out of myself.

Fourteen – Mario

SUNDAY EVENING, I HEADED over to Ava and Dad's with a clear head. After agonizing over the reason behind this invitation for days, I decided that Jayden was right. This was a good thing. Continuing to pine for a woman I couldn't have would only drive me crazy. Meeting someone new was just what I needed to start to move past these feelings. And since she was such good friends with Ava, no doubt she'd be a good woman.

Armed with a bottle of wine, I knocked on the door, prepared for anything.

"Babe, could you get that?" I heard Dad yell.

A few moments later, the door eased open and there she was. Damn her for looking so good.

"Hey, Mario," Ava greeted me, smiling.

I nodded. "What's up, Ava."

"Come on in."

I stepped inside, noticing the delicious aromas in the air. Ava must have cooked, because Dad's culinary skills pretty much ended at thaw, heat, and serve.

Handing her the bottle in my hand, I removed my leather jacket. "You like white wine, right?"

"I love it. This is so sweet of you, Mario, thanks."

"Least I could do."

She eyed me. "You look so..." Biting her lip, she seemed to lose her train of thought momentarily before catching herself. Blushing, she cleared her throat. "You look great."

"That's nice of you to say." I didn't want to return the compliment, even though it definitely applied.

"You want me to take your coat?"

"Nah, I got it."

"You know, Vera likes white wine, too," she hedged. "Let me go ahead and introduce you; she's in the kitchen."

Shrugging, I kept my face even. "Cool."

She grabbed my wrist. "What do you think about peach cobbler? You like peach cobbler?"

"It's all right. Apple is my favorite, though, if I'm gonna eat it."

"Well, Vera's might just make you change your mind. You're gonna love *her* peach cobbler. That woman can bake her ass off."

She certainly wasn't wasting any time hyping her girl up. If I didn't know better, Ava looked a little nervous. Anxious, even. I didn't know if it was because she was afraid I wouldn't like Vera, or if she was afraid I would.

Leading me into the kitchen, she went straight over to a woman who was folding some napkins at the counter. As soon as she heard us, Vera whipped around, a huge smile on her face.

"Vera," Ava grinned, "This is Mario."

"Hey Mario!" Vera greeted me, way more excited than necessary. She stepped forward and eagerly took my hand, shaking the hell out of it. "It's so nice to meet you!"

"You, too. Ava tells me you make some bomb peach cobbler."

"Would you like some now? I can fix you a bowl of it."

"Oh uh, that's all right. I can wait."

"I'll make sure you get some first, okay?'"

My hopes for hitting it off with Vera were already starting to deflate, but I told myself to chill out. We just met; maybe she was only acting so eager because she was nervous. That was understandable.

"I'm gonna go see if Harper is ready to eat," Ava announced. "You two stay here and get acquainted."

She scurried out of the kitchen, and I turned to Vera with a tight smile. She was already eying me with a semi-creepy grin on her face.

"So," she began, "You're Harper's son, huh?"

Wow. "Yep. Ava said you two have been friends since you were kids?"

"Yeah, eighth grade. She helped me when someone knocked me over and spilled all my stuff out of my bag. It was super embarrassing and I was crying my eyes out, but she made me feel better. Helped me get cleaned up, made me laugh; even shared her Skittles with me. We've been best friends ever since. She's something else."

I told myself not to let that story make me any more enamored with Ava. It was hard, though.

"Yeah, it sure sounds like it."

"So do you wanna have kids someday?"

How the hell did we jump to *that*? "Yeah, someday."

"Do you mind me asking how old you are?"

"I'm thirty-six."

"Nice. I can't believe someone as handsome as you has never been married or has any children by now. Y'all are almost a rare breed."

"I guess. Those are things I wanted to hold off on until I was ready for them, that's all."

"That's great. Me, too!" Vera exclaimed. "Do you think you're ready now? I know I am. We're around the same age; not getting any younger, you know."

I regretted agreeing to this. Ava didn't say anything about her friend being on some husband-snagging mission.

As politely as I could, I endured the rest of this interview (because that's exactly what it felt like) until we were thankfully interrupted.

"Everette!" I exclaimed, way more excited to see him than I normally would've been. My granddad and I got along fine (and for whatever reason, he always insisted I call him by his first name), but I would've been happy to see anybody right then if it got me out of this mind-numbing conversation.

"Hey, boy," Everette greeted me as he always did. We shared a brief hug before he turned to Vera. "Who do we have here?"

"This is Vera, a friend of Ava's. Vera, this is my grandfather, Everette."

"It's nice to meet you," Vera quickly greeted, offering her hand.

"The pleasure is all mine, pretty lady." Everette lifted his fedora with one hand and brought her hand to his lips with the other, kissing it as he eyed her. She grinned.

Taking this opportunity to excuse myself, I hurried out of the room, leaving the two of them alone. I was already ready to go, and seriously thought about making up an excuse to do just that. Vera seemed like a nice woman, and she was pretty, but she was a little too eager for me. I could smell her desperation about as strong as I could smell the meat loaf in the oven. And she was a little too thin for my taste, anyway.

I wandered out to the living room, watching YouTube videos on my phone, frowning and rubbing my chin like I usually did when I was concentrating on something. I'd been thinking about starting a channel of my own so I was getting a feel for how other travel vloggers did theirs.

Suddenly I paused, frowning. It sounded like Ava and Dad were arguing. It was faint, since they were upstairs, but I definitely heard it.

"Why didn't you tell me you invited him?" Ava hissed.

"Why should I?"

"Because I made dinner for four, not five. A heads-up would've been nice."

"It's my dad, babe. I didn't think I needed to run it by you."

"Of course you didn't. You and I are finally on speaking terms again, Harper; this is the kind of stuff that makes me wanna go back to the silent treatment."

"Okay, I'm sorry; I should've told you he was coming. But you don't have to worry about having enough food; he's probably not gonna eat much of anything, anyway."

"Well, he can have some of yours, if he does. And if what happened last time he was here happens again, I'm checking him, Harper, and I don't care if you don't like it. I'm just letting you know now."

What happened last time?

"Can you stop thinking the worst and let's just have a nice evening?" Dad pleaded. "He already apologized for that, remember?"

"Uh-huh."

My curiosity was immediately on ten. What did Everette do to piss Ava off so much?

I acted like I hadn't heard anything when they both came down the stairs a few moments later. Dad and I greeted each other with a fist bump, and made small talk while Ava checked on things in the kitchen. I wanted to ask what Ava was upset about, but I couldn't do that without admitting I'd been eavesdropping.

Thankfully, the dinner kicked off not too long after that. Of course, Ava suggested I sit next to Vera, who scooted her chair unnecessarily close to mine and shot me this lovesick smile.

"You want me to fix your plate, Mario?"

"I can do it. Thanks, though."

"You sure? I don't mind."

"Yep. Totally sure."

"Y'all got any more of this meatloaf? Looks like I just got a sample size," Everette joked, holding up his nearly empty plate.

"You can have mine, Pops," Dad quickly spoke up, nervously glancing at Ava as she shot him a look. "I'm saving room for dessert, anyway."

"Oh yeah, that peach cobbler in there," Everette commented, handing his plate to Dad. "It sure did smell good."

Vera beamed. "I hope everyone likes it. And I made two pans, so there should be plenty if you want seconds." She glanced at me.

"Or thirds," Dad joked, though that was a possibility with him. "Nothing like homemade cobbler."

"You always did have a sweet tooth. Do you bake?" Everette asked Ava.

"I'm decent at it. Not nearly as good as Vera, though."

"Thanks, girl," Vera smiled, throwing another anxious glance my way.

I gave her another tight smile, silently reminding myself to tell Ava not to bother ever trying to set me up again after this.

The dinner continued, with everyone talking about what was going on in their respective lives. When it got around to me, I told them about my latest trip to New Orleans, of course leaving out my encounter with Celine before I left.

"New Orleans sounds like such a fun city. I've never been," Vera commented. She gave me another one of those looks. "I'd love to go one day. You know, with someone that's been there and knows their way around."

"You should. Maybe y'all can go on a girls trip or something," I replied, dodging her obvious request for an invitation. "I know I won't be making it back there for a while, myself."

"Speaking of trips," Ava excitedly perked up, wiping her mouth with a napkin, "Harper and I are going out of town tomorrow. Finally having that honeymoon."

I wondered if anyone else noticed how uncomfortable Dad automatically looked.

"Where y'all going?" Everette asked.

"Tennessee. Our flight leaves at two o'clock."

"Flight?" Everette looked at Dad, shocked. "You gettin' on a plane?"

Dad hesitated, then nodded, determined. "Yep. It's really important to Ava so I want to do this for her. For *us*." He took Ava's hand, and she smiled at him appreciatively. "And it's just to Tennessee so we won't be up in the air but a minute."

"Wow, good for you, Dad," I commended him, meaning it. I knew how planes freaked him out. "I'm glad y'all are finally getting away together."

Dad smiled while Ava gazed at me, then caught herself, looking at her plate guiltily. Dad didn't even notice. "Me, too."

A little later, we moved on to dessert. Vera sprang from her seat to go help Ava dish it up in the kitchen (and I'm sure some girl talk was shared, also), and Vera came back with a heaping bowl of warm peach cobbler for me. It was enough for two people.

"Wow, trying to fatten me up, huh?" I joked, knowing I couldn't eat all that. I enjoyed dessert but not *that* much.

"Just want to make sure you're satisfied," she replied, momentarily touching my arm. A pleased look crossed her face when she felt my bicep. Subtlety wasn't her strong suit at all. "There's ice cream in there, if you want some."

"Oh no, I'm good with this, thanks."

"I'll take some ice cream," Everette spoke up.

"Me, too!" Dad was already digging into his dessert. "Vera, this is some of the best cobbler I've had *anywhere*!"

Grinning proudly, Vera stuck her chest out a little bit. "Thank you, Harper! There's plenty more. I'll go get your ice cream."

"Girl, you don't have to do that. I'll get it," Ava offered, starting to get up.

"No, no; stay there. I got it."

We all sat around stuffing our faces and talking for a while longer before people finally started getting up. Ava sent everyone to the living room, saying she'd clear all the dishes herself. Dad didn't need to be told twice. Vera trailed behind him, still riding high from all of his praise about her cobbler. Everette stepped outside to smoke a cigarette, and I went to the restroom, taking my time.

This evening was as good as over for me. I had no interest in Vera, which was the whole point of my being there. And despite myself, I was still too attracted to Ava. I'd done a good job of keeping my attention elsewhere and not focusing on her too much, but I wasn't foolish enough to think I was over her. Any time her and Dad showed any kind of affection towards each other, even if it was just holding hands, a pang hit my chest. And while I was glad about Dad facing his fear of flying to please Ava, the thought of the two of them on their honeymoon, *doing what honeymooners do*, didn't sit well with me. Straight up, I didn't want her to go. But I knew that was a selfish thought I'd have to keep to myself.

Before I totally bummed myself out, I decided to go ahead and get out of there. Since the kitchen was closer, I was just gonna poke my head in and let Ava know I was leaving, but stopped when I heard she wasn't in there alone. Not able to resist, I stopped and peeked around the arched doorframe, surprised to see Everette was standing rather close to her. Both of their backs were to me.

"What do you need, Everette?" Ava asked, inching away from him. "I told you I don't need any help cleaning up."

"Just wanted to keep you company," Everette replied, closing the brief gap between them. "It's not right for you to be in here doing all this by yourself."

"I don't mind." Ava stepped away again.

"*I* do." He eyed her hungrily. "I've been wanting to tell you how good you look tonight."

What the hell? Was he flirting with her??

Ava looked at him, her expression anything but flattered. "Please go back into the other room, Everette. Or leave."

"Why, baby? I just paid you an innocent little compliment."

"Because I asked you to, that's why. I'm not comfortable being in here with you alone."

I felt my fists balling up all on their own.

"You don't have to be afraid of me, baby," Everette persisted, a look in his eyes I'd never seen. He licked his lips, and my ire flared like a water-doused grease fire. "I'm not gonna hurt ya."

"We've already had this discussion and you said you respected it. Or were you just fronting because Harper was there?"

"He's not gonna mind us getting *closer*." He advanced on Ava, who had moved to the other side of the kitchen. "You saw how mad at you he got when you fussed about my flirting before. He'll believe whatever I tell him."

I seriously wondered if I was dreaming. I'd never seen my granddad in this light before, and in that moment, I hated him.

"You need to back up, Everette!" Ava exclaimed strongly, holding her hand up. "I'm not playing!"

"Better lower your voice. Wouldn't want Harper to hear us in here, would you?"

"I don't give a damn! Father-in-law or not, I *will* knock you out with something if you're not outta my face in the next two seconds!"

Clearly not taking her seriously, Everette chuckled. When he suddenly reached out and snatched her closer to him by the waist, drawing a frightened shriek from her, that was it. I charged into the room ready to beat some ass.

"Hey, back up, man!" I ordered, grabbing his shoulder and pushing him away from Ava, stepping between them. I felt her grip the back of my shirt. "You're not gonna put your hands on her while *I'm* here!"

Everette looked shocked, apparently forgetting that other people were in the house. "Look, boy, I don't know what you think you saw, but-"

"Don't even try that. I ain't Dad. Plus, I heard her tell you to back up off her. That smooth talk won't work on me."

"So you just gonna talk to me any kinda way, huh? I'm still your granddaddy, boy, even if..."

I frowned. "Even if what?"

He glared at me for a moment before shaking his head. "Nothing. Forget it."

"Look, I don't know what's up with you and right now, I don't care. But you need to roll. *Now*."

We stood there, angrily staring each other down. I was just itching for him to make a move. I loved my granddad, but I was more than willing to fight him right then. I didn't take well to a man disrespecting *any* woman, but seeing it happen to Ava set off a whole new level of rage within me.

Finally, he stepped back, holding his hands up. Dammit.

"I'll go," he acquiesced. He looked at Ava, who was still holding onto my shirt from behind. "I apologize."

"Bullshit. You've already proven your words don't mean anything." She stepped around me, her voice strong. Looked him right in the eyes. "So just get out."

Pursing his lips, Everette looked at the both of us before leaving the room, tipping that tired fedora like he always does.

As soon as he was out of the room, I turned to Ava, putting my hands on her shoulders. "You all right?"

She released a shaky breath and clutched my arms, the weight of the situation apparently hitting her. Looking up at me gratefully, she shook her head. "Not really. I can't believe he came at me like that. He's flirted before but never tried to put his hands on me."

"Well, when I came out of the bathroom and heard you two in here, I knew something didn't seem right. So I just hung around the corner, just in case."

"Thank God you did. I really appreciate it, Mario, because who knows how all of that would have turned out. I would've tried to knock the hell out of him, but I'm not foolish enough to think I can easily overpower a grown man."

"Thankfully it didn't come to that."

"*This* time. What about next time? What if he comes by here when I'm by myself? There won't be anybody to stop him then. And you heard him, what he said about Harper; he wasn't wrong. Harper *would* believe whatever Everette told him; he'd probably think I was lying just because I don't like his dad." Her breaths started coming quicker and tears welled in her eyes. Her hands flew around in the air in front of her. "What if Everette forces himself on me next time? What if I can't fight him off? What if-"

"Ava, shhh...calm down, sweetheart." I pulled her close to me, because I could see she was losing it. She held onto me tightly, and I could tell she was really afraid of what she was saying actually happening. It only made me want to do anything I could to protect her. If it was up to me, I'd have her pack a bag right then and get in my car so I could take her away from there. "Whatever I can do to keep that from happening, I will. Nothing is going to happen to you as long as I can help it, Ava." I smoothed her hair as she buried her face in my chest. Hearing her cry and feeling how she clung to me made me want to rip Everette's limbs off.

She sniffled, then looked up at me. "You really mean that, don't you?"

I admit, I got lost in those brown eyes of hers for a minute. Emotion flooded me and I gripped her a little tighter. "More than I've ever meant anything."

We stood there looking at each other, and I wondered if she wanted to kiss me as much as I wanted to kiss her. If anyone were to walk in at that moment, it would've been hard to explain how close we were standing, wrapped in each other's arms and sharing a gaze that was clearly not a platonic one.

I cleared my throat and made myself step back before I lost my head. We were in my Dad's house, with him in it.

"Let me go find Dad and tell him what's going on," I finally offered, reluctantly dropping my arms.

Ava sucked her teeth. "Don't bother. He's not gonna believe me, anyway."

"I was right here, Ava; I heard everything that went down with you and Everette. He can't lie his way out of it."

"You would think that I wouldn't need a witness. Hell, even if Harper *did* believe it happened, he'd just brush it off, making excuses for Everette and somehow twisting it into being *my* fault. It's sad that my own husband won't take my side on something like this." She shook her head, looking off to the side. "Damn, what kind of family did I marry into?"

"No, Ava," I quickly refuted. I didn't want her thinking I was like them. "Please don't think like that. We're not perfect at all, but I hope you don't start lumping us all together."

A few thoughtful moments passed before she finally looked back up at me. "I know you're different, Mario," she assured softly. "You're amazingly different."

I actually felt relieved. "I'm glad you think so."

"You're actually not like Harper at all," she continued. "Y'all don't look or act alike. Come to think of it, I could say the same about Harper and Everette. The women in your family must have some strong genes."

"I suppose. I never knew my grandmother and you might as well say I never really knew my mama, either, since she died when I was so young. Can't even say I've seen any pictures; Dad said they were all destroyed some kind of way."

"What? That's crazy."

"Very. It's always just been us three dudes. Look, you want me to go get Vera?"

"No, that's okay. I'm just gonna hang in here and get myself together. And speaking of Vera, I take it you aren't that interested?"

"To put it nicely."

She threw her hands up and shrugged. "Well, I tried."

Was that a smile tugging at the corner of her mouth?

"She's nice but she's just...not for me."

"I respect that. I know she can try a little too hard at times. Hopefully one day she'll meet the right man."

"I'm sure she will. Are you sure you're okay?"

"I will be. I just need to be alone for a little bit."

"All right." I held out a chair at the kitchen table, then got her a beer from the refrigerator. She smiled at me gratefully.

"Thank you so much, Mario," she smiled. "I can't tell you how much I appreciate you being here for me."

"My pleasure." Resisting the urge to lean down and kiss her forehead, I just gave her a nod and left the room. My head was spinning a little bit. This had been one crazy evening.

Despite Ava's claims that she was fine, I knew she was still a little shaken up so I figured I'd go find Vera or Dad and have them keep an eye on her, without saying anything about what went down with Everette. I was still tripping over seeing him step to Ava like he did. Everette had always considered himself something of a ladies' man, but I didn't think he'd ever try to force himself on anyone.

After making sure Everette had actually left, I went looking for Vera. I figured Ava would want to see her more than she'd want to see Dad right then. Since no one was in the living room, I did a quick scan of the rest of the downstairs but didn't find her or Dad. Frowning curiously, I headed upstairs. I couldn't imagine Vera would have left without a word to Ava. But why would she be upstairs?

I wasn't five steps down the hall when I heard Dad's voice coming from the guest bedroom. Maybe he had gone in there to take a call or something. The door was ajar, and I started to knock on it when I heard Vera in there with him. Stopping, my suspicion antennae shot up and I couldn't help but peek in. I guess this was just my day for being nosey.

"You've been so sweet to me tonight, Harper," Vera commented, standing a little too close to him. She looked up at him with a look I recognized instantly. "I appreciate it."

"Oh, well, I really didn't do anything special," Dad shrugged, his hands in his pockets. Her closeness clearly didn't bother him. "You asked for a tour of the house, so I gave you one."

"Yeah, but you probably would rather be with your guests."

"My dad and my son aren't guests. I'm sure Ava is keeping them entertained."

"So..." Vera eased even closer, "You don't mind being up here with me?"

"Nah. Why would I?"

Damn, Dad was clueless sometimes.

Vera smiled and placed a hand on his arm. "I'm glad to hear that, Harper."

"Good."

They stood there for a couple of moments, her hand lingering while she looked at him flirtatiously. The same way she was looking at me just a couple of hours before. I guess she just latched on to any man that was nice to her.

"I'm glad I came tonight," she stated, her hand slowly traveling up his arm. Dad didn't bat an eye. "We haven't really gotten acquainted before now."

"Yeah, I know. Glad you were able to come. You're good people."

"You really think so?" She stepped closer. Her breasts were practically pressed against him. Biting her lip, she boldly placed a hand on his chest.

Seeming to finally wake up to what was going on, Dad cleared his throat and took a small step back. I noticed he didn't remove her hands from him, though. "We should probably head back downstairs."

"Why?" Vera pulled his hand from his pocket and grasped it in hers. "Like you said, Ava is keeping Mario and Everette entertained. And this isn't so bad, is it?"

Dad looked at her and seemed to become transfixed or something. "No. It's not bad at all.'

That was apparently the go-ahead Vera needed. She slid her arms around his neck and kissed him. And I don't mean a peck, either. The tongue came quick and it came aggressive. I just stood there with my jaw on the floor, appalled at this woman's gall. This was supposed to be Ava's best friend?

What blew my mind even more, though, was that Dad seemed to have no problem kissing her back. He was holding her around the waist, moaning and enjoying it right along with her as they started inching towards the bed.

When I saw Dad end up on top of Vera and her legs immediately clamp around his waist, I turned away. I didn't need to see any more. Part of me wanted to go get Ava while the other part wanted to make sure she never knew anything about this.

I'd had more than enough drama for one evening. Deciding to just get the hell out of there, I tiptoed towards the stairs right as I heard the door to the guest bedroom close.

And lock.

Fifteen – Ava

I NEVER SAID ANYTHING to Harper about Everette coming on to me. Partly because I wanted to just forget about it but mostly, I didn't think he'd believe me, anyway. And even if he did, he'd just make excuses for him. I had to make myself put that out of my mind or else I'd never get on that plane with him to Tennessee.

Thank God for Mario. If he hadn't come in when he had, there's no telling what Everette would have done. At least I had one witness who was on my side. Being in his arms made me feel so safe, and the way he stood up for me to Everette, his own grandfather...it did something to me. I felt closer to him, and I didn't mind it. There's nothing like someone unconditionally having your back like that.

By the time I had gotten myself together, Mario had left, Harper was in the shower and Vera was rushing out, saying there was something she had suddenly forgotten about that she had to take care of. She was acting rather strangely, but I just figured I'd find out what was going on with her later. I guessed she wanted to get out of there since Mario was gone; she probably sensed he wasn't that into her. I'd go over there and cheer her up when Harper and I got back; might even take her a bottle of wine for letting her get her hopes up.

Thankfully, I felt a lot better by the time I woke up the next morning. I was looking forward to this trip with Harper. So much had been going on lately that I felt we needed this time away together. We could just focus on us, with no distractions.

And it would be good to put a little distance between me and Mario for a while.

It was barely seven o'clock in the morning when I sprang out of bed, excited like a kid on Christmas. Harper's side of the bed was empty. After going to the bathroom and washing my face, I headed downstairs, where I found Harper in the kitchen standing at the counter eating a huge bowl of cereal. Him and those Cheerios.

"Good morning!" I greeted cheerfully. I went over to give him a hug, but since he made no move to stop eating, it ended up just being around his waist. "You're up early."

"Mornin'. Yeah, I have some stuff I need to do."

I paused in opening the refrigerator. "Like what?"

"Just some errands I gotta run, that's all." He kept his eyes on his bowl.

"How long is that gonna take? I want to be at the airport no later than noon."

"Don't worry about it, babe. I'll be done in plenty of time."

"Good." I pulled out the chocolate milk. "I am so glad we're going on this trip. I'm so excited!"

"Yeah, me too."

He sounded anything but excited, but I figured he was still a little nervous about flying.

"Did you finish packing?"

"Almost."

"You might ought to do that before you head out on your errands, just in case. I'm gonna go ahead and put my suitcase in your truck before you leave so it'll already be in there when you come back to get me."

"Actually, babe, I'm gonna need to meet you at the airport. It'll just be easier since a lot of the stuff I need to do is over that way, anyway. Won't make much sense to come back over here."

I stopped sprinkling salt into my chocolate milk. "Wow, so we're not even riding together?"

"It's just to the airport, babe. We'll still be getting on the plane together. Just take an Uber so you won't have to worry about parking."

Telling myself to let it go, I forced a smile. "Okay. You're right, the actual trip is the most important thing. I wanted us to leave here together and all that but if you have stuff to do, it is what it is."

"That's my girl." He placed his empty bowl in the sink and came over to kiss my cheek. I grabbed his shirt as he started to turn away and slid my hands around his waist, smiling up at him.

"Wanna meet me upstairs?" I asked flirtatiously. I slid a hand between us, massaging him through his jeans.

He bit his lip, then stepped back, looking away. "I can't, babe. I need to get out of here if I'm gonna make it to the airport on time."

I peered at him curiously. He seemed different all of a sudden. "What's wrong?"

"Nothing," he replied quickly. "Um, I'm gonna go throw the rest of my stuff in my suitcase real quick then head out. I'll see you this afternoon."

"Okay."

He was already halfway out of the room. This flight really did have him on edge. I couldn't help but smile at the effort he was making for me, though.

I went on about my day, making sure I had everything together for the trip. On an impulse, I made a quick run to the mall to get a sexy negligee and a couple of cute bra and panty sets to wear for Harper, already picturing the look on his face when he saw them. I couldn't *wait* to get to Tennessee!

The day seemed to drag. I was grateful when Trish called, wanting the rundown on the previous night's dinner.

"Go ahead and tell me how everything bombed last night," she joked.

"Nothing bombed, girl, hush," I laughed. "But I can't say that Mario and Vera hit it off like I hoped they would."

"Quit lying. You didn't hope they would."

"Whatever. He wasn't interested."

"Did he say why?"

"He said she wasn't for him. He probably thought she was trying a little too hard."

"Oh lord," Trish sighed. "I'm not even surprised. What did her eager ass do, offer to run him a bath or something?"

"They were alone in the kitchen for a while so I didn't hear their conversation, but I know at the dinner table she kept offering to fix his plate. She *did* come across a little thirsty."

"That's our girl. Have you talked to her today? I bet she's probably bummed."

"I tried to call her a little while ago but she didn't answer. She rushed out of here last night before we got a chance to talk. I was too upset about what happened with Everette at the moment, anyway."

"What are you talking about? What happened with Everette? That's Harper's dad, right?"

"Yeah. Basically, he pushed up on me in the kitchen, and said Harper wouldn't believe me if I told him about it."

Trish gasped loudly. "*Girl, you lyin*!!"

"I wish I was. But I swear on my parents' graves."

"What did he do??"

"Said a bunch of inappropriate stuff and refused to leave when I asked him to, following me around the kitchen. When he grabbed my waist, though, I thought I was going to lose it. Thank God Mario came in."

"Mario?"

"Yeah, apparently he had heard us in there and was listening to the entire thing. When Everette started to take it too far, Mario charged in and got in his face, telling him to step off. I've never been so glad to see someone in my life."

"Girl..."

"Yeah, girl."

"So Mario came to your rescue? That's hella romantic."

"I don't know about it being romantic. It was certainly chivalrous."

"I doubt chivalry was his motivation, if he's feeling you like you're feeling him. Is he?"

I hesitated. Trish still didn't know about the intimate moments Mario and I had shared. I wanted to think she would understand, but she was a happily married woman, herself; maybe she wouldn't respect the loss of control I seemed to have around Mario. She might think I was supposed to resist, no matter what. It's not like she'd be wrong. But everything isn't as black and white as that, as I was learning.

"I don't know," I finally answered her.

"Are you sure?"

"I can't speak for someone else's feelings, Trish."

"Girl, please. You can tell if someone is feeling you like that. The way he looks at you, the things he shares with you, the things he does for you. I think threatening to knock his own granddaddy's head off to defend your honor qualifies as an act of love. And I don't mean the familial kind."

Before I lost my nerve, I decided to go ahead and let her know the real deal. If I was going to confide in anyone about this, it would be Trish.

"Mario and I have kissed," I blurted out. "A couple of times."

"*What??*" I had to hold the phone away from my ear because she was so loud. "When was this?? And why are you just now telling me?"

"It's not exactly something I want to shout out, Trish. I mean, I'm married to his father. It's not my shining hour."

"Girl, you know you don't have to be ashamed to tell me anything. I'm not gonna judge you. What, you think I'm some kind of Girl Scout?"

"It's not that...not really. I guess it's mostly that I'm trying to accept how much I *don't* regret it. I've never been a cheater in my life. But the more I'm around Mario...the more I want to be. And that scares me."

"Wow, girl, I had no idea it was *that* deep for you," Trish admitted sincerely. "I thought you just had a little crush on him 'cause he was fine. But you sound like you're in love."

"At times I feel like I might be," I admitted for the first time, even to myself. "But I *shouldn't* be. I'm married to Harper. And despite the troubles we're having, I want to at least be able to say I tried to make our marriage work. That's why I'm looking forward to this trip so much; hopefully it'll help us connect some more. We need that."

"Ava," Trish hedged carefully. "I respect where you're coming from. But you can't force something that isn't there. You've been saying this same stuff for a while now and clearly, things haven't gotten any better. If it's not working with Harper, there's no shame in admitting it. People get married too quickly every day of the week."

"But I want to make sure that's all it is, and that it has nothing to do with any feelings I have for Mario," I countered. "Harper at least deserves my sincere effort. He's got his flaws, but he's been good to me. For the most part, at least. I can't forget that."

"I just don't want you to waste months with the wrong man because you feel guilty or obligated. You'll just start resenting Harper after a while. I know you don't want to hurt him, but you're not doing him any favors staying with him when you're in love with somebody else, regardless of who it is."

I knew Trish was right. But I was determined to do whatever I could to improve things between me and Harper. In the back of my mind, I still hoped that being able to do that would wipe out any feelings I had for Mario, even though I knew that was a long shot.

After a while, it was finally time to head to the airport. I tried to call Harper to make sure he couldn't come back and pick me up, just in case, but he didn't answer. I requested an Uber and felt my excitement start to reignite. Everything that happened the previous night had made me temporarily forget about how much I had anticipated this trip, but now that it was actually time to go, I felt giddy again. It was time to officially put all of that drama with Everette and Vera and Mario out of my mind and concentrate on having a wonderful honeymoon with my husband.

I was supposed to meet Harper at the gate, and I wondered if he was there already. I'd sent him a couple of texts on the way to the airport and he hadn't responded to those, so I figured (hoped) it was just because he was navigating his way through the unfamiliar airport and trying to calm his nerves, which were no doubt raging. I was totally prepared to comfort him and soothe him and put him at ease as much as I could, even if that meant getting him a little drunk. The fact that he was even getting on the plane at all filled me with a lot of hope about our relationship, and I was going to do everything I could to make it easier for him.

After checking in, dropping off my bag, and going through security, I started heading towards the gate to meet Harper. My skin was actually tingling, I was so excited. The grin was already plastered on my face as I weaved around slow-moving people, saying a quick 'excuse me' whenever my haste caused me to bump into one of them. As I got closer to the gate, I started looking for Harper's large frame, though my being so short didn't help with trying to see over the people in front of me. A lot of people were traveling that day so it was rather clogged.

When I finally made it to the gate, I didn't see Harper anywhere. Glancing at my watch, I shook my head. Of all times for him to run late. I started to pull my phone out to call him when there was a tap on my shoulder.

My jaw hit the floor when I saw Mario standing there.

"Mario? What's up? What are you doing here?" I asked, looking around as I adjusted my purse strap on my shoulder.

The expression on his face was uneasy. Almost pained. "I'm here to catch a flight."

"Yeah? I didn't know you were going out of town today, too. You didn't mention it last night."

"I know..."

"Decided to take a trip at the last minute or something?"

"You could say that. Ava-"

"Have you heard from Harper? I thought he'd be here by now," I asked him, standing on my tiptoes as I slowly turned around, perusing the bustling crowd. "Did y'all ride together?"

"No, we didn't. Ava, look, I hate having to tell you this, but...Dad's not coming."

My eyes snapped to him. "What?"

"I'm so sorry. He said the thought of flying just freaked him out too much. Said he even had a nightmare about it."

My purse fell to the floor as I tried to keep my emotions in check. I felt like the wind had just been knocked out of me. Everything in me wanted to scream. "He didn't mention any of that this morning! I *just* saw him a few hours ago and he was saying he'd meet me here!"

"I know..."

"He didn't say anything to *me* about any nightmares! He was talking like it was all good and we were all set! So, what, he was lying right to my face, knowing full well he had no intention of coming??"

"He wanted to, Ava. I know you might not believe it right now, but he didn't intend to stand you up."

"But that's exactly what he did! This was supposed to be our honeymoon, and he bails on me? Doesn't even have the courtesy to call and let me know himself that he changed his mind? You knew about all of this before I did?? When did he call you??"

Mario hesitated, clearly knowing I wouldn't like this answer. "Late last night."

"*What??!?*"

I was practically screaming, but I didn't care. Composure wasn't happening right then. I could not believe Harper had left me hanging like this!

"Ava, please try to calm down!" Mario begged, reaching out for me. He was a little hesitant, as if he was afraid I would swing on him or something. He gently pulled me to him, easing us over to the side. "I know you're thrown for a loop right now, and there's nothing I can really say in Dad's defense-"

"No, there *isn't*!" I adamantly concurred, leaning back to give him a look warning him not to try. "There is absolutely nothing either one of you can say to justify any of this!"

"I know. I wouldn't even insult you by acting like there is."

"What are you even doing here, then? You came all the way to meet me at the gate just to tell me Harper wasn't coming? Why didn't you just call?"

"He, uh...he wants me to go in his place."

"Are you fucking serious??" I exclaimed, breaking free of his grasp. "He sent you to go on our *honeymoon*?"

"Ava, I know this is crazy, but-"

"Crazy isn't even the *word*, Mario! It's bad enough that he ghosts me like this, but he actually expects me to agree to go anyway with *you*? Is that supposed to make me forget about him standing me up??"

"He said he wants you to still have a good time, and he wanted me to make sure you did. Look, I told him this was jacked up. If it makes you feel any better, I'm not thrilled about this, either. It's only because Dad damn near begged me to come that I'm even here. Well, that and I didn't want you here by yourself going crazy wondering what was up."

I didn't allow myself to stop and wonder what was behind Mario's displeasure over this situation. All I could think about was putting my hands as far around Harper's throat as they could go and squeezing until all the feeling in my fingers went out.

"I'm leaving," I announced abruptly, snatching my purse from the floor and turning away. "Where is Harper? Just *wait* until I find that bastard!"

"I don't know where he is, Ava," he insisted, gently grabbing my arm. When I shot him a look that clearly relayed my disbelief, he looked me right in the eyes. "I swear to God; I wouldn't bullshit you right now. But I'd be willing to bet anything he's not sitting at the house. It wouldn't surprise me if he's hopped in his truck and escaped down the road somewhere."

"I don't *believe* this!" I covered my face with my hands, unable to stop the angry tears. Collapsing onto the closest chair, I just sat there and cried, my tears falling to the floor. I was pissed, but I was also hurt, not to mention embarrassed. I just could not believe that Harper was doing this to me. As nervous as I knew he was about flying, the last thing I expected him to do was leave me hanging at the airport like an abandoned child.

After a moment or two of looking at me helplessly, Mario sat next to me. "Ava, I am *so* sorry," he stressed again, his voice full of conviction. "I wish there was something I could say to make you feel better about all this. I...I *hate* seeing you cry."

"Well, I don't know what else to do right now," I whimpered, wiping my eyes with my fingertips.

"You have every right to be upset."

"Upset is a major understatement."

"What can I do? Tell me what I can do to help you right now and it's done."

"Nothing, Mario," I shook my head sadly. My energy had officially run out. I slumped in the chair, my purse hitting the floor again. "There's nothing you can do. I appreciate you coming here to tell me what's going on, but right now I just want to get out of this airport and go find the strongest alcohol in the city."

"I don't think you should be alone right now."

"Well I wouldn't be good company to anybody in this frame of mind, Mario. I'm not feeling very pleasant."

"I get that. Look, as crazy as it sounds, how 'bout you and I go ahead on this trip together? We're here, we've got the tickets, they've already started the boarding call. Let me try to cheer you up."

"Don't even bother. And I'm sure you have other stuff you could be doing besides babysitting me."

"I'm not babysitting anybody. You deserve to get away for a minute and clear your mind of all this nonsense. And you and I both know nothing good can come of you sitting at home alone getting toasted. And even if Dad *were* there, you're in no frame of mind to deal with him."

He was right about that. I'd probably try to stab Harper if I saw him right then.

"Come on," Mario persisted, putting a warm hand on my back. "Don't let Dad keep you from enjoying a trip you've already paid for. And as for me, I'll get my own room. Let me at least try to show you a good time, Ava. I want to do that for you."

When I dared to look over at him, he looked so genuine and sincere that I felt myself calming a tiny bit. Mario really seemed to want to make me feel better, as futile as it seemed right then. And I appreciated his willingness to be there for me like that. But even with my head as jacked up as it was right then, I knew him and I going away together alone wasn't the best idea, especially with me being so angry at Harper. Who knows what I'd let myself do in the name of spiteful revenge?

"I should try to call him," I finally decided, pulling my phone from my pocket. "I'm sure by now he knows I've probably figured out what's going on. Maybe he'll at least tell me in his own words why he did this."

Mario looked skeptical, but he kept his mouth shut. He just motioned for me to go ahead, sitting back in his chair and watching me intently.

I dialed Harper's number, praying I'd hear his voice. Yes, I was pissed at him, but I had to believe that he would at least give me the courtesy of an apology, if nothing else. He wouldn't send me off on what was supposed to be our honeymoon with his son without a word.

I couldn't have married that much of a punk.

But apparently I had, because that call and the one I made right after that were sent right to voicemail. Wow.

I just sat there looking at the phone in utter disbelief. All I could do was bite my lip and try to keep the next wave of tears from falling. I felt something in me shift.

"Ava?" Mario said gently. I felt his hands on my shoulders. "They're calling our flight again. I'll understand if you don't want to get on this plane, but I really hope you do. You coming?"

Not letting myself think about all the reasons this wasn't a good idea, I shot out of the seat. If Harper wanted me to go away with Mario, then he only had himself to blame for whatever happened when I did.

"Yeah. Let's go."

Sixteen - Mario

THERE IS NO WAY I COULD have predicted any of this. Not in two million years.

When Dad called me the night before and asked me to go on this trip in his place, I really thought he was joking. Because there was no way any man would so willingly send his wife off on a romantic trip with another man, son or not.

"Wait, you're serious?" I asked when I realized he wasn't laughing along with me.

"Yeah, I'm serious, son," Dad glumly replied. "I'm embarrassed about this, but I just can't make myself get on that plane tomorrow. I just had a nightmare about the plane going into the ocean."

"What ocean? You're going to Tennessee. It's an hour-long flight."

"Still. The flight being short doesn't mean it can't crash and burn."

"See, thinking like that is what's freaking you out. The odds of that happening are super slim, Dad. Flying is perfectly safe. Safer than driving, actually."

"Can you just do this for me, son?" he finally pleaded, apparently tired of defending his fears. "I need you there to look after Ava."

"Speaking of Ava, where is she?"

"She's asleep."

"So you got up in the middle of the night to call me about this without talking to her? That's not cool, Dad."

"I can't look her in her face and disappoint her again, Mario. She's been upset at me enough lately, and I know how much she's looking forward to this."

"And you think bailing on her without a word at the last minute is going to help any? She has to come back sometime; you'd still have to answer to her for this."

"But by then she'll have cooled down, thanks to *you*," Dad countered. I guess he just had this all figured out.

"I'm not comfortable with this. It's not like she'd agree to go with me, anyway. This is supposed to be your honeymoon, man. There's no way she's gonna go for this. And I don't blame her."

"Convince her. Say or do whatever you have to to get her on that plane. By the time y'all get back, I'll be ready to talk to her."

As much as I wanted to just say no and hang up, I kept picturing Ava at the airport, alone, not knowing what happened to Dad. She'd call him, his punk ass wouldn't answer, and she'd no doubt call me next. I wouldn't want to leave her hanging, knowing full well why she was calling. So either way, Dad was putting me in a difficult position.

"I really don't like this, Dad," I pressed. It was taking all of my restraint not to tell him what I *really* thought of him right then. "Do you even realize the position you're putting me in?"

"I know, son. I know. And I'm sorry but...this is the only way I can think of to handle it."

"How about just being straight up with your wife?"

He sighed. "Look, I'll owe you big for this. Please just do this for me, son."

It was my turn to sigh. He sounded so anguished that it was hard to flat-out refuse him. "This is *so* jacked up, Dad. Ava doesn't deserve this."

"I know she doesn't."

"And what kind of marriage do y'all have if you can't even talk to each other?"

He sighed again. "Mario..."

"All right, I'll consider it if you tell me something."

He perked up. "What? Anything."

"What the hell were you thinking letting Vera kiss you like that last night?"

The line went quiet and I wondered if he'd hung up. "You, ah...how do you know..."

"Because I saw y'all, Dad. I had come looking for you and saw Vera make her move, and you didn't do a damn thing to stop her. Matter of fact, you seemed to help yourself, too."

"Damn," he muttered.

"I mean, you didn't really try to be discreet with it. The door was half open. What if Ava had come up there instead of me, huh?"

"Mario, I know how that must've looked. And I admit I...I got caught up in the moment. I'm not proud of it, but it was a one-time thing that's *not* gonna happen again. And for the record, I did tell Vera she was wrong for hitting on me like that."

"You mean after you boned her?"

"*What?* Who said I -"

"Y'all were on the bed, Dad. Then you closed and locked the door. I don't claim to know everything but I'm not an idiot."

"Okay, I was tempted. But we did *not* have sex. Just...a lot of heavy petting and hunching."

Hunching? Now there's a word I haven't heard since high school. "Wow, Dad."

"I'm not trying to make excuses. But you've never lost your head and did something you usually wouldn't have?"

I stopped cold. Images of me and Ava at her front door and on my couch started flashing through my brain like a slide show. If I concentrated hard enough, I could still feel her lips on mine. It was a hard reminder that I really didn't have any moral high ground to stand on when it came to this; I wasn't any better than Dad. Honestly, I was worse because my kissing Ava wasn't a one-time thing, and I had ached to be with her like that again more times than I could count.

Finally, something Dad and I had in common.

Coming to this realization is what ultimately made me say, "Send me the information."

Dad sounded more relieved than school kids on a snow day. "Thank you, son! Show Ava the best time you can, okay?"

"Yeah."

Now, I had to focus on making sure Ava had at least a decent time on this trip to Tennessee. She'd been thrown for a major loop, and I hated having to be the one to break the news to her that Dad was a no-show for their honeymoon. She rotated between being pissed, being confused, and being just plain distraught. It wrenched my gut to see her like that, especially when she got to the distraught part. As much as I might've been able to relate to Dad when it came to what happened between him and Vera, I still couldn't get with him punking out on Ava like he was. I mean, he could've at least taken her call, shot her a text, *something*.

After I finally convinced her to get on the plane, she didn't have much to say. I didn't try to engage her in conversation. I just let her feel what she needed to feel, opting to wait until we were in Tennessee to start my spirits-raising mission. I was still trying to figure out how I was going to get her mind off of Dad long enough to enjoy herself for a couple of days.

The flight was over in no time, and when we got to the hotel, we hit the first snag.

"I'm sorry, sir, we don't have any other rooms available," the hotel clerk informed me. "We're all booked up."

Wonderful. "All right. Thanks." I turned to Ava. "I'll check around to other hotels in the area and see if I can get a room at one of those."

Ava pursed her lips, then shook her head. "You don't have to do all that, Mario. It's not necessary."

"I have to find some place to stay."

"You have a place to stay. Just stay in my room. It's fine."

"I don't want you to be uncomfortable."

"It's not like you're a stranger. And there's no need in going through the trouble of searching for a room in a different hotel when there's more than enough room in mine."

Even though no one there knew us, I still glanced around before stepping closer to her.

"Are you *sure*?" I eyed her pointedly. We hadn't discussed either of the kissing sessions that had gone down between us, but I was sure she hadn't forgotten them. Us sharing a room seemed to just be asking for trouble. Delicious trouble, but trouble nonetheless.

"Yes," she eyed me back, apparently getting my message. "We both know what the deal is. We know why we're both here."

My eyes roamed her face for a moment. There was no flash of flirtation, no hint of a smile, no whiff of coyness. Neither of us planned this. She wanted to be there with Dad and I wanted to still be at home watching movies and eating my Thai leftovers.

"If you're sure," I finally acquiesced. "I appreciate you being so generous. And I have no problem sleeping on the floor."

Ava just nodded, thankfully not insisting I sleep in her bed with her. I think we both knew better than that.

I followed her to the room, noting the king size bed as soon as we walked in the door. Ava must have told them she was going to be there on her honeymoon, because there was a slew of rose petals strewn everywhere and some champagne chilling next to a platter of fresh fruit. Ava just stood looking at all this, and I could tell she had temporarily forgotten requesting it.

"Great," she muttered under her breath.

"Do you want me to have them send someone to come get all of this out of here?"

"Yeah. Well, no. No, it's okay."

"You sure?"

"Yeah, it's fine. I'm actually glad to see the champagne. Don't be surprised if I drink most of it."

Not sure if she was joking or not, I suppressed the chuckle that almost escaped and put my bag on the armchair in the corner of the room.

"Have at it," I told her. "In the meantime, I'll take care of all these rose petals..."

She looked at me gratefully, giving the first small smile of the day. "Thanks, Mario."

"No problem."

I went about gathering all the rose petals from the floor and the bed while she grabbed the bottle of champagne, not even bothering with glasses and taking it right to the head. Once the bed was clear, she settled in the middle of it with the fruit platter, sitting cross-legged and looking more adorable than I wanted to admit.

"Want some?" she asked me, referring to the fruit.

"I'm good."

"Come on, I can't eat all this by myself."

Relenting, I tentatively sat on the edge of the bed as she slid the platter between us. Neither of us said much as we snacked. I wanted to cheer her up, but I didn't want to act like the events of the morning hadn't happened. And I didn't know her quite well enough to be able to gauge her moods yet.

"I appreciate you convincing me to come, Mario," she said after a while. "I actually already feel a little better, just being in another environment."

"I'm glad to hear that."

"I'll deal with Harper later but for the time being, I just want to forget he exists. While we're here, can we agree not to talk about him?"

I held up my hands. "Whatever you say."

"Good." She popped another piece of pineapple into her mouth. "I just want to put home and anything to do with it out of my mind for a while."

"Understood." While I was agreeing with her wishes, part of me felt bad for keeping what happened between Vera and Dad from her. I felt she should know what kind of person her friend was.

But I had to wonder what my motivation would be for telling her. Was it just about wanting her to know the real deal, or did some part of me want her to get even more upset with Dad? I wondered if this was something she would leave him over or if she would give him another chance, especially considering the fact that she'd been unfaithful, herself.

Just thinking about all this was making my head hurt, and I decided to adopt Ava's philosophy about just putting all that out of my mind during this trip. I'd drive myself crazy if I didn't.

"Here," she said, offering me the bottle of champagne. She'd killed most of it, but had apparently saved a little for me. I took the bottle without a word and drained it, following her lead.

"Thanks," I said, setting the empty bottle on the nightstand.

She burped, then looked at me, clearly embarrassed. "Wow, excuse me..."

"Good stuff, huh?" I smiled, trying to put her at ease. "You want me to call for some more?"

She relaxed a little bit. "Nah. If I'm gonna get drunk, it's gonna be on something more fun than champagne."

"Well, I'd ask if you were hungry but with the way you devoured this fruit..."

"I didn't *devour* it."

"Girl, this platter is empty."

"You ate some, too!"

"Not nearly as much as you did."

"Well, I started first. And I didn't have much of a breakfast this morning."

"Hey, you don't have to justify anything to me. It's your world right now."

"My world, huh?" Ava leaned back on the bed pillows, her hands behind her head. "I don't hate that."

"Shocker."

Ava looked at me and chuckled. "Whatever!"

I caught her bare foot as she tried to kick me, and proceeded to tickle her. She squealed and tried to scoot away, and I grabbed her leg and yanked her closer. I'd never heard her giggle so much, and I couldn't help but grin at the sound of it. Of course, it just made me want to tickle her more.

"Mario!" she exclaimed, trying to squirm away from me again. "I can't take anymore!"

"Aww, sure you can," I teased, continuing the torture.

"Mario!"

"Yes?"

She shrieked and exploded into another round of giggles when I moved to the back of her knee. I loved seeing her like this. She rolled away, or at least tried to, and I yanked her back once again. She was laughing so hard she started hiccupping, which only made me bust out laughing.

"Mario," she gasped, managing to sit up. She tried to grab my hands, which of course, I evaded. That led to her trying to tackle me, which was comedy in and of itself due to the hold I had on her legs. The empty platter got kicked to the floor. We play-wrestled and tussled for a while, with me taking any and every opportunity I could to get more tickles in. Ava's face was turning red from laughing so hard.

When her hands slipped underneath my arms, she discovered something that I'd hoped she wouldn't: I was ticklish, too.

"Oh it's *on* now!" she declared, diving on me. Now *I* was trying to get away from *her*. And she was a relentless little devil. She was clearly trying to pay me back for all the playful torture I had put on her. I hadn't been tickled in years, and my stomach was hurting from laughing so much. Not that I minded.

Eventually, though, I had to exert my superior strength and tackle her, putting her on her back. She wasn't about to have me piss my pants from laughing.

"I've got *you* now," I informed her, pinning her wrists above her head. We both tried to catch our breath as I hovered over her. "You're not gonna keep messing with me, woman!"

"You started it!"

"No, *you* started it by trying to kick me."

"That...whatever!"

"Uh-huh. *Whatever.*"

"Don't think this means you won," Ava stubbornly retorted. "I know your weakness now."

"And I know yours, so watch yourself. You're *way* more ticklish than I am."

"Not *way* more..."

"Yes, *way* more."

"Well...so? I can still get ya."

"Try it and see what happens, woman!"

We both busted out laughing. I didn't release my hold on her, and it wasn't too long before we both realized the position we were in. I made the mistake of looking into her eyes, and she was already looking at me. Our smiles started to fade, and I became very aware of the feeling of Ava's body underneath mine. Another kind of aching began to take root in my stomach, and I knew if I didn't move right then, something would start that we might not be able to stop.

I let go of her wrists and backed off of her, moving to the opposite side of the bed. She sat up, adjusting her shirt and looking away.

"You wanna get outta here?" I asked, trying to avoid an awkward moment.

She looked at me gratefully. "Yeah, we can do that."

I hopped off the bed, then paused.

Ava looked concerned. "What's the matter?"

"Is that rain I hear?"

Ava stopped to listen, then padded over to the window and opened the curtains. Sure enough, it was pouring down rain outside.

"Well, isn't this awesome?" she droned sarcastically.

"That's crazy. It was bright and sunny just an hour ago."

"Yeah, I know. Well, I don't know about you but I'm not trying to go out in that."

"No arguments here. Hopefully it'll pass by tomorrow. In the meantime, though, we can order some dinner later, watch some movies, *or*..." I went to my bag and pulled out a deck of cards. "I can kick your ass in some Uno."

She brightened. "Oh no, when it comes to Uno, I am the undisputed guru. Don't even do that to yourself, trying to challenge me on that."

"Well bring it, then, if you think you got it like that!"

That kicked off a Uno game marathon that went on for the next three hours. Any time either of us won a game, the other immediately challenged them to another. Neither one of us were willing to concede our self-appointed Uno titles. And we were talking *much* junk, too, laughing as much as we were clowning.

"You can put down all the Draw 4's you want, you're *still* not gonna beat me!" she announced. I just gave her a mocking snicker as she snatched four cards from the deck.

"Whatever you have to tell yourself to feel better. You *do* realize I've won the last two games, oh thou guru."

"That means nothing. You probably have some marked cards in this ancient deck of yours."

"Oh that's the route we're going, accusing me of cheating? I don't need to cheat, baby; my skills are more than enough."

"Cocky ass."

"It ain't cocky if it's correct."

"You can be correct and cocky. It's all in the delivery."

"My delivery has been on point. You might need to work on yours."

"I'm all good over here. You just draw these cards," she taunted, sticking her tongue out at me as she dropped her own Draw 4 bomb.

I sucked my teeth. "Whatever."

"Yeah, *whatever*."

This just continued, us going back and forth at each other. At some point we ordered dinner, and ate it on the floor while we took a break from our Uno battle to watch some episodes of *Wild n' Out*. Ava hadn't seen the show before but ended up laughing at it more than I was.

"Oh my gosh, where has this show been all my life??" she exclaimed.

I laughed. "It's been coming on for years. You're late."

"Well, they've certainly got a new fan now. Most of the time when I'm at home and watching anything its movies or *Frasier* reruns, so no wonder I hadn't seen it."

"I feel ya. I love me some movies, too. I've had more than my share of Netflix and chill nights. Though can you still call it that when you're by yourself?"

Ava burst out laughing. "Silly!"

"I'm just saying. We all know what *Netflix and chill* means."

"You're just doing it in the literal sense. So yeah, it counts."

"Good to know. Not that I was gonna stop either way."

Ava just shook her head as she playfully bumped her shoulder against mine. We looked at each other and laughed, as if on cue. I couldn't remember the last time I felt so in sync with someone.

We sat there on the floor watching the show and talking for another hour or so. When Ava started to yawn, I began cleaning up our dinner trash and gathering the Uno cards. It had been a long, emotional day, and I wasn't surprised it was finally starting to catch up with her.

"Go on to bed, Ava," I gently ordered, helping her off the floor. "You're about to fall over down here."

"I'm not," she protested, her words betrayed by another huge yawn.

"No need in trying to fight it. It's damn near midnight. Get some rest. We can have plenty more fun tomorrow."

"I guess I just don't want the evening to end," she admitted, looking at me.

I returned her look. She wasn't by herself; this had been one of the best evenings I'd had in a long time, too. And I couldn't help but love that I'd shared it with her.

"I know," I finally replied. "I don't, either. But we're gonna have more time. Go on and get ready for bed."

"Okay."

She got some clothes from her bag and went into the bathroom to shower. Since the room had a small couch, I thankfully didn't have to sleep on the floor. I was getting the spare blanket and pillow out of the closet when Ava emerged from the bathroom smelling like lemongrass in a nightie that stopped somewhere near mid-thigh. Damn her.

When she looked at me shyly, I had to remember that she probably didn't have anything tamer than that to wear to bed. This *was* supposed to be a romantic getaway with her husband, after all. I wouldn't be surprised if her suitcase was full of racier nighties and those matching bra and panty sets women liked to wear. Imagining Ava in sexy lingerie was starting to make everything on me turn to cement.

"Um," I shook my head, trying to jar those thoughts, "You all done in there?"

"Yeah."

Grabbing my toiletry bag and some clothes, I hurried into the bathroom, closing the door behind me with a deep breath. I got into the hot shower, fighting off fantasies of Ava joining me. I was still trying to wrap my mind around the fact that I was there at all. Taking my dad's place on his honeymoon with his wife who was like a walking piece of forbidden fruit, who was right outside the door half naked in a king-sized bed? It was like a punishment and a reward mashed together.

I took my time, hoping that Ava would be asleep by the time I got out of the shower, but no such luck. She was lying on her side, tracing designs on the bedspread with her finger. A pink silk scarf was now covering her head, bringing her cuteness level up even more. She eyed me as I stepped into the room.

"You take long showers."

I shrugged lightly. I wasn't about to admit I'd just been stalling. "Sometimes, yeah."

"You tired?"

"A little bit."

"Hmm."

I went and put my clothes away, feeling her eyes on me. Usually I just went to bed in some boxers, but in the spirit of modesty, I wore basketball shorts and a t-shirt.

Ava stayed quiet as I fixed up the couch. As tired as she seemed earlier, she was wide awake now. I tried to stay focused on what I was doing, because I was having a hard enough time keeping my thoughts in check.

Finally, I turned out the lights near the couch and tried to get comfortable.

"Good night," I called out.

"Good night."

Ava still hadn't turned her bedside lamp off, so a faint glow still washed over me. I squeezed my eyes shut and threw an arm over my eyes, trying to block out everything. I figured Ava was one of those people that liked to sleep with a light on.

Eventually, though, she killed the lamp and the room went dark. The only light in the room was from the thin sliver between the curtains; I could barely see my own hand in front of my face. Ava's lemongrass scent had wafted over to where I was, and it was just like another layer of torture.

Why did I agree to come on this damn trip again?

I don't know how much time passed in silence before Ava's soft voice stilled my restless thoughts.

"Mario? You awake?"

I thought about pretending I wasn't, but decided against it. "Yeah."

"Can I bother you for a favor?"

Immediately sitting up, I looked towards her voice. "What do you need?"

"Can you come hold me?"

My dick immediately jumped and I pressed a hand against it, trying to calm myself. Being close to Ava like that would be dangerous, and I knew it. But I couldn't resist her.

I threw the blanket off me and headed over to the bed. Didn't say a word as I gently lifted the covers and slid underneath, easing closer to where Ava was. I wrapped an arm around her from behind, and she immediately held onto it, pulling it tighter. When she scooted her ass closer to my crotch, my eyes closed and I had to bite my lip and summon all the strength I could. She felt amazing in my arms. Her skin was so soft, and she smelled *so* good...after a mere minute, I was going crazy.

But I eventually made myself calm down. Our breathing fell into rhythm as we just laid there in the dark. I wondered what she was thinking right then, but didn't have the balls to ask.

At some point, Ava turned so she was facing me, wrapping her arms around my waist and pulling me closer. She buried her face in my chest and sighed, sounding frighteningly content.

I tried to ignore how natural it felt, laying with her like that. And the emotion that was warming my skin as I did so. When she fell into a deep sleep, looking fresh-faced and peaceful, I couldn't help but hold her tighter, knowing I wasn't going to forget how I felt right then.

Seventeen – Ava

WHAT HUSBAND?

I was glad Mario was there in Tennessee with me, despite how everything had gone down for him to end up there. I'd called Trish to let her know we made it safely, (and tried to call Vera but she still wasn't answering), but other than that, I just wanted to forget everything from home. And Mario was doing a great job of helping me with that.

Waking up in Mario's arms was something I knew I couldn't afford wanting to get used to. But it felt *so* nice. Even when he was asleep, Mario held onto me, and I loved that. He just made me feel so safe and protected; I found myself not worrying about anything when I was around Mario. Somehow, I just knew he'd have my back in whatever came up.

Thankfully the rainstorm had passed sometime during the night, so we got dressed and headed out to enjoy the city together. We went on a food tour, went bowling, and took an excursion train. Mario took lots of pictures, which would no doubt end up on his blog. By the time we treated ourselves to way too many sweets at Magpies Bakery, I was wiped.

"It's a good thing I had the sense to wear sneakers today," I said, trailing behind Mario as we left the bakery. "My feet are screaming right now."

"Is that why you're walking so slow?"

"That's exactly why."

"Here, hop on," he instructed, turning his back to me.

Not hesitating at all, I jumped onto his back, holding onto him as he hooked his arms under my knees. I tried to ignore how good he smelled as we continued down the sidewalk.

"You two are so cute together!" an older lady exclaimed as we approached her. She eyed my wedding ring. "How long have you been married?"

"Just a few months," I quickly answered with a grin, before Mario could say anything.

"Oh! Newlyweds! I loved my newlywed phase! Isn't it just wonderful?"

"It sure is!"

I wished I could've seen the expression on Mario's face.

When we got back to the hotel, it happened again. The same front desk clerk from the day before nodded to us as Mario carted me through the lobby.

"Good afternoon, Mr. and Mrs. Downing."

"Good afternoon!" I replied, grinning. Again, Mario didn't comment.

It wasn't until we were in our room that he asked, "What are you doing?"

I shrugged innocently, even though I knew what he was talking about. "I don't know what you mean."

"Yes you do, Ava. What's up with pretending like we're married?"

"I don't think that's what I did. And, *technically*, we *are* Mr. and Mrs. Downing."

"That's splitting hairs and you know it, but that doesn't explain away the lady on the street. You flat-out lied to her."

"Okay, fine," I threw up my hands. "I didn't plan on doing that; it just came out. What, are you upset?"

"No, not upset. Just wondering why you did it."

"It doesn't mean anything, Mario. Just having a little fun. And I didn't see you jumping in to correct me."

He paused, then gave a convicted shrug. "True enough."

"Why didn't you say anything, if you have such a problem with it?"

"Who said I had a problem with it?"

I looked at him, and he was gazing at me so intensely I had to quickly avert my eyes.

"Umm..." I couldn't seem to find words all of a sudden. "You, uh, you hungry?"

"We just ate."

"Oh yeah."

"What's the matter?"

"Nothing," I replied quickly, even though my insides were flaming. "Nothing at all."

"You wanna chill and then go do something else? I heard someone say something about some live music somewhere around here."

I really would have preferred to stay in the rest of the night, but with the way I was feeling right then, us alone in a hotel room wasn't a good idea.

"Sure, that sounds good. Let me just go take a shower real quick; I'm kinda sweaty from all the walking around today."

"Take your time."

I tried to gather myself as I grabbed my stuff and went into the bathroom. As I started the shower, I thought back to how easily lying about being married to Mario had been. I figured it was all because I was so pissed at my own husband that I was so willing to pretend I was married to someone else. That had to be it.

My imagination started running off like a child in the mall, and I began imagining Mario and I as a couple. We certainly had a lot in common, and we got along really well. And attraction wasn't an issue. It just made me wonder what would have happened if I'd met him before Harper. Would I have even given Harper a second look? I knew what answer I was leaning towards, even though I didn't want to admit it to myself. I didn't even feel guilty about claiming Mario as my husband, even in jest. Honestly, I was in no hurry to get back home and deal with Harper and whatever excuses he'd try to give for ditching me. I didn't miss him, even a little bit. And what's worse, I didn't care to make myself try to.

I tried to push those thoughts out of my mind as I showered and got dressed. Mario was showing me a great time, and I just wanted to enjoy it.

And that's exactly what I did. After Mario took his own shower, we went to a nearby place where a long, lanky woman perched on a stool sang and played the guitar. She sounded great, but I have to admit my attention wasn't on her; it was on the man next to me. I wanted to hold his hand, but I didn't. I wanted to keep looking over at him, but I didn't. When I leaned into him, though, he automatically put an arm around me, and I started grinning and blushing like a schoolgirl.

It was pretty obvious that I had a crush on Mario. But it was becoming more obvious that it had grown into something deeper than that.

All I could wonder was exactly how he felt about me.

After enjoying the music for a while, we took a leisurely walk. No destination in mind, just walking and enjoying each other's presence. We talked about our childhoods; he shared what little he knew about his mother, and I told him about the rather strained relationship I had with my parents before they died. At some point, he reached over and took my hand, and there came the grinning and blushing again. I didn't know if it was the atmosphere or if it was just Mario, but he was doing something to me I wondered if I was ready for. I was actually starting to dread going back home; I just wanted to stay there with Mario.

It *had* to be my jumbled-up emotions.

As much as I tried to tell myself that, the feelings didn't diminish or dissipate for the rest of our time in Tennessee. Whether we were out and about or just chilling in the hotel room, I felt myself wanting to get closer and closer to Mario, in every way. I ached to know where he was, because we had yet to really talk about any of this; our kisses, the obvious feelings we had for each other, anything. But I admit, I was too shy to broach the subject. If my feelings for him greatly outweighed his for me, I'd be humiliated. How could I look him in the eye after that?

On our last night there, Mario took me to a really romantic dinner and told me to order whatever I wanted. We each agreed to order for each other, and we *had* to eat whatever we got. That in and of itself was fun for me, because he was so willing to try something new. Lord knows I got tired of the same basic stuff I had at home all the time because Harper never wanted to venture past the familiar.

"Have you enjoyed yourself these past few days, Ava?" Mario asked, gazing at me.

Smiling at him, I nodded. "I really have. Best few days of my life."

"That's what I wanted to hear."

"Thank you so much, Mario. You really did make me feel better after everything that happened. I honestly wish we didn't have to go back home tomorrow."

"Well," he reached across the table and took my hand, "The night's not over yet."

The look in his eyes made my heart light up. It wasn't lust; he wasn't looking at me like he wanted to rip my clothes off. It was deeper than that, and I felt it. I was feeling the exact same way, and I wondered if he could see it in my eyes like I could see it in his.

Everything around us faded out as we continued to gaze at each other. I suddenly hated that we were in a crowded restaurant. I wanted to be alone with him. More than anything.

I was over the guessing and wondering and speculating; I needed to know what this was. It was past time we had that talk.

When we got back to our room, I didn't waste any time with preamble.

"Mario, we need to talk about what we're doing."

He was removing his wallet and keys from his pockets, and looked at me intently. I had a feeling he knew what I was referring to but he still asked, "Meaning?"

"Meaning *us*. The times we've kissed, how well we vibe...I don't think I'm being presumptuous to say we have some feelings for each other that go deeper than just a harmless crush. I mean, am I wrong?"

Sliding his hands into his pockets, he turned his body towards me. "You're not wrong at all."

My breath hitched with relief. "So the question now is...what do we do about it?"

He started slow-walking towards me. "What do you *want* to do about it?"

My mouth opened, but nothing came out for several moments. "I don't know."

"You know when we get back home, it's gonna go back to how it was before."

"I don't want to think about that."

He stopped in front of me, looking right into my eyes. "Me, either."

God, he smelled good. He looked amazing. And being so close to him was making every inch of me sing.

"Mario, when I agreed to come on this trip with you after Harper ditched me, I was determined to just have a good time in spite of him. But this has felt like more of a honeymoon than it probably would have felt like with Harper, and I can't lie to myself about that. I've...I've loved being here with you like this."

"Me, too." Mario took my hands and gathered them against his chest. "I haven't given any thought to anything or anyone but you."

"Really?"

"Really. Ava...I absolutely have feelings for you. As much as I've tried to avoid it and deny it, I've fallen for you, hard. I know I shouldn't and I'm wrong for it, but that's just the real. And it kills me knowing that this time tomorrow, you'll be back in that house with my Dad and I'll be going home alone."

My knees were actually weak. It was a huge relief knowing that this wasn't one-sided.

"I've fallen for you, too," I admitted, finally. "Ever since the first time we met-"

"I knew I was in trouble," he finished. "Since the first time I laid eyes on you, you've had me, Ava. And part of me resents my dad for meeting you first."

"Mario..."

He leaned in and kissed me, as if he was done trying to let his words convey the message. I eagerly returned the kiss, savoring his lips and touch in a new way now that I knew his feelings matched mine. Our arms slid around each other tightly as the kiss deepened. I couldn't get close enough to him.

His hands cupped my bottom, and my feet came up off the ground, my legs wrapping around his waist. He slowly walked over to the bed, our kiss continuing, my hands caressing his face. That hot ache had spread over my body like a delicious rash that only Mario could soothe. I wanted this man in every way I could have him, consequences be damned.

He laid me down and climbed on top of me, bringing his lips back to mine. It just felt so right, him covering me like he was. Unlike the other two times we kissed, our hands began to acquaint themselves with each other's most private areas, and I wanted to scream at how good it felt. Neither of us was in a rush, even though I wanted to beg him to get inside of me. I loved how he took his time; how he caressed my body and savored every new part he discovered.

My hands were already underneath his shirt, and his were under my dress. I didn't even try to contain my moans and gasps of pleasure. His lips and fingers were sending me to the moon.

Eventually, my dress was on the floor, topped by his shirt and pants. Our underwear soon followed. Usually I'm pretty self-conscious when a man sees my naked body for the first time, but I didn't feel any of that with Mario. Being there with him like that felt like the most natural thing in the world.

"Damn, baby," he whispered, his eyes drinking me in. "You are so *fucking* sexy."

His appreciation for what he saw was evident, and it made me feel like the sexiest thing walking. I grinned, returning his lustful looks with some of my own.

"Not nearly as sexy as you," I countered. "And I'm gonna take full advantage of having you all to myself tonight."

Rolling on top of him, I went on my own slow exploration of that beautiful body of his. I was gonna make *sure* he didn't forget me.

I lingered on every sensitive spot I found, swirling my tongue over his dark skin as if it was coated in chocolate. As anxious as I was to get to the next part, I was so enjoying getting to savor him like this. Every time he shuddered or hissed or whispered how good something felt, it just spurned me on. And when I saw just how much he was working with below the waist, I took it as a personal challenge to get as much of it into my mouth as I could.

"Ava, *shit*!" he yelled, grabbing my short hair.

"Mmm-hmmm..."

"*Damn*, baby..."

"You like it?"

"I *love* it...*damn*, I love it!"

"Mmmm..." I dove back in, even more energized than before.

Several times he tried to push me off because he was getting close to the mountaintop, but I wasn't moving. I didn't care if my jawbone fell off, I was going to make him cum in my mouth. When his legs started shaking and clenching, I knew he was close. I swear, I've never heard a man scream so loud.

"*AAAUUGHHH SHIIIIIT!!!*"

Not gonna lie, I loved making him scream like that.

But before I could pat myself on the back too much, he was flipping me over and exhibiting his own sexual torture. My smugness melted away like butter on a scorching skillet as his tongue pleasured my breasts so good that an orgasm hit me before I could do anything about it.

"*Oh my god!*" I shrieked, caught off guard. I had never, ever cum that quickly before.

Mario wasn't about to stop, though. He kept right on with it, bringing that taser tongue down my body until he got between my legs. Now *my* legs were shaking.

I braced my feet against his shoulders, steeling my body for the next wave of shudders. My knees fell open, not having the energy to stay up. His hands squeezed up and down my hips and thighs as he feasted on me, taking his time and going so tortuously slow that I wanted to pull my own hair out. It felt *so* good. My hands clawed at the wooden headboard, not able to inch away because he had my thighs in a vise grip, and I was speaking so much profanity-laced gibberish that I didn't even recognize my own voice. Then the next orgasm hit me like a ten-foot wave.

"Mario!"

I swear I blacked out for a second. It felt like every cell on my body was bursting in a million little fireworks. I managed to sit up on my elbows, looking at him in amazement.

"So this is what the beginning of a new addiction feels like," I marveled, only half-kidding.

He smirked, tongue-kissing the inside of my thigh. "You flatter me."

"I didn't know you had it like that."

"I could say the same about you," he replied, pushing himself up on his fists and crawling closer, his gold chain dangling. His lustful eyes bored into mine. "But I hope you're not done."

The way he was looking at me had me transfixed for a second. All I could manage was a small shake of my head.

He dove for my lips, sharing my taste with me as he lowered his body onto mine. We kissed languidly as I wrapped my legs around him, reminding myself that this was a one-night thing that I better enjoy every second of. The thought brought tears to my eyes, but it increased my intensity. I didn't want a break. My hips lifted against him impatiently, anxious to feel him inside of me.

"Now, Mario," I gasped against his lips. My short nails dug into his back. "Please, *now*."

Without another word, Mario slid inside of me slowly, letting me adjust to his size. The speed steadily increased, our slick bodies moving against each other with a frightening familiarity. His thumbs wiped my tears but he didn't ask what I was crying about; I think he already knew. He was looking pretty emotional himself, but he didn't stop. Not until both of us felt that sweet release, mine coming before his.

"Ava, *baby*..." he cried out, his eyes squeezing shut as he shuddered on top of me, then dove in for an urgent, sloppy kiss. His hold on me tightened. "God*damn*!"

We clung to each other until our screams and heavy breathing died down, his forehead pressed against mine.

"You need me to get up?" he softly asked after a few moments. "Am I too heavy for you?"

"No," I quickly replied, holding him tighter. "I don't want you to move."

He lifted his head and smoothed the sweaty hair from my forehead, looking tenderly into my eyes. "I can't tell you how many times I've imagined this."

I smiled. "Me, too. I kinda feel like I'm dreaming right now."

"My feelings for you are very real, Ava. I really hope you believe that."

"I believe you," I assured him, caressing his face. "I'm right there with you."

"So you love me? 'Cause I damn sure love *you*, Ava."

There went another wave of tears. "Mario...I absolutely love you, too."

We kissed deeply, his hand palming my face, and I tried to keep the sadness from overtaking my body. Who knew when or if Mario and I were going to be together like this again? All I was sure of was that this was the man I wanted. *Needed*. Mario and I just made more sense. *Why* didn't I meet him first??

"How in the world are we gonna handle this when we get back home?" I asked after the kiss tapered off and a moment of thoughtful silence passed. "I don't want to go back to pretending."

"I don't either, baby. But unless we're gonna tell Dad everything, we'll have to. Are you ready to do that?"

"Not really, but I'm even less ready to be without you." I looked at him helplessly. "After this time we've spent together...I can't imagine..."

"Ava," He took my face in his hands. "Believe me, I know. I'm in no more of a hurry for you to go back there with...*him*. But until we're ready to come clean about all this, we have no choice."

I closed my eyes, knowing he was right. As much as I wanted to be with Mario, I knew I wasn't ready to tell Harper the truth. Regardless of anything, I still cared about the man. I didn't want him to suffer because I realized too late that we just weren't right for each other, but I also didn't want make myself miserable by staying with him out of pity or guilt. No, at some point we'd have to tell him. I just didn't know when or how.

Mario and I continued to hold each other, talking and musing, before we made love again. I didn't want the next day to come but eventually, it did. I dreaded it, but at least I woke up to it in Mario's arms.

Eighteen - Mario

SO...WE WERE BACK HOME.

I hated dropping Ava off at Dad's house. The thought of him touching her made me want to punch something. But until Ava was ready for us to tell Dad the truth, I'd just have to deal with it.

I should have felt guilty for falling for Ava, and even more so for making love to her, but I didn't. Dad asked me to accompany her to Tennessee to cheer her up, not take her to bed. And it didn't matter that he only did that out of guilt for bailing on her, because I only agreed out of guilt for kissing her. This was just a jacked-up situation all around, and I knew the shit was gonna hit the fan at some point.

Everything in me wanted to call Ava and check on her, make sure she was all right. I could only imagine how things were going between her and Dad. He was there when I dropped her off, and it was obvious she wasn't thrilled to see him. This agreement Ava and I had about keeping what happened in Tennessee between us and acting like nothing happened was going to be way harder than I thought.

As I unpacked my bags, I wondered how the hell I was going to pull this off. We'd been back in town two hours and I missed her like crazy already. I wanted her there with me, not with Dad. When she got out of my car earlier, she told me she loved me, and I could tell that she was fighting back tears. It was like a punch in the gut.

"Damn," I whispered, dropping onto my bed and putting my head in my hands.

AFTER A FEW HOURS OF moping and resisting the urge to text Ava, I responded to some comments on my blog and checked my social media. I didn't pay much attention to it when I was in Tennessee. I uploaded the pictures from the trip with Ava, but had no plans of posting them. Those were just for me.

I couldn't help but smile as I scrolled through them. Ava looked so carefree and happy; I was glad I was able to help her feel like that, given how upset she had been over Dad standing her up. Even though I had only been there as a stand-in, it was the best trip I'd taken. Out of all the places I'd been, who would have thought a trip to Tennessee would be at the top of the list.

But it was all because of Ava.

I was still smiling and reminiscing over the pictures when I got an instant message from Mikki.

Hey ~ Mikki

I closed it without responding. Mikki and I didn't have anything to talk about. But of course, that wasn't the end of it.

Can we talk? ~ Mikki

Sighing, I knew she would just keep messaging me until I responded. Or try to show up at my damn door, not that she'd be able to get up there.

Already frustrated, I banged out a quick reply, pounding my keyboard way harder than necessary.

About what? ~ Mario

A bout how we left things ~ Mikki
Nothing to say about that ~ Mario
I think there is ~ Mikki
Mikki, I'm busy ~ Mario
Can I come over? I miss you ~ Mikki
No ~ Mario
I'm sorry for what I said. You're a good man and I don't wanna lose you ~ Mario
You never had me ~ Mikki
Don't be like that. You got me over here eating all this ice cream... ~ Mikki

Before I could respond to that, she sent me a picture of her, topless. She was holding a container of Ben and Jerry's and her breasts were covered in whipped cream. Her legs were spread to the camera and her hair was falling over her face, giving the camera her best seductive look.

I rolled my eyes. It was like she didn't listen to a word I ever said to her. You would think after I told her the main reason I didn't want to be with her was because she was all about sex, that she would come at me with something more genuine instead of a staged picture where she was offering up her titties as a treat.

Not even bothering to respond, I deleted the picture and the conversation, then blocked her. Mikki was fun while she lasted, but my attention was elsewhere now.

THE NEXT DAY, I WAS really trying to work out my frustration during my morning workout. When I'd woken up in bed alone, it sent my mood to hell. I was cranky and irritable because my woman wasn't there with me, and I didn't feel I could reach out to her like I wanted to.

I wondered how Dad tried to talk his way out of this one. Standing her up for their honeymoon was a big thing, and I was sure Ava wasn't going to fall for one of his sob stories. I figured he'd try to say how he was traumatized by planes or something like that, laying it on thick so she'd feel sorry for him. Either that, or they weren't talking at all.

It wasn't too long until Dad called me, needing an ally. I should have known it was coming. Plus, he wanted a report on how the trip went.

"Did she have a good time?" he asked me. I could hear the anxiousness in his voice.

"Yeah." My tone was casual. "She managed to put you ditching her out of her mind and enjoy herself."

"You didn't have to say it like that."

"I'm just calling it like it is, Dad. That's what you did."

"I was hoping she had such a good time that she wouldn't be so angry when she got back," he admitted. "But she's still mad at me. Hasn't said a word to me since she got back. You know she slept in the guest room last night?"

I was glad we were on the phone because I wouldn't have been able to hide the grin that shot across my face if we were talking in person.

"I had no idea, Dad. I haven't talked to her since I dropped her off."

"Damn. I mean, I know I messed up but I thought she'd cut me a little slack."

"Dad, be for real. You stood her up for your honeymoon. And what's worse, you let her think you were going when you knew you had already asked me to go in your place. She was blindsided at the airport. That's a little bit more than *messing up*. She's not gonna cut you any slack on that."

"Well, can you talk to her? Try to make her see my side?"

"With all due respect, I don't want to get involved in y'all's stuff anymore. I tried to tell you to just be straight up with her but you weren't trying to hear me. I've done enough, going on your honeymoon for you. I hate to say it but you're on your own with this one."

"Come on, son..."

"Dad, I don't know what makes you think she'll listen to me on this, anyway."

"She likes you. I can see how you two get along. Having somebody with such a good head on their shoulders vouching for me should score me some points."

"And you don't think she'll just consider me too biased to listen to and tell me to kick rocks?"

"She wouldn't do that. Not to you. Especially if you showed her as good a time on that trip as you said."

"Like I said, Dad, you're on your own. Sorry."

Dad sighed, but there was no way I was going to agree to convince Ava to forgive him. While I wasn't necessarily rooting for them to stay at odds, I wasn't going to help them mend fences, either. Hell, I thought Ava had every right to be upset at Dad, and I'd think that even if I didn't want her for myself. But I didn't want to tell him flat-out that I was on her side and not his.

"Okay, fine," he finally conceded. "I guess this *is* something I should try to fix on my own."

"Yep."

"Oh, and I think I might have another issue."

"What?"

"Vera."

I cocked a brow. "What *about* Vera?"

"I think she might become a problem."

"Why? What did she do?"

"She's been calling, texting. Talking about she thinks she might have a crush on me. Saying how much she enjoyed what we, um, did upstairs in the guest room."

"Wow, really?"

"Yeah. She even came by here. I figure it's because she knew Ava was out of town."

"She really *is* shady. What happened when she stopped by? I hope you slammed the door in her face."

"Maybe I should have, but I let her come in since she said she just wanted to talk. It turned out to be a bad idea, though, 'cause she made another pass at me."

"Aww hell. You stopped it, though, right?"

Silence.

"Dad?" I called out. "You *did* stop her, didn't you?"

"Okay, we *did* kiss for a little bit," Dad finally admitted. "But that's it. I stopped it at that."

"Really? No *hunching* this time?"

"That's not funny."

"Are you attracted to Vera or something? Why do you keep giving in to her?"

"She caught me in a weak moment. I was feeling sorry for myself over Ava and Vera was talking about how good a man she thought I was and could see herself falling for someone like me, and it was nice to hear right then. I think she had been drinking."

"Regardless, you need to let Ava know about it."

"Are you serious? She's pissed enough at me as it is. She'd probably move out if I told her I made out with her best friend."

Good. "She needs to know what kind of woman Vera is."

"Well, she's not gonna find out from me. I'm worried about fixing our marriage, not saving their friendship. All me and Vera did was kiss; it didn't mean anything. I know I don't want Vera. Not even a little bit."

"And you don't think she's gonna catch a conscience and tell Ava herself?"

"I doubt it. Not when she was begging *me* not to tell her."

"This is quite a mess you're in, Dad. I hope you can find a way out of it."

"You *sure* you don't wanna talk to Ava for me? Hell, I'll pay you."

"Not gonna happen."

"Fine."

Would I have helped Dad out in some way if Ava was just another woman and not someone I was in love with? Maybe. Lord knows I'd bailed him out of sticky situations before. But this time was different. It was hard enough for me to act like there was nothing between Ava and I; I couldn't make myself try to convince her to forgive her husband, even if he *was* my dad.

And yeah, trying to get him to tell her about Vera might've been a little selfish. Maybe if Ava knew about him and Vera fooling around, that might be the justification she needed to finally leave him. Then I'd be right there for her to turn to because naturally, she'd need a place to go. She sure as hell wouldn't go to Vera's, her friend Trish had a family so she wouldn't want to impose on her, so that left me. And over time, we'd just get closer and closer. After a while had passed, we could announce our feelings for each other. Dad wouldn't be the wiser because, well, he usually wasn't.

I wasn't proud of myself for scheming like this, especially against my own father. But I'd never been in love like this, and I wanted Ava with me more than I wanted to let Dad keep living a lie. He clearly wasn't ready for a wife, and if he was, Ava wasn't the right woman. They weren't compatible; he had to see that. Eventually, I believed he would.

I had to let Ava take the wheel on this and tell him in her own time. We'd tell him together, if she wanted. There was no telling how Dad would react to this and I didn't want her to face him alone. I was in this as much as she was.

Patience wasn't my strong suit, but I'd wait for Ava. She was worth it.

Nineteen - Ava

AFTER WHAT FELT LIKE a thousand calls, I finally caught up with Vera.

"Girl, where have you been?" I exclaimed. "I've left you a bunch of messages."

"I know. I'm sorry."

"You ran out of my place the night I introduced you to Mario and I haven't heard from you since. Are you mad at me 'cause that didn't work out?"

"Oh, no. I mean, I *was* a little bummed about it at first, but not too long after that I met someone else. And anyway, it's not your fault that he wasn't interested."

"I'm so glad to hear you say that. I was feeling a little responsible for you being so upset, even though I did try to talk you up to Mario."

"I know you did. And I appreciate it. Mario is a looker, but I'm not even thinking about him anymore. This new man is *so* much better for me."

She sounded absolutely giddy. But then again, she always sounded like this when she met someone new. I could only hope this time didn't turn out like all the others, for her sake. She deserved the happiness she was chasing after.

"Well, I must say, you sound a lot happier than you have in a while," I told her. "I'm so glad to hear it. Where did you meet this new man?"

"Oh...nowhere special. It was kind of a chance meeting."

"Aren't those the best kind? I told you, it's when you're not really looking that you find somebody."

"You're right. Because I certainly wasn't expecting to come across him when I did."

"What's his name?"

"Uh," Vera's voice faltered a little bit. "I don't wanna say. Not yet. Until I know we're solid, I'd rather just keep him to myself. Trying to go about this in a different way than all the others, you know?"

"I guess I can understand that. Well, Vera, I am so thrilled for you. Seriously. You deserve someone who makes you this happy."

"Thank you, Ava. I really think I've found him this time. I've never felt so in tune with anybody. And the way he kisses and uses his hands..."

"Oh, y'all have taken it there already?"

"Well, not all the way. It certainly wasn't because I didn't want to, though. It's been *too* long since I've gotten some. You know what it's like when you feel like you want to explode from wanting someone so badly?"

Boy, did I. It had been almost a week since my trip with Mario and I was going crazy from missing him so much. All I had were the memories of us in Tennessee, especially that last night. There were more than a few times where I thought about making a beeline to his condo and jumping into his arms, leaving my clothes on the floor.

"Yeah, I do," I answered simply. There was no way I could tell her about me and Mario, at least not right then. If her and this new man ended up going the distance, then I could tell her. But I didn't want her thinking I had anything to do with Mario not being interested in her.

"We need to grab Trish and have a girl's night soon," Vera suggested. "Get a few bottles of wine and some junk food and sit around and talk about people for a few hours."

"Sounds like fun; we absolutely need to do that soon."

We talked for a few more minutes before Vera had to go. I hung up the phone and sighed, happy for my friend and praying that it turned out the way she hoped this time.

VERA'S BUDDING NEW relationship was some welcome good news, because things certainly weren't any better between me and Harper. From the minute I got back from Tennessee, he started trying to plead his case, telling me all this bullshit about how he got so freaked out about the plane ride and didn't know how to tell me. No matter how real his fear of flying was, there was no excuse he could give me for handling it how he did. And I was no more ready to forgive him than I was when I went to Tennessee.

"Babe," Harper called out to me as I started to head upstairs after dinner. I had made myself a duck breast with roasted vegetables and polenta while he heated up a frozen pizza. "Ava."

Ignoring him, I sauntered up the stairs. He was right on my heels.

"Ava, come on," he pleaded as he watched me get a nightgown out of the dresser. "You're sleeping in the guest room again? When are you gonna talk to me? It's been days."

I slammed the door shut and went into the bathroom to get my body wash.

"We can't fix this if we don't talk," he declared when I re-entered the bedroom. "Even if you cuss me out, it'd be better than this."

I cut my eyes at him, but said nothing.

"I said I was sorry. What else do you want me to do?"

"I'll tell you what you can do," I finally responded, stopping at the doorway. "You can leave me alone."

"For real? We're just gonna go on like this?"

I was already out of the room.

I'm sure Harper really was sorry for what he did. But I was just over it. I was over *him*. There had been too many times of Harper shoving me and what I wanted to the side, and I had no reason to think it would change. Even if Mario wasn't in the picture, I wasn't gonna keep living like this.

Over the next couple of weeks, I threw myself into my work, holing myself in the office with the door locked so Harper wouldn't bother me. He was home a lot more, and I was hoping he'd go on another road trip so he could get out of my hair for a while. But he was on a mission to get back on my good side.

"You want to go out to dinner tonight?" he asked, ambushing me when I came out of the office to go to the bathroom. I could hear the desperation in his voice. "Anywhere you wanna go."

"No." I started to walk by him.

"Ava." He grabbed my arm, stopping me. "I'm trying, here."

I eyed his hand. "I've told you about grabbing me like this. But you've already proven that you don't listen to me so

I shouldn't be surprised." I yanked my arm free and glared at him.

"Well, you keep ignoring me."

"That's your justification for grabbing on me when I've repeatedly asked you not to?"

"I cannot believe you're being so stubborn about all this. Isn't a wife supposed to forgive her husband when he makes a mistake? I'd forgive you if *you* messed up."

I immediately thought of Mario, even though he was anything but a mistake.

"This has nothing to do with being stubborn, Harper. You lied to me then stood me up on our honeymoon and sent someone else in your place, and didn't have the balls to talk to me when I tried to call you. And you think because you said you're sorry, I'm just supposed to get over it. Well, it doesn't work like that."

"I don't expect for you to just get over it."

"Yes you do, Harper. You want to be done with it and you want me to be done with it so you don't have to feel guilty anymore. Well, too bad."

"I want us *both* to be done with it. I want us to be good again."

"And I wanted to go to Tennessee with you. But we clearly don't always get what we want, do we?"

I left him standing there and went on to the bathroom. Even if I was inclined to go ahead and forgive Harper for this latest indiscretion, I honestly didn't see myself getting over it. I didn't even look at him the same way anymore. And I certainly didn't want him touching me.

Maybe I was a hypocrite for condemning Harper for not being honest with me regarding the trip when I hadn't been honest with him about Mario, but I could take solace in the fact that I sincerely tried to make our marriage work. How many times had I held my tongue or let things slide to keep the peace? Time after time, I tried to squelch any budding feelings for Mario and concentrate on Harper. I wanted us to work. But now I realized I was just trying to force something that wasn't there, like Trish said.

Later that night, I was in the office working when Harper yelled to me from downstairs.

"Ava!"

I sighed. He didn't know anything about letting me have my space. Why couldn't he show me this much attention when things were good between us?

Pushing away from the desk, I trudged out of the room, stopping at the top of the stairs. Harper was standing in the middle of the living room, where he had laid out a blanket, a bottle of soda with some plastic cups, and a bucket of chicken. Maybe he was trying to use humor to get back into my good graces because this had to be a joke.

He looked up at me hopefully. "Have dinner with me? You've been up in that office all day."

I cocked a brow. "Seriously? Is this really your idea of something romantic?"

"I don't have fancy tastes, you know that."

"It has nothing to do with being fancy. But you should know me well enough by now to know that big bottle of cola and some KFC isn't gonna appeal to me. This is a classic Harper meal, which is just another example of the problem."

"What? What does this have to do with the honeymoon? I thought that was what you were mad at me about."

I heaved a deep sigh as I peered at him intently. He just had no idea.

There was no need in this going on. It was time I finally told him the real deal.

"Okay, look," I began, coming down the stairs. "We need to talk, Harper."

He looked uneasy. "Don't you wanna eat first?"

"No, I don't wanna eat first. Sit down, Harper."

He slowly sat on the couch while I took the armchair, telling myself to choose my words carefully.

"Let's be real with each other," I said gently. "This isn't working."

His eyed widened slightly. "What do you mean? *What* isn't working?"

"This," I emphasized, waving a hand back and forth between us. "Us. We need to just stop kidding ourselves."

"Ava! Are you giving up on us? Just like that?"

"It's not 'just like that', Harper. I've tried."

"We haven't even been married a year yet!"

"Well, we got married quickly so this is in right in line with that. And I'm not trying to spend years going through the motions, especially when I see no evidence of it getting any better. We...just aren't right for each other, Harper."

He looked at the ground. "You don't love me?"

"Yeah. I love you. But that doesn't mean we belong together. Sometimes love just isn't enough."

"What if I said I'd go to counseling?"

I shook my head. "I hate to say it but I wouldn't believe you. You'd probably say whatever you felt you needed to say to get me to change my mind, then I'd get my hopes up and make an appointment, trying to convince myself this time will be different. But it'd only be a matter of time before you'd flip the script on me like you usually do, giving me some reason why you don't believe in therapy or something like that. And I'm not putting myself through that."

"Babe, don't leave me, please," he begged, grabbing my hand tightly. He didn't notice my wince. "I know I can be difficult but I'm trying to be the kind of man you want. Can't you just give me some more time?"

"I don't have any more time, Harper." I gently pried my hand free.

"So I'm a little set in my ways; you know I mean well. I haven't had a wife in years and years; it's just taking me a little while to get used to it."

"I'm not trying to sit around waiting for you to get the hang of marriage, Harper. Maybe I'd buy that excuse if we were in our twenties, but we're too old for this. Just like we're too old to be jumping into marriage before we really knew each other." I looked into his sad face. "I can't keep living like this."

Crestfallen, he looked away. I could see the glassiness in his eyes. It didn't make me feel good to hurt him like this, but being with Mario in Tennessee made me realize that I was wasting my time with Harper. Part of me already knew that, but I had repeatedly tried to convince myself otherwise.

Speaking of Mario, I knew I needed to take that opportunity to be honest about my feelings for him. Harper deserved to know the whole truth.

"I know this is probably the last thing you expected to hear," I began. "And it's not the easiest thing for me to say. But you need to know-"

"Please," Harper held up his hand, his face still turned. "I get the message."

"No, Harper, it's something else-"

"Ava, can you at least give me some time to process *this* bomb you just dropped on me before you pile on? I already feel like I've been kicked in the gut."

I pursed my lips. "I'm sorry."

He looked at me, his eyes slightly red. "Can you *please* give me another chance? Whatever you say to do, I'll do it. I don't wanna lose you."

I briefly covered my face with my hands. Of course this wasn't going to be easy. "Harper, please don't do this to me. In a couple of months we'd be right back where we are now. Like you said, you're set in your ways. You're not willing to make any changes for me, and a marriage can't work like that. Let's just face facts and let it go."

A single tear rolled down Harper's cheek, which I had to admit made me a little sad. I'd never seen him cry. But I'm sure there was plenty more about Harper that I had yet to find out about. That's how it went when you jumped into a marriage without taking the time to get to know each other first.

Figuring I had said enough for the moment, I stood up. Harper just stared at the bucket of chicken on the floor as

I quietly headed back upstairs, relieved that I'd at least told him part of what I needed to tell him. I would have liked to have gotten the truth about me and Mario in, too, but I could understand him needing time to process my telling him our marriage was over.

Once I was back in the office, I closed the door and leaned against it, releasing a shaky breath. That hadn't been easy, but it had to be done. Maybe things would start to get a little better now.

WHEN I CAME OUT OF the office a while later, Harper was gone. I checked every room in the house, but his truck was missing from the driveway. The picnic he had prepared was still in the middle of the living room floor. Part of me wanted to call and make sure he was okay, but I figured he deserved to have some space. I *had* just dropped a bomb on him, even if it wasn't the biggest one I had to drop.

I put away the picnic items, then fixed me a peanut butter and jelly sandwich and a bowl of blueberry pie ice cream. As I ate, I wondered how all of this was going to play out. Would Harper grant me a divorce, or would he keep trying to get me to change my mind? Now that I'd told him I wanted out, I really just wanted to be done with it.

After I finished eating, I cleaned my dishes and headed back upstairs to get ready for bed. The light on my phone was flashing, indicating I had a message. I was thrilled to see it was Mario. We hadn't communicated much since returning from Tennessee, since we had agreed to lay low for the time being. And just speaking for myself, talking to Mario would only make me want to be with him. But I missed him something terrible, which was part of what spurned me to go ahead and be honest with Harper.

I miss you so much. Just wanted to let you know I don't regret anything we did and everything I said in Tennessee still stands. Can't wait to see you again.

I read the message several times, grinning harder each time. Flopping onto the bed in the guest bedroom, I typed out a reply, wiggling my toes happily.

Can't wait to see you, too. I certainly don't regret anything either. Wish I was with you right now. By the way, I started to tell Harper about us but he stopped me. But I did tell him I wanted out of our marriage.

M ario immediately responded.

How did he take it? ~ Mario

*N*ot great but it could've been worse. I'll try to tell him *the truth about you and me another time soon. He needs to know. ~ Ava*

Let me be there when you do that. You shouldn't have to bring that to him alone. We're both in it. ~ Mario

I appreciate that. Can't say I'm looking forward to that conversation. ~ Ava

Neither am I. But if we want to be together, he needs to know. ~ Mario

You're right. I certainly want us to be together. ~ Ava

That's what I wanna hear. Where is he now? ~ Mario

He left outta here and I don't know where he is. Hopefully he won't be too upset when he gets back. You don't think he'd do anything crazy, do you? I'm a little worried about him. He was pretty upset. ~ Ava

I'm sure he just needed to get away and get his head together. ~ Mario

You're probably right. ~ Ava

Are you okay over there? ~ Mario

I'm good now. :) ~ Ava

We continued communicating for a while before my eyes started getting heavy. After exchanging 'I love yous', I plugged my phone into the charger, put it on the nightstand, turned out the light, and snuggled under the covers with a goofy smile on my face. I couldn't help but feel I was a little closer to being with the man I really wanted to be with.

It was a little after four in the morning when Harper got home. I'd always been a rather light sleeper, and my eyes opened slightly when I heard the alarm beeping, indicating the front door opening. Not thinking anything of it, my eyes drifted closed and I burrowed deeper into the covers.

Pretty soon, the guest room door banged open. My back was to the door, and I turned slightly to see Harper's huge frame in the doorway. I could smell the alcohol from where he stood.

"Harper?"

He didn't say anything for a few moments, and I turned away from him again, closing my eyes. Maybe he just wanted to be near me or something. I figured he'd just stand there for a while and then make his way to his room and sleep it off.

But all of a sudden, the comforter was being yanked off me. Harper roughly grabbed my shoulder and jerked me onto my back. I could barely make out his face in the dark, but I could see his eyes well enough to know they held an expression I'd never seen before. They looked...crazed. Fear shot through me like a comet.

I tried to ease away from him, but he wasn't having that. He had a grip on my arm that made me grit my teeth in pain.

"What are you doing?" I exclaimed, kicking at him. "You're hurting me!"

Ignoring my pleas, his other hand reached under my nightgown and ripped my panties off. He was already naked, apparently having prepared for this violation. I was screaming and trying to get away, but whatever Harper had spent the evening getting hammered on had temporarily erased any compassion I thought he had.

He jammed himself into me, not caring about my screams of pain. His large body had me pinned, and I cried and begged him to stop while he just grunted and breathed his alcohol breath into my face, his sweat pouring onto me like a salty waterfall.

"Harper, please stop," I pleaded, my tears streaming into my ears. "Don't do this, please!"

"Shut up!" he grunted, increasing his force. He was pounding into me, clearly punishing me for telling him our marriage was over. And when his hands closed around my throat, I panicked, honestly thinking he was gonna try to kill me. But thankfully he loosened his grip almost as quickly as he applied it, opting to grab a tight handful of my hair instead, which still hurt like hell but at least I could breathe.

After he was done with that position, he roughly flipped me over and shoved my head into the bed as he re-entered me, no gentleness to be found. His left hand held my hip while his right hand slapped my ass as hard as he could, almost as if he was trying to see what could make me scream in pain the loudest. This had to be a nightmare.

When he finally got enough, he yanked me back onto my back, sticking his tongue deep into my mouth. I was too disgusted and distraught to kiss him back, but either he didn't notice or he didn't care. He just continued to practically swallow my face, his teeth clanking against mine. Both of his hands grabbed my breasts so hard I thought he was trying to rip them from my body. I pushed against his shoulders, but it didn't do any good. He was like a boulder.

Thankfully, this part only lasted a minute or so before he suddenly passed out, collapsing next to me. I just laid there, his body partially draped across mine, crying and too scared to move. As much as I tried to convince myself that this was all just a bad dream, I knew it wasn't. My husband had just raped me.

Harper was out cold. I slowly eased myself from underneath him, grabbing my torn nightgown when I was finally free. Covering my bruised body, I snatched my phone and charger from the nightstand and hurried from the room, going to put on the first pair of sweats and sneakers I could find. Then I grabbed my keys and my purse and got the hell out of there.

Twenty - Ava

I KNOW I MUST HAVE looked a mess when I slinked into the police station. My hair was sticking up all over my head and my face was red and puffy from all the crying. But no one really batted an eye. I guess seeing a disheveled woman in the middle of the night was old hat to everyone in there.

"Can I help you?" a woman asked me. She was blonde, but that's all I could register about her.

"I'd like to speak to someone," I said in a low voice, leaning a little closer to her. "I want to, um, file a report against my, um, husband."

"Do you need to see a doctor?"

"No," I quickly replied. Clearing my throat, I briefly looked at her before looking away again. Her eyes were green. "No, I don't."

"Okay," she nodded, unnerved. "Have a seat over there and an officer will be right with you."

Sniffling, I nodded and headed over to the wooden bench against the wall, scooting as far into the corner as I could. I hastily wiped my eyes as I glanced around me. For it to be so late, there were quite a few people milling around. There was a woman with a black eye, a pair of teenagers and an older gentleman, an elderly woman with a horribly bad wig, and a man who was clearly high on something. None of them really paid me any attention.

I pulled out my barely-charged phone that was still attached to the charger and started to call Mario. Hearing his voice would no doubt make me feel at least a little better. But I ended up stuffing my phone back into my purse, hastily tucking in the dangling cord on top of it. Calling him could wait. I still felt like I was in a daze, and my head was killing me. I rested it against the wall and closed my eyes. Pretty soon I began noticing the conversation going on near me, between the older man and the two teenagers.

"I tried to tell you she was no good," the teenaged girl hissed in a not-subtle whisper. "But noooo. You just *had* to let her back in the house."

"She's your mother. I had to give her another chance," the man justified.

"You've already given her a *hundred* chances," the teenage boy reminded him. "She does the same crap every time."

"And she just did it again," the girl chimed in. "Stole all our stuff—including Grandma's jewelry—while we were gone, slashed your tires, tried to *fight* me-"

"And she used my social security number to open a bunch of accounts and stuff," the boy added. "And let's not forget all the crap she did to *you*, Dad."

"Guys, I don't need a rundown of everything your mother did," the man said, his voice tired. His body was slumped, the weariness of whatever they were dealing with evident. "I'm well aware."

"Well, I just wish you would think of *us* first instead of her for once," the girl snapped, folding her arms. "I'm sick of her making our lives miserable."

"If you let her come back again, I'm moving out," the boy announced emphatically. "I don't even consider her my mother, anyway. A real mother doesn't do that kind of stuff to her kids."

"You know she has a problem. We can't turn our backs on her," the man protested.

"I don't care, Dad. She doesn't give a damn about us. I'm done giving a damn about her."

They continued to go back and forth, and I looked down at my wedding ring, twisting it around my finger. My eyes roamed around me again and suddenly, I no longer wanted to be there. I don't know what it was, but hearing that family and what they were dealing with gave me some warped renewed sense of strength. That in no way meant that I was forgiving Harper or giving him a pass for what he did, but I just had a strong urge to get out of that police station right then.

Standing, I slung my purse over my shoulder and quietly walked out. Maybe it was stupid not to fill out a report, but for the time being, I was following my gut.

As I got back into my car, I started to call Trish to let her know I needed to come by. I wasn't quite ready to let Mario know about this yet. But when I thought about it, Trish would take one look at my face and know something was wrong. Same with Vera. They'd try to pry the details of what happened out of me, and I really didn't want to talk about it yet. And if they happened to see any of the bruises that had surely appeared on my body by then, they'd call the police on Harper themselves. Or Trish would send her husband over there with his rifle.

I couldn't handle a bunch of commotion right then. All I wanted to do was get my head together in peace and process what happened, and figure out what I wanted to do about it. I'd have a clearer head after a few hours of sleep.

So I went and checked into the Holiday Inn, bruised, spent, and confused.

MY PHONE WAS BLOWING up.

I'd turned it on vibrate after I checked into the hotel so I could get some rest, burying myself under the covers and drowning everything out. But now the constant sounds of the phone vibrating on top of the nightstand were breaking into the temporary peace I had managed to force. Groaning, I reached over and blindly grabbed it, bringing it underneath the covers with me. My eyebrows shot up at the number of missed calls and messages from Harper, Mario, and Trish. Harper must have sobered up and freaked out, wondering where I was, and called Mario and Trish looking for me.

Not ready to deal with them yet, I pushed the phone aside and closed my eyes, burying my face in the pillow. When I had gotten undressed and dared to look at my bare body in the mirror, I gasped at the bruises that covered my arms, hips, and right side of my butt. I had expected some bruising given how hard Harper had grabbed and slapped my body, but actually seeing the bluish-purple spots right in front of me only cemented how real all of this really was. Maybe some part of me held out hope that it wasn't quite as bad as I remembered, or even still that I was dreaming all of this. But those bruises wiped all that out.

Eventually, I sat up and rubbed my eyes. I still wasn't quite ready to deal with all of this, but I knew I couldn't put it off forever. I didn't want Mario and Trish worrying about me so I figured I could at least let them know I was okay. Harper could go to hell.

I called Trish first.

"Girl, where the hell are you? Harper called here, waking everybody up and freaking out, saying you were nowhere to be found."

"I'm fine. I'm sorry he bothered y'all like that."

"Hell, when I tried to call you and got no response I got worried, myself. Where are you?"

"I'm at a hotel."

"Why? What happened?"

"I'd rather not get into every little detail right now but let's just say things got very heated between me and Harper last night. He didn't...react very well after I told him I thought we should split up."

Trish gasped loudly. "You did?? You actually told him you wanted a divorce?"

"I had to. We don't belong together. And what happened last night only cemented that for me."

"Does this have anything to do with Mario?"

"That's another thing I'll have to catch you up on later but yes, it has a lot to do with Mario. I'm in love with him, Trish. There's not a doubt in my mind that he's who I want to be with. But even if he wasn't in the picture, I certainly don't want to be with Harper anymore."

"Ava," Trish's voice was stern, "Did he do something to you? And do not lie to me or tell me you don't wanna talk about it."

"Trish..."

"If you don't want to get into the details right now, I'll respect that. But I at least need to know this much. Yes or no; did Harper put his hands on you?"

I *didn't* want to get into this right then, but I wasn't about to lie to my homegirl. Not about this.

"Yeah, he did," I admitted, my voice low. It was almost like I was worried about the people in the next room hearing me or something. "But please understand, that's all I have the energy to say about it right now, okay?"

"All right," Trish conceded, though I knew she was probably about to burst with all the questions she wanted to ask, as well as from anger. "I'll leave it alone for now, as far as asking you to talk about it. But are you *sure* you're all right? That's the main thing I'm worried about right now. We'll deal with Harper's ass later."

"I'm not great but I'm as well as I can be right now."

"Well, that's a mild relief. Does Mario know about any of this?"

"No. I haven't talked to anyone since I left the house. I'm gonna call him next."

"And why the hell didn't you come over here instead of going to a hotel?"

"Because I wasn't ready to explain why I was showing up at your door in the middle of the night. Not to mention you have a husband and kids; I didn't want to disturb y'all like that if I didn't have to. I just needed to get my head together."

"I get it, but you know you can come here any time you need to. Leroy wouldn't have a problem with that, especially under circumstances like this."

"I appreciate it, girl."

"I'll let Vera know you're all right. I had called her to see if you were over there or if she knew what was up. I wonder why Harper didn't call her like he called me."

"Who knows."

"Yeah. Well, go ahead and call Mario 'cause he needs to know what's going on. Keep me posted on where you are."

"I will."

"What do you want me to tell Harper if he calls back?"

"I'm sure you don't need me to tell you what to tell him."

"I didn't know I had free reign to speak freely. Now that I know I do, say no more."

I couldn't help but chuckle. Trish was the best friend a girl could have.

"Trish, girl," I shook my head, the tired smile still on my lips. "I just love you."

"I love you too, girl."

Ending that call, I took a deep breath as I dialed Mario. I could only hope that he didn't take it personally that I opted to go to a hotel instead of going to his place.

"Ava?" His voice sounded worried.

"Hey," I greeted softly.

"Baby, what's going on? Dad's been calling me every two minutes, asking if I know where you are."

"Yeah, I, um...we had a big fight when he got back last night and I left."

"Where are you?"

"At a hotel."

"Why didn't you come over here?"

"I was pretty messed up and just wanted to be by myself."

"You were driving around while you were that upset?"

"It wasn't really an Uber kind of situation. But I'm all right."

"Come over here, Ava. I don't like you being alone right now. And what the hell happened with Dad? He's losing his damn mind, wondering where you are."

"I told you, we had a fight."

"The last time you left out of there it was because you found out some stuff about his past and he brushed it off. Was it something else like that?"

"Hmph, I *wish* that was all it was," I grunted, picking at the bedspread.

"What aren't you telling me, Ava?"

I wouldn't be able to hide what Harper did from Mario for long, but over the phone wasn't the way to let him know. And now that I was talking to him, I wanted to be with him. If for nothing else than to just lay on his chest and feel his arms around me.

"Let's just say it was really bad, Mario. I'll tell you more later but right now, I'm gonna get myself together and get out of this hotel."

"You going home or you coming here?"

"I'm coming there. I still don't want to see Harper. And if he calls you again, just let him know you've heard from me and he needs to give me some space. Though I'm sure he'll try to act like he doesn't know why."

"All right. Just get here as quickly and safely as you can. We'll deal with whatever comes next together. I just want to see with my own eyes that you're good."

The times I wished I'd met Mario before Harper increased by ten. "Okay. I'll get over there as soon as I can."

"Be careful. I love you."

Maybe it was because it was still so new coming from him, but hearing that made me smile. Hard. "I love you, too."

Anxious to be with my man, I hurried to gather my things. Harper had left me several messages, as well, but there was no way I was calling him back. None of the messages mentioned anything about what happened last night, so I was sure he'd say he didn't remember any of it, or worse, deny it.

Less than an hour later, I was at Mario's. He hugged me tightly as soon as I was through the door, and I winced slightly due to my body still being sore.

"I'm glad to see you," he said, looking me over with concern.

"Believe me, I'm glad to see you, too. You have no idea."

He took my hand and led me to the couch. "Still not ready to talk about what happened?"

I shook my head. "Not yet."

"I'll respect that. Do you need anything? You hungry?"

Really, I wanted to take a shower but if I did that and Mario saw my bare body, there would be no way to explain the bruises without straight-up lying. It's not like I was naturally clumsy and able to pass it off on that, and he probably wouldn't buy that, anyway, given the placement and severity of the bruises. Mario was far from an idiot and I'd rather tell him nothing at all than try to insult his intelligence.

"I wouldn't mind something to eat," I admitted.

He jumped up to fix me something, asking what I wanted. When I said I didn't care, he heated up the leftovers from the Greek dish he had experimented with the night before, and I marveled a little too enthusiastically about how good it was. I just needed to focus on something that had absolutely nothing to do with Harper or what happened with him the night before, and Mario's cooking was as good a subject as any.

After I ate, we continued to talk about everything but what was at the forefront of both of our minds. I knew Mario wanted to know everything, and I appreciated him being patient and not pressuring me for details. This was all new territory for me and I was just flying by the seat of my pants as far as how to deal with it. Might not have been the best way but it was the best I could do right then.

Eventually, I got tired of talking and laid my head on Mario's shoulder. Getting the message, he put an arm around me and we just sat there together, quietly. My hand was on this thigh, rubbing it mindlessly back and forth. I eyed my movements, watching it get closer and closer to his crotch as if I had no control over it. When I gently grabbed his manhood through his pants, there was a sharp intake of breath, and his hand gripped my sweatshirt.

Not letting myself think about it, I sat up and kissed him abruptly. I just wanted some intimacy with him, as if that would help erase the violation I'd endured the night before. Mario kissed me back, following my lead. My hand was still holding his dick, but I wasn't trying to take it much further than what we were doing. I just wanted to be close to him, and feel something other than pain for a while.

Twenty-One - Mario

AVA ENDED UP STAYING with me for the next two days.

Something was up. It felt like she was glad to be there with me, but she seemed different. There was a distance there that usually wasn't. She took a shower but locked the door while she was in there, keeping me out. When I offered to give her a t-shirt of mine to put on, she insisted on either her sweats or a pair of pajamas. And it was like pulling teeth to get her to sleep in my bed with me; she was going to sleep on the couch. We kissed some, and some very light petting, but that's where the intimacy stopped.

I didn't want to push her for details, but it was clear that this latest fight with Dad was different from the others. She'd told me that she let him know she wanted out of the marriage and then he left the house; apparently the shit hit the fan whenever he got back. But what could he have said to make her run off to a hotel in the middle of the night?

Dad was still calling me, asking about Ava's whereabouts. Ava had already told me that I could tell him she was there, but to let him know that she did *not* want to see or talk to him. Dad wasn't quite satisfied with that, though.

"Why are you trying to keep her away from me?" he demanded.

"I'm just respecting Ava's wishes, Dad. Whatever went down between you two really shook her up and she needs some time."

"So we had a fight. I don't get why she keeps running off like this. She's too much of a drama queen."

I could feel my ire ignite, but tried to keep my temper in check. I was still just supposed to be the impartial go-between; cussing Dad out in Ava's defense might make him suspicious. "So you had *nothing* to do with any of this, huh? This is all on her?"

"I'm just saying. She's a grown woman but can't stay and face her issues with her own husband. She sneaks out while I'm asleep and then I have to go looking for her."

Taking a beat to calm myself, I replied, "Well, you know where she is. I'm taking care of her. And until she's ready to talk to you, you should just ease up and give her the space she needs."

Dad was quiet for a moment. "What did she tell you?"

"She only told me y'all had a fight. I don't know anything else."

"Did she blow it up and try to make it sound worse than it was? Did she blame it all on me?"

My fists were balling up all by themselves. "I have no way of knowing if she's blowing anything up. I wasn't there to see whatever happened. But again, all she said was y'all had a bad fight."

"Well, when is she planning on coming home?"

"I don't know."

"So she's just gonna stay over there with you?"

"If she needs to."

"What if I don't feel right about that?"

"You felt right about sending me on your honeymoon with her. Don't see what the problem would be with this."

It came out snide, but I didn't try to take it back. The fact that Dad was acting so insensitive and blameless was getting on my nerves. True enough, I didn't know *what* their fight was about, but I knew Dad. He had a tendency to not take accountability for his part in things. I didn't know if it was his stubbornness keeping him from taking any blame, or if he was actually delusional enough to think he didn't have any.

"I don't appreciate you throwing that in my face," he growled, testiness in his voice. "This doesn't have anything to do with that."

"Dad, I'm not trying to go back and forth with you about this. Ava is still very upset and doesn't want to see you right now. That's it."

He sucked his teeth. "Whatever."

"And I'd think you'd rather her be here with me than off in a hotel by herself like she was the night after y'all fell out."

"Why didn't she go to Trish's? That's where I got her from that other time."

"Trish has a husband and kids. Ava didn't want to impose on them like that. It's just me here."

"Fine. I guess it's not enough that somebody's been following me lately and I damn near got ran off the road twice in the last few days. Not to mention one of my accounts getting hacked. Now I've gotta deal with this."

Maybe it was because I was so annoyed that his words barely registered. I didn't even blink. "You don't have to *deal* with anything. I've got Ava."

"I'm not crazy about it but I'll ease up. For now."

"Good. And, Dad?"

"What?"

"I'm not trying to be nosey but I'll ask you since Ava doesn't want to talk about it yet...what happened?"

"She basically told me she wanted a divorce," Dad eagerly answered. I wonder if he thought this would make me empathize with him. "Just out of the blue. I was trying to make things right between us and she walked around here ignoring me for days, sleeping in the guest room. Then, just like that, she tells me she doesn't think this is working and wants out."

I frowned. Ava had already told me about this part, but she didn't say they fought about it. She said he got upset, then left. She was there alone texting back and forth with me while he was gone. So whatever went down between them had to happen whenever he got back.

But of course, I wasn't supposed to know all this.

"That's it? That's all that happened?"

"Isn't that enough?"

"Just doesn't seem like the 'bad fight' that Ava said it was."

"I told you, she's a drama queen. She drops that kind of bomb on me but then she's the one to shut *me* out? Hmph," Dad sucked his teeth again. "Women."

Either Dad was leaving a lot of stuff out, or Ava was greatly exaggerating what happened. And I hate to admit it, but knowing Dad, I believed it was the former.

"Hmm," I finally grunted. "Okay, then."

"It really hasn't even hit me yet, I don't think, the fact that she wants to leave me," Dad continued. "But she has to come home sometime and whenever she does, hopefully I can get her to change her mind. This is just a bump in the road, that's all. Did she think marriage was always gonna be easy or something? This isn't one of those movies she likes to sit up in the bed and watch. I thought she was more mature than this."

Shaking my head, I knew it was time to end this call. There was only so much downtalking about Ava I was going to be able to tolerate before I lost it.

"Well, everything will turn out like it's supposed to," I managed to say without anger. "And like I said, I'm taking care of Ava so you don't need to worry about that."

"I appreciate it. Put in a good word for me, son."

Not a chance in hell. "Bye, Dad."

I was more curious than ever about what actually had gone down between Ava and Dad. Ava wasn't acting like herself and I had a feeling Dad wasn't being completely forthcoming. If I didn't know better, I'd wonder if Dad...nah. I didn't even want to think that. Dad had his flaws, but he wouldn't go *there*.

Ava emerged from the bedroom, up from her nap. She looked adorable in my plaid pjs that were way too big for her. Combing through her disheveled short hair with her fingers, she looked around the room, then at me.

"Hey," I greeted her.

"Hey." She rubbed her eyes. "You were just on the phone?"

"Yeah." I tossed my phone onto the couch. "It was Dad."

"Ugh." Ava rolled her eyes. "He just won't take a damn hint."

"I set him straight. Told him he needed to ease up and leave you alone for a while."

"And you think he'll actually do it?"

"Sure. He might not *like* it, but he'll do it."

"If you say so."

"You want something to eat? I made some sweet potato waffles."

"Ooh!" Ava's head snapped to me, automatically intrigued. I chuckled. "For real?"

"Yep. I got some of that chicken sausage you like, too, if you want some of that."

"Okay, Mario, I already wasn't in a hurry to leave, but you're making me want to start claiming spots up in here."

I laughed. "I've already claimed it for you, baby. And for the record, I don't *want* you to leave."

"Awww, sweetie!" she gushed, walking over to me with her arms out. I received her hug, glad I could make her smile. "Thank you so much for everything you're doing for me."

"My pleasure. I'll do whatever I can for you."

"I know. And I appreciate it."

Taking her face in my hands, I kissed her, loving it more each time I got to do it. I meant what I said about not wanting her to leave. Despite the reason she was there, it just felt right, us being there together.

"Come on," I said, putting an arm around her. "I'll fix you a plate."

"You don't have to. I can do it."

"I know you can. But you won't. Let me pamper you, woman. You don't think you deserve that?"

She looked up at me and grinned, and a bolt of emotion shot through me. The love I felt for Ava was enough to freak me out, because I'd never felt it on that level for any other woman. But instead of running from it, I was enjoying it. I was starting to hate the thought of Ava not by my side.

"You twisted my arm," she joked. "Just don't be getting me all used to this kind of thing and then fall off when you think you've got your hooks in me."

"Please. I'm too grown for that bullshit."

I fixed her a plate, underestimating how much she would eat because she went and got three more waffles on top of the two I initially gave her. And she killed *all* the chicken sausage.

"Damn!" I marveled when she was finally done. "You want me to defrost the pork loin in the freezer and stick a dozen biscuits in the oven?"

"Maybe for dinner," Ava quipped, winking at me.

"I knew you liked to eat but didn't know you could put it away like *that*. I'm not mad at it, though. I think it's hot."

"Yeah? Well, you know what they say," she teased, rubbing her bare foot against my leg. "Women who eat a lot make the best lovers."

"I have never heard that before in my life."

"It's true, though."

"You're a damn good lover, so I'm inclined to believe it."

This was my aim, to keep her mind off of her drama with Dad. She'd have to face him eventually, but I wasn't going to rush her to do it. Just like I wasn't going to rush her to tell me everything that happened between them that night. I knew I'd find out the truth soon enough.

We just spent the day chilling together. Watching movies, trading college stories while she helped me fold some laundry, eating junk food. We even traded advice about work; I showed her the ideas for my YouTube channel that I was working on and she made suggestions on how to punch it up, and she bounced ideas off me for an article she was working on. She finally seemed at ease and relaxed.

We curled up on my old recliner, her on my lap, sharing a bowl of popcorn while we binged-watched *Frasier*.

"It's crazy how much we both love this show," she commented, giggling. "My friends surely don't get the appeal."

"It's just one of the many things we have in common, baby. I told you we were soul mates."

"Yes, we are." She pecked my lips before turning her eyes back to the screen. We were watching the episode where Niles had to watch his beloved Daphne get engaged to another man right in front of him. It made me think of how I felt whenever I had to see or hear about Ava and Dad together.

We just sat there cuddled up together, laughing and talking about what we were watching, both loving having someone to do that with. I really felt like Ava was my best friend as well as the love of my life. And I loved that.

I rubbed her thigh through her pjs. "Babe."

"Hmm?"

"You remember the first time you came over here and you asked if this chair had sentimental value?"

She turned to look at me. "Yeah..."

"Well, it does. This is the only thing I have of my Mama's." I played with the hole in the arm. "Dad had it in storage for years and was gonna get rid of it; he actually didn't want me to keep it."

"Why?? I'd think he'd want you to have something of hers, since you didn't get much time with her before she passed."

"You would think. But he gave me some bullshit excuse about making a clean break, not that I listened to him. We had a pretty big fight about it, actually."

"Wow, Harper actually did that? I can't believe that he would have such a problem with you keeping this."

"Yeah. Held a grudge about it for a while, too. Almost as long the one he kept when I quit playing ball." I felt my anger flare up, as it usually did when I thought about this. Those were not good times between me and Dad and I tried not to think about them too much. "Anyway, that's the deal with the chair."

After gazing at me for a moment, she moved the bowl of popcorn to the end table before straddling me, wrapping her arms around my neck. I hugged her back tightly, closing my eyes.

"Thank you for sharing that with me," she said softly. "It means so much that you did."

I waited until she pulled back before I looked right into her eyes and replied, "You mean so much to *me*, Ava. You're everything to me."

Looking like she was about to cry, she grinned and leaned in for a long kiss before curling up in my lap, holding onto me tightly.

"You're everything to me, too, Mario."

We stayed like that through three more episodes.

She went to sleep not too long after that, and after I worked on my blog for a while and returned some emails,

I joined her. I loved how she immediately snuggled up to me when I got in bed. For a while, I just laid there in the dark, admiring her as she slept. She looked so peaceful, and innocent. The urge to protect her grew the longer I gazed at her.

Even if it was from my Dad.

AND SPEAKING OF DAD, guess who showed up at my door early the next morning?

"Are you kidding me?" I droned, wiping my eyes as I stood in the doorway. He was standing there with a bouquet of roses and a teddy bear like it was Valentine's Day or something. "I thought you said you were going to give Ava some space, Dad."

"I did."

"It hasn't even been a full day. And I know she didn't tell you to come over here."

"Look, I miss her, all right? I don't like being in that house alone."

"So call Everette."

"I haven't even been able to get in touch with him lately. I guess him and that lady he was seeing have really been hitting it off. But I don't want him there, anyway; I want Ava."

"Well, Dad, Ava has already said that she didn't want to see you. Not respecting her wishes isn't the best way to get back on her good side."

"Did she eat already? I can go get her a biscuit or something from McDonald's."

I resisted the urge to roll my eyes. "She's still asleep. And *I'm* gonna fix her breakfast."

"Well, maybe I can eat with y'all."

"Dad, I have to say, man...you're sounding real desperate right now."

"I want my wife home with me. There's nothing desperate about that."

"Harper?"

Ava stood behind me in another pair of my pajamas, one of my wave caps on her head, looking anything but pleased.

Dad was no more pleased to see her adorned head to toe in my clothes. He frowned. "What is that on your head?"

"Why are you here?" she demanded, ignoring his question. "What part of *I need space* don't you get?"

"I left you alone all day yesterday. And that was after you'd been over here a day already. And why do you have on his pajamas?"

"Would you rather I walk around naked?"

Dad's face actually turned red a little bit. "Can we talk, babe?"

"You can go ahead and stop calling me that. And no, we cannot."

"Seriously?"

"Did you really think some fake flowers and a re-gifted teddy bear were going to soften me up? Yeah, I recognize it," she continued at his shocked look. "You got that thing for free when you subscribed to some magazine."

Coughing and clearing my throat to hide my laugh, I held up my hands. "I'm gonna go in the other room and let y'all handle your business."

"You don't have to do that, Mario," Ava immediately protested.

"It's cool. You do whatever you feel is necessary." Which I hoped was slamming the door in his face, but I kept that thought to myself. I moved towards the bedroom, stopping next to her. "I'm right back here if you need me," I assured her in a low voice.

"Thanks," she looked at me gratefully before turning her frown back on for Dad.

I went into my bedroom and closed the door, resisting the urge to stand there and eavesdrop. Whether I liked it or not, they were still married. Only the two of them knew what had really driven her out of that house. So I had to step aside and let Ava handle it as she saw fit, without hovering over her.

I turned on the TV, trying to further fight the temptation to listen to them. I could hear their voices, but couldn't make out what they were saying. Even without hearing the exact words, though, I could tell the conversation wasn't peaceful. Ava's voice steadily got louder, and eventually, so did Dad's. I moved towards the door just in case I had to go get in between them, because it sounded like it was getting pretty heated. But after a few minutes, their voices calmed down to a low murmur. I sat on the bed, expecting Ava to come through the door any minute and say she had sent Dad on his way. All I could hope was that he hadn't upset her so much that she wouldn't be able to enjoy the rest of her day with me.

Eventually, my bedroom door eased open and Ava stepped in. Closing the door behind her, she looked at me with an expression I couldn't quite read.

"Everything okay?" I asked, sitting on the edge of the bed.

She turned her eyes away. "I'm gonna go home with him, Mario."

It sounded like the last thing she wanted to say. It was certainly the last thing I wanted to hear. Hell, it was the last thing I was *expecting* to hear, considering how pissed she still was at him. I had to check myself because I immediately started to ask what the hell she was doing.

Looking at my hands, I asked, "Why?"

"Because I can't put it off forever. I have to deal with our issues, and I can't really do that while I'm over here."

Nodding slowly, I just twisted my lips to keep from cussing. "I see."

"This doesn't mean I've changed my mind about anything," she insisted, coming to stand in front of me. She grabbed my face, lifting it and waiting for me to look at her. "You're still the man I want to be with. But we're never going to be able to enjoy each other and have a relationship like we want until I close this chapter with Harper."

"All right."

"Mario, please tell me you understand this."

"Yeah, I get it."

Her eyes pleaded with me. "Really?"

"Yeah, Ava. I can't say I'm thrilled about you leaving with him, but you're right about us not being able to really be together while y'all are still up in the air."

She only looked mildly relieved. "I'll keep you posted on everything."

"Are you planning on telling him about us?"

"I honestly don't know how I'm gonna handle all of this. While I *am* still upset at him, I can't forget that I betrayed him, too. So I want to at least try to give him some modicum of closure. But trust me, I made it clear that this doesn't mean he and I are good or that we're reconciling. He's deluded enough to think he can change my mind, but that's not happening."

"If you say so."

She gasped. "Mario!"

"I'm sorry, I'm trippin'," I checked myself. I was mad, but I knew I couldn't be mad at her. We both knew she'd have to go back over there sometime. And I tried to focus on the fact that the sooner she closed things out with Dad, the sooner she could come to me.

I took her hand and kissed it, holding it tightly in mine. "Do whatever you need to do. I'm not going anywhere."

Smiling, she pulled on my hand, urging me to my feet. She slid her arms around my neck, holding me tightly. I closed my eyes as I buried my face in her neck, a pang hitting my chest. Even though I knew better, I felt like I was losing her and the thought made me ache.

"I better go," she eventually whispered, easing back. I just nodded and dropped my arms from her waist, letting her start gathering her things. She slid my wave cap from her head and asked if I could step out while she changed back into her sweats. I looked at her, frowning slightly.

"Harper is still here, sweetie," she reminded me, her voice hushed. "You can't very well stay in here with me while I change clothes. How would we explain that?"

"Damn, my bad; you're right," I quickly said, clearing my expression. I hadn't even thought about that.

I started towards the door, but stopped. I walked quickly over to her, pulled her to me, and laid a deep kiss on her, glad that she was returning it with as much intensity as I was giving it.

Finally, I left the room so she could get changed. Dad was sitting on the couch in the living room, twiddling his thumbs nervously like an anxious teenager waiting on his first date. He shot to his feet when I entered the room.

"Is she ready?"

Goodness gracious. "She'll be out when she's done, Dad. She's changing clothes."

"Oh." He sat back down.

I sat on the other end of the couch and mindlessly watched television. Didn't try to make any small talk because I didn't have anything to say. Regardless of the reasoning or his right to do so, I hated that Dad had come over there after Ava. I hated that she was going home with him. I hated that she wasn't really mine like I felt she was.

Thankfully, Ava emerged, dressed in her sweats, her short hair brushed back from her face. I swallowed upon seeing her, but quickly turned my eyes back to the television. I didn't want to see her leave with him. It was taking all my restraint not to get up and leave the room.

"Thank you for everything, Mario," she said to me, her voice soft. I could feel her looking at me. "I appreciate it."

"No problem."

"See you later, son," Dad called out, opening the door. "I appreciate you looking after my wife."

All I could do was tap my fist against my temple and force myself to glance over at him, my eyes like slits. "Yep."

Dad walked out, with Ava trailing behind him. She looked at me regretfully as she closed the door behind her.

As soon as the door closed, my head fell against the back of the couch, feeling like I'd just been kicked in the chest.

"SO," JAYDEN SAID, "YOU boned your stepmother."

I'd called him and asked him to meet me at a bar so I could drink my sorrows away (though that's not what I said to him). I hadn't planned on telling him about what happened in Tennessee yet, but after a couple of Hennessey and Cokes, everything came out.

I cut my eyes at him as I slammed my glass to the counter. "Real funny."

"Okay, my bad. I guess I shouldn't mess with you right now."

"Please don't."

"Are you *sure* you've fallen for her like that and it's not just infatuation?"

"No, man. I'm old enough to know the difference between being infatuated and being in love. And I'm in love with Ava."

"And she's in love with you?"

"Yeah. She says she is."

"I get that you can't help who you for fall for but, *man...*" he whistled. "You couldn't have picked a more inconvenient woman."

"You don't have to tell me. Things would be so much easier if I had fallen for Mikki or somebody else. But like I told you, Ava had a hold on me since we first met. I tried to fight it, deny it, ignore it, all that, but it didn't work. And when we went to Tennessee together, that just cemented everything."

"And your dad has no idea?"

"No. I love my dad but his head seems stuck in the sand half the time."

"How in the world are you gonna handle this, man?"

"I don't know. I'm letting Ava lead on this. However she wants to handle it, I'm with it."

"I can't imagine your dad is gonna just step aside and let you have Ava like that. Even if she doesn't want to be with him anymore, he won't take it well at all when he finds out she wants to be with *you*."

"I know. But that's just the reality of all this."

"And you're not worried about how it's going to affect your relationship with him?"

"Of course, I've thought about that a lot. But honestly, the thought of losing Ava hurts more than the thought of being on the outs with Dad. It's not like it would be the first time. If anything, I resent him for meeting her first."

"Man...I hope she's worth all this. Because there's no way this can end well."

"I know." I took a long swig of my refreshed drink. "Trust me, I know."

We stayed at the bar a while longer before Jayden drove me home, not trusting me to drive myself. I just flopped onto my bed, staring up at the ceiling. I would've given anything to know what was going on over at Dad and Ava's. For the hundredth time, I checked my phone for any texts from her, but there were none. This was going to require more patience than I had.

I couldn't even believe I was in this situation. Dad and I never had similar tastes in women before. The few times he did date anyone after Mom's death, it was always with some nondescript, plain jane-type chicks that were closer to his age. And they were never around for very long.

I recalled a time when I asked Dad why his brief courtship of a lady had ended so abruptly. It was literally a case of here one day and gone the next, which was strange to me because they seemed really into each other. But he had been tight-lipped, not wanting to share the details with me. Something about that whole situation seemed off to me, but I couldn't pry anything out of him as to what really went down. Not that we usually really made a habit of confiding in each other; like I've said, Dad and I were never terribly close. We got along, but that was about it.

When I really thought about it, I felt like there was a lot I didn't know about Dad. Like the whole thing with his sexual assault case from back in the day; I'd been just as shocked as Ava was to find out about that. Hell, even the fact that he'd married Ava in the first place, seemingly on a whim. Being impulsive wasn't really a trait of Dad's.

And don't even get me started on this latest fight between them. I still felt like Dad was hiding something, and

I didn't feel good about it. There was just a bad feeling in my gut that I wouldn't like what I would hear if I learned those details.

When it really came down to it, I began to wonder *just* how well I knew my own father.

TWENTY-TWO – AVA

PREGNANT.

Fuck.

The last thing I expected when I went to the doctor was to hear that I was pregnant. I thought I was just stressed or had caught a bug or something. But life was throwing me yet another curve ball, right to the face.

I wasn't thrilled about this. Being a mother had never been at the top of my life wish list. Whether it was due to the strained relationship I had with my own mother or if it was just something I never really wanted, I wasn't sure, but knowing that there was a baby cooking inside of me didn't fill me with joy. Especially since I wasn't entirely sure who the father was.

Depending on how far along I was, it could be Mario *or* Harper. I recalled when Mario and I were in Tennessee, and how things went down our last night there. We had gone a few rounds, and protection hadn't been used during all of them. And Harper certainly wasn't thinking about protection when he was raping me.

Speaking of that, it was something I had yet to address since agreeing to go back home with Harper. Strangely, I wasn't very afraid of a repeat performance. I was still sleeping in the guest room, and I made sure to keep the door locked. But even if he broke the door down and tried it again, I had a knife under the pillow ready for him. And this time, I wouldn't punk out about turning him in.

I'd gone back home with Harper so we could finally close out our marriage and move on from each other, but now Harper was playing the avoidance game. The day after I got back home, he went out on the road. He wouldn't take my calls or return my texts. It really amazed me how childish this grown man was turning out to be. The more I got to know him, the more I realized marrying him had been a major mistake.

Well, I wasn't going to sit around and wait for him to start acting sensible. While he was gone, I went ahead and contacted my lawyer. I already knew an annulment was out of the question, and alimony wasn't going to happen, either. I didn't need that, anyway. Money had nothing to do with why I married Harper and it wouldn't be a factor in my leaving him. All I wanted was to be done.

As promised, I let Mario know everything I was doing. At least, as far as the stuff with Harper. I didn't say anything to him about my positive pregnancy result. I was going to tell him, but not over the phone. And really, I wanted to establish who the father was first so I could tell him everything up front. Part of me worried about how he'd react. We hadn't seriously discussed children, or the possibility of having any together. He knew about my childhood and the fact that I felt my parents resented me for jacking up my mother's insides and making it impossible for them to have any more kids. But that was it.

Trish was constantly checking on me, which I appreciated. (And I had a strong suspicion she was behind Harper's tires being slashed right before he left, but she tried to act like she didn't know what I was talking about). Vera had gone scarce again, and this time I didn't have the energy to find out why. I loved my friend, but it was always something with her. And I had plenty of my own stuff to worry about.

"Are you sure you're okay, being back in that house with Harper?" Trish asked me over the phone one day.

"Yeah, girl, I'm fine," I assured her. "Especially since Harper is out on the road. He's been gone for days."

"He's *still* gone? What, did he think getting you back in the house was all it would take to make everything okay with y'all again?"

"Who knows what he thought. It doesn't matter, anyway. I didn't come back to reconcile. So his being gone is actually a blessing because it means I can do what I need to do without interference."

"What did you do?"

"Called my lawyer and asked him to draw up some divorce papers. And I'm about to go get some boxes and stuff so I can start packing my things."

"Oh, so you ain't playin', huh? That's my *girl*!"

"Absolutely not! I meant it when I said Harper and I are done. And I'm trying to move on from him as quickly as I can."

"Well, I'll come help you pack, if you need me to. And we can borrow Leroy's truck to move your stuff."

"I appreciate that, girl. I'll certainly let you know."

"You gonna move in with Mario?"

"Honestly, we haven't talked about that, but I doubt it. At least at first. I don't want to make the same mistake with him that I made with Harper, as far as moving too fast. I want us to take the time to continue getting to know each other and build our relationship, and be sure this is something that will last. I sincerely love him, but I've learned my lesson about jumping the gun."

"I feel you on that."

"And anyway, Mario and I have more pressing things to worry about."

"Like what?"

"Like this baby I'm carrying."

Trish screamed loudly, causing me to pull the phone from my ear. "You're *pregnant*??"

"Yeah. Found out yesterday. I was super tired and stuff so I went to see if maybe I'd caught some kind of virus, or if the stress from everything going on was just making me sick. But nope. Got a bun in the oven."

"Wow," Trish marveled. "How are you? How do you feel about this? I know you've kinda been on the fence about being a mother."

"Right, exactly. I'm not great but not terrible. Having kids wasn't anywhere on my agenda any time soon, if it was on there at all, but especially not now. Hell, I've already had one miscarriage, back in my twenties."

"Oh yeah, I forgot about that."

"Yeah. So I'm not over the moon about this but I'm not devastated, either. It's just crappy timing."

"How far along are you?"

"Girl, I don't even know. I'm gonna have to go back to find all that out. When they told me I was pregnant, I was too shocked to even ask; I just walked out. But I need to know because that's the only way I'm gonna know who the father is."

"Oooooh girl!" Trish exclaimed. All this drama was probably like candy to her. "You're not sure whose it is??"

"No. It could be either Mario's or Harper's. I hope to high heaven it isn't Harper's; I just don't want him having any ties to me."

"Yeah, I want his ass gone, too. He's still acting like he didn't do what he did?"

"He still hasn't apologized or even acknowledged it. But of course, he's barely been here since I came back. Whatever."

"Whatever? You're just letting it go?"

"I didn't say all that. It's just not the main thing I have to worry about now."

"I guess. Well, *I'm* certainly not letting it go."

I paused. "What did you do, Trish?"

"I'm not admitting a damn thing. But I *did* tell you that we'd deal with Harper's ass and I meant it."

"Trish..."

"*Anyway.* You need to find out who the father is and let them know so everything can be out in the open. You don't need to be stressing about anything right now."

"True. I'm gonna find out. I've already made an appointment for next week."

"Good. I'll go with you, if Mario doesn't."

"I appreciate it. I'll probably want you to go with me 'cause I don't want Mario thinking I've slept with Harper or anything."

"What? Doesn't he know what Harper did?"

"No," I replied, hesitating. "Not yet."

"Why not??"

"I wasn't ready to talk about it when I was over there. And I'm sure he won't be thrilled about my waiting so long to tell him."

"You know he won't. And he shouldn't be. If y'all are gonna be in a relationship, you can't be keeping stuff like this from him. It's just too big."

"I know. At the time, I told myself I just didn't want to think about it. Mario made me feel so much better that I wanted to keep that feeling going. But I'm gonna tell him everything as soon as I find out."

"Good."

After talking to Trish, I really did begin to worry about how Mario would react after finding out I didn't tell him about Harper violating me. I'd told Trish, however vaguely, but I hadn't told him anything. I'd drastically underplayed what happened; not to protect Harper, but to give myself some relief. I could only hope Mario saw where I was coming from with that and not take it personally. Outside of Trish (and to a slightly-decreasing extent, Vera), he was the only one I trusted.

HARPER FINALLY CAME home, and before I could say anything, he announced that he wanted to have a family dinner.

I admit, that stumped me a little bit. "Um, what?"

"I want to have Pops and Mario over for dinner."

"Why?"

"Because I think it would be nice to do; have one last dinner all together before things start to change."

"You mean before I divorce you?"

He frowned slightly. "You don't have to be ugly about it, Ava."

"Well, being patient and understanding hasn't gotten me anywhere. You come get me from Mario's and then you dash out of town for days and ignore my calls. Now as soon as you walk in the door, you're talking about a damn family dinner. No, thank you."

"Come on, what's the big deal?"

I cut my eyes at him. "You know, I'm really getting tired of you saying that to me. You being so dismissive of my feelings is partly how we got where we are now."

"I'm not trying to be dismissive. I just don't understand why we can't do this."

"I don't want to. Is that easy enough to understand?"

"Ava...okay, look, I know I'm not the best at handling difficult situations. I usually just run from it or push it aside; I get that. Rushing out of town and ignoring your calls was wrong. Shouldn't have done that."

"Yeah, you always recognize you were wrong *after* the fact. At least, most of the time. But you don't seem to try very hard to make yourself not do it again."

"Did it occur to you that I might've needed the time on the road to think about all this?"

"No."

"Well, I did."

"And how hard is it to tell me that, Harper? I can't read your damn mind."

"I know that..."

"Our crappy communication is *another* reason why we didn't work."

"Are you gonna run down the list or are we gonna talk about this dinner?"

"There's nothing to talk about. I already said no."

He looked dumbfounded. "Are you seriously gonna refuse something so minor? What do I need to do to make this happen?"

Eying him for a moment, I turned and stomped up the stairs, grabbed the divorce papers, and stomped back down and over to him. Holding them out, I challenged, "Sign these and I'll do it. If you refuse, so will I."

Harper stared at the papers for several long moments. I knew he didn't want to sign them. Just like I knew his abrupt road trip was mainly a stalling tactic; he'd hoped that I would have changed my mind about leaving him by the time he got back, or at least softened some. But it backfired, only making me want to get out of there faster.

I could almost see the wheels churning in his head, trying to think of a way out of this or to at least prolong it.

"Will you at least stay here until we have the dinner?"

I wasn't thrilled about it, but I agreed. "Fine. But I'm still sleeping in the guest room and you are not to come in there under *any* circumstances. If you do, all bets are off. You clearly can't be trusted."

He frowned. "What does *that* mean?"

"Harper, this whole innocent act is getting a little old. Why don't you just admit to what you did?"

"What in the world are you talking about?"

I peered at him. He looked genuinely clueless. It dawned on me that maybe he *didn't* realize what he did to me that night. He'd clearly been drunk. He'd passed out right after. Not that that excused anything.

I'd let him know everything about that night. *After* he signed those papers.

"Just sign, Harper," I finally demanded.

"Okay," he finally conceded, slowly taking the papers. He patted his pockets and looked around blindly. "I don't have a pen, though..."

Anticipating this, I handed him the pen I'd been holding in my other hand, eyeing him pointedly.

"Thanks," he grumbled. He trudged to the couch, pulled the coffee table closer to him, leaned over and scratched out his signature on the all the marked lines. Dude didn't even have enough sense to read through it first.

I stood over him, watching to make sure he was actually signing his name and not some nonsense that would nullify the documents. He held them up to me when he was done, looking at the ground. Without a word, I took them and headed upstairs.

If a family dinner was my charge for getting out of this house, I'd gladly pay it.

HARPER WANTED TO HAVE this dinner the following weekend, but I wasn't falling for that. In all that time he might conveniently have to go on the road or something, and try to hold me to our arrangement of me sticking around until he got back and could reschedule everything. Nope.

"This needs to happen in the next couple of days," I demanded. "We're not gonna drag this out."

"Babe – I mean, Ava," he corrected when I shot him a look, "I just figured the weekend would work better with everybody's schedule, that's all."

"Harper, we're talking about two people here, not a multitude. Mario works for himself and Everette is retired. The only issue would be if Mario is out of town. *Is he?*"

Of course I already knew he wasn't. Harper hesitated before grudgingly answering, "No."

"So then there should be no problem with them coming at any time. Just stress that it's important that this happen as soon as possible."

"And what if they ask why it's so important?"

"Tell them the truth or make something up. I don't care. Just make this happen ASAP."

Both Mario and Everette agreed to come the very next night and apparently, Everette was bringing a guest. I'd already given Mario the heads-up about all of this, so he was ready whenever. He wanted to move things along as swiftly as I did, though there was still the matter of telling Harper about our feelings for each other. We discussed going ahead and revealing it at this dinner, but decided against it, not wanting to give Harper any reasons to contest anything. After the divorce was final would be best.

The next night, Mario showed up first, and I had to stop myself from jumping into his arms. It felt like I hadn't seen him in months, and it had only been a little over a week.

Settling for a chaste hug, I savored the brief exchange. If I could have gotten away with pulling him into the hall closet and making out with him for a few minutes, I would have. I needed to be close to my man again. His cologne was already bringing me close to a mini orgasm.

"I've missed you," he whispered in my ear before pulling away.

"Me, too," I mouthed back, not knowing where Harper might be lurking. I didn't want to take any chances.

"You okay?"

"Yeah. I'll be better once this evening is over with."

"Where's Dad?"

"In the kitchen, last I saw. I told him I wasn't cooking anything for this so he's taking care of dinner."

"Guess that means we're having cereal, then, 'cause we both know Dad doesn't cook."

I giggled. "He ordered takeout."

"Oh okay. Good."

We stood there gazing at each other longingly, our smiles fading slightly. Everything in me ached to kiss him until my lips were numb. Seeing him just made me realize how much I'd missed him. The only thing that had kept me from being miserable since coming back to Harper's was the determined task of preparing to leave so I could be with Mario.

Mario started to say something else when Harper ambled into the foyer where we were still standing. His eyebrows shot up when he saw Mario.

"Oh hey, son. When did you get here?"

"Just a minute ago. What's up, Dad?" They bumped fists.

"Getting dinner together."

Mario sniffed the air. "What did you get? Barbecue?"

"Yeah. I was gonna just get a few pizzas but figured I'd spring for the good stuff. And it's not just meat; I got sides, too."

"Nice." Mario nodded approvingly, as if Harper had really gone the extra mile with that.

Subtly rolling my eyes, I glanced at my watch. "Where's Everette, Harper?"

"I don't know. He said he'd be here."

"Maybe you should call him to make sure."

"Pops keeps his word. He probably had to go pick up that lady friend of his."

"Oh, Everette's bringing a date?" Mario asked, mildly surprised.

"Apparently so," I shrugged.

"Have y'all met her?"

"Nope. But I figure she's gotten her hooks into him because I've hardly been able to get in touch with him for weeks now. He's always *busy*," Harper commented. "I personally can't wait to see this woman that's got Pops' nose so open like it is. I think he said her name was Paula."

With fortuitous timing, there was a brief knock on the door. Since Mario was closest to it, he stepped over to answer it, taking a peek through the peephole first.

"You've gotta be shittin' me..." he muttered in disbelief, still looking.

Harper frowned. "What's wrong?"

Mario just glanced back at both of us before wordlessly opening the door. Everette stepped through, gold tooth gleaming, holding the hand of his mysterious lady friend. But both my and Harper's jaws dropped when we saw who it was.

"Vera??"

Twenty-Three – Mario

WELL...THIS JUST GOT interesting.

Even more so when Vera couldn't contain her excitement about another new piece of information.

"What the hell do you mean, you're *engaged*??" Ava exclaimed.

"She's gonna be my wife," Everette confirmed, pulling Vera closer to him by the waist. They were both grinning something terrible. "I can't wait."

Ava looked absolutely dumbstruck, like she couldn't even gather any words to say. When I glanced over at Dad, he didn't look too thrilled, either. I figured it was because Everette didn't know about Vera pushing up on him, but part of me wondered if maybe Dad was jealous. Vera apparently had *some* effect on him, since he'd succumbed to her advances twice. Maybe he didn't want his dad with her, even though he didn't necessarily want to be with her himself. Some of us dudes were funny like that.

"I swear, I am just the happiest woman alive!" Vera squealed, looking at Everette dreamily. She grabbed his face and planted one on him, and Ava, Dad, and I immediately turned our heads, not wanting to see that.

"Well," Ava said after a few awkward moments, clearing her throat. "Let's, uhh...let's eat, shall we?"

She hurried out of the foyer, looking a little dazed. I wanted to follow her, but I hung back, resisting the urge to watch her walk away.

"I'll help you bring the food in, Dad," I offered.

"No need. We're doing this buffet-style."

"Buffet?"

"Yeah. That way everybody can just get what they want."

What a lazy way to put on a dinner, I couldn't help but think. *Have someone else cook it* and *have everybody serve themselves.*

But whatever. I shrugged it off and followed him. It's not like the food was my main reason for being there, anyway.

Everyone filed into the kitchen, grabbed their plates, and filled up. There was barbecued chicken, corn on the cob, baked beans, potato salad, and rolls. I'm surprised Vera didn't bring that peach cobbler she was so proud of, but she was probably too over the moon about finally getting a man to bake.

When we all took our plates to the dining room, Vera wasted no time speaking up.

"I know this comes as a surprise, Everette and I being engaged," she said, the smile still plastered on her face. "We've been so wrapped up in our own little world for weeks, just enjoying each other. And since this was where we met, we figured this was the perfect place to make the announcement."

Dad was giving them the side eye, and I could tell Ava had to force herself to speak.

"This *does* come as a big surprise," she admitted. "I mean, it's great to see you so happy, but this was just the *last* thing we were expecting..."

"Oh, I know. I'm sorry I've been so scarce these past few weeks. I just wanted to enjoy my snuggle bunny, here. Plus, there was a lot going on with the move and all."

"*What* move?"

"With Everette. I had to put some of my things in storage-"

"Wait...you've *already* moved in together?"

"Yeah!" Vera didn't seem to notice Ava's incredulousness. "I moved in a couple of weeks after we met at the last dinner here. We wanted to be in the same space as soon as possible. Why wait, right?"

Ava was looking at her as if she'd lost her mind. I was already convinced she had.

"Vera, I don't want to be a downer or anything, but isn't that a little fast?"

"I know it *seems* fast, but it just felt right. There's not a doubt in my mind that this is what I want."

"All right, well...I guess you know what you're doing. If you're happy, I'm happy for you."

Dad shook his head as he raked his fork through is baked beans. Vera looked at him, then at Ava.

"Look, I want to have full disclosure," she proclaimed, holding her hands out. I noticed her engagement ring flash in the light. It was some kind of yellow diamond. I wouldn't be surprised if she fainted when Everette gave it to her. "Let's get everything out on the table."

"What are you talking about?"

"Ava, you're my best friend. And I'm not proud of this, but..."

Oh hell...

"Harper and I have had...an encounter. A couple of them, actually."

Dad's head snapped up, his eyes bugged in panic. He then glared at Vera, as if trying to send her the message to shut up.

"What *kind* of encounter?" Ava asked, her eyes narrowed suspiciously.

"I made a pass at him," Vera admitted clearly. "We kissed and did some other stuff, but that's as far as it went. That's another part of the reason I've been avoiding you; I couldn't face you after that."

Ava's eyes turned to Harper, who looked like he wanted to get up and run from the room. Everette didn't look surprised at all, so I guess Vera had already told him about all this.

Her eyes fixated on the table, Ava didn't speak. Vera looked pensively at Ava, waiting for her reaction. It was the first time the smile had left her face since she arrived. I eyed Ava myself, wondering just how upset she was going to get over this.

Clearing her throat, Ava dabbed her mouth with a napkin and stood.

"Excuse me," she mumbled, leaving the room.

Dad, Everette, Vera, and I all exchanged worried glances, though all for different reasons, I'm sure. No one bothered to fill the silence with meaningless conversation; we just picked at our food, ready for anything. Ava could've just needed a minute or she could've been outside busting Vera's car windows. Or Dad's.

After a couple of minutes, Dad looked at me. "Son, maybe you should go check on her."

"Why me?"

"You're the only one here she wouldn't cuss out right now."

"Maybe we need to just give her a minute, Dad. She probably just needed to throw some cold water on her face or something."

"It's kinda freaking me out how calm she is. I just don't want her to-"

Ava came back in, and Dad clamped his mouth shut. She didn't look at any of us; she just re-took her seat and took a long gulp of her iced tea. Vera was still looking at her, clearly nervous. I don't know if she *really* thought it through before deciding to make this little admission.

I figured I'd have to be the one to say something first. Nobody else seemed to have the nerve.

"Ava," I hedged. "You good?"

Ava shrugged and took a bite off her corn cob. "As well as I can be after hearing about my best friend putting the moves on my husband. And him apparently letting her."

Even though I knew Dad was still Ava's husband, that didn't mean I liked hearing her refer to him as such. I tried not to take this to mean anything; Ava had made it perfectly clear that she was done with Dad. Even so, though, it was a fight keeping the frown off my face.

"Ava, I'm sorry," Vera said, sounding sincere. "Please understand, I was in a bad space when I did that. I didn't even feel like myself. And when we were here last time and Harper had been so nice to me...I let myself read more into it than was there."

"Uh-huh. And the second time?"

"The second time, I'd just had a disagreement with Everette and I thought he was gonna dump me. I came over to talk to you, but you were out of town. And I looked at Harper and just...wanted to make myself feel better." She put a hand to her chest. "I'm so sorry. I know there's no excuse, and you have every right to be angry. I just hope you can realize the place I was in and forgive me."

"Realize the place you were in?" Ava scoffed, shaking her head. "You know what, Vera? I figured you were a little jealous of me after I got married, but I didn't think your desperation would make you actually do something like this. We've been friends since we were kids, but you wanted a man more than you wanted to be loyal to me."

Vera hung her head.

"But whatever."

Vera's head snapped up. Dad finally dared to look right at her; his face had been averted ever since she came back into the room.

"What do you mean, whatever?" Vera hesitantly questioned.

"You're gonna reap what you sow. Especially now that you're marrying Everette."

Everette, who had just been sitting and enjoying the show of all this, sat up in his chair. "What?"

"What do you mean by *that*?" Vera asked, glancing at her future husband. "If you're trying to freak me out, I already know all there is to know about Everette."

"Oh yeah?" Ava looked back and forth between Vera and Everette, slightly amused. I wondered if she was going to tell

Vera about Everette nearly accosting her in the kitchen last time. "Well, I guess we'll see."

Dad still hadn't said anything in defense of himself, and I had a feeling he wouldn't. He probably thought the fault all landed on Vera, since she's the one who initiated everything. The fact that he went along with it (and even enjoyed it) wasn't supposed to matter. So why bother apologizing?

Ava glanced at Dad, probably thinking the same thing I was. She certainly knew him well enough to know his aversion to taking accountability. Remembering that made me breathe a little easier. There was no way she was going to reconsider her decision to leave him, especially after this.

"Nothing to say, boy?" Everette asked Dad pointedly.

Looking flustered, Dad stopped nervously stuffing his face and put his fork down. Taking his time swallowing, he glanced around the table before finally looking at Ava.

"I should've, um...I should've told you about all this," he mumbled.

"But you didn't," Ava snapped.

"It's not exactly the easiest thing to bring up. I was embarrassed..."

"Just save it, Harper." Ava pushed her plate away. "By now, it doesn't change a thing. You should've gone ahead and fucked her when you had the chance to."

Dad's face flushed, and Vera gasped. I wanted to smile, not because it was funny, but because it was just further reassurance that Ava was still mine.

"Ava-"

"Nothing you can say right now, Harper. In fact, maybe it's *my* turn to make an announcement."

Everyone turned to her curiously. Part of me started to feel a little nervous. *Surely* she wasn't about to tell everyone about our relationship? Was she that miffed at Vera and Dad that she was willing to do a tit for tat? Top their news with some of her own? I tried to send her a signal that now was *not* the right time for this, but she wasn't looking at me, either.

"What announcement?" Dad asked pensively.

Ava actually looked a little smug when she proclaimed, "That I'm pregnant."

"*Pregnant??*" everyone yelled. Any other time, that probably would have been hilarious.

"Oh my god, me too!" Vera squealed, apparently not able to hold it in. She clapped her hands gleefully. Nobody seemed to hear her, though.

The whole vibe of the room changed. Dad looked shocked but that only lasted for a second before his expression morphed into vein-bursting anger.

"How the hell are you pregnant?" he roared at Ava, shooting up from the table so fast that his chair fell over. Everette quickly stood, and then Vera.

"How do you think?" Ava shot back at him, undeterred by his anger.

I was thrown for a loop myself, and I felt my own anger shoot up. My hands were actually shaking. Why the hell was I just hearing about this now?

And more importantly, whose baby was it? I had to imagine that if it was mine, she wouldn't have picked this moment to just blurt it out like she had. So that had to mean that she slept with Dad sometime recently, and the thought of that made me want to tear the room up.

But if I flipped out like I wanted to, everyone would know something was up between me and Ava.

"Nah, you're gonna have to come with something better than that," Dad retorted angrily, standing over Ava. "Because if you're pregnant, that had to mean that you cheated on me!"

Oh shit...

"Now, y'all just need to calm down, here..." Everette tried to soothe the situation.

"Forget that! Is that why you're pushing me to get a divorce??"

"Divorce? You're getting a divorce??" Vera gasped.

"What makes you think it's somebody else? Maybe it was the night you *raped* me!" Ava yelled, standing toe-to-toe with Dad.

"*Excuse me?!*" Being calm was out the window. Now I *was* about to tear something up, namely Dad's face.

I stalked around the table headed straight for him, but Ava quickly scurried between us, bracing her hands against my chest.

"What??" Vera and Everette exclaimed.

Dad's anger faltered. "What? What are you talking about? There's no *way-*"

"Wait a minute! Is *that* what happened the night you ran out to a hotel in the middle of the night?" I clarified, looking accusingly at Ava. She never said anything about him doing *that* to her!

"Yes, it is," Ava confirmed, looking at me with eyes that begged for understanding.

"I don't appreciate you lying on me," Dad growled, grabbing her arm. I immediately yanked his wrist towards the ground, wishing I could snap it in two, then pushed him back. He looked at me in shock. I'd never put my hands on him like that.

But he was gonna get a lot worse if he kept grabbing on Ava like that.

"Nobody's lying about anything, Harper. You came in my room drunk and forced yourself on me. My body had all kinds of bruises. You have no idea how close I was to reporting you to the police!"

"You're crazy!"

My head was spinning, hearing all this. So that explained why she would only wear sweats or pajamas at my place and wouldn't let me see her shower or change clothes.

"If you're pregnant, it ain't mine," Dad declared. "It can't be!"

"How can you be so sure?"

"Because I ain't never been able to have kids! I'm infertile and always have been!"

"Whoa, whoa, *what*??" I exclaimed angrily, as a collective gasp went up around the room.

"Damn!" Dad muttered, banging a fist on the table so hard the plates jumped. He looked at me regrettably. Clearly, he hadn't meant to blurt that out but there was no way he could take it back now.

Everette wedged himself in between us, keeping an eye on me because I was breathing *fire*.

"Before things go too far here, let's take a minute and calm down..."

"Fuck that! Too late for that!" I spat, my eyes fixated on Dad, who was doing the eye-avoiding thing again. "What the hell do you mean, you're infertile and always have been? How am I your son, then?"

Dad was looking at Everette, likely wanting him to bail him out. But Everette shook his head.

"He deserves to hear it from you," he told him. "He should've heard it years ago."

All of his earlier bravado and anger now melted into fidgety nervousness, Dad ran his hands down his face. He switched his weight back and forth, his pressed-together hands tapping his mouth, trying to work up the nerve to say the now-obvious out loud.

Finally he said it. "You're adopted, Mario."

I blacked out and just started swinging.

Twenty - Four - Ava

SO THIS IS WHAT GETTING punched felt like, huh?

After Harper dropped the bomb about Mario being adopted, all hell broke loose. Mario just lost it and went after Harper with both fists. Harper actually started fighting back, Everette tried to break them up, Vera started screaming, and I got punched in the back of the head. I don't know whose fist delivered the blow, but that mug *hurt*.

I fell to my knees, wincing from the pain, and crawled away from the melee. I didn't care if they busted everything in the room up; all I wanted was to get out of there and find the strongest Tylenol in the house.

"Ava!" Mario called out when I eased out of the room. By the time I pulled myself to my feet, Mario was by my side.

"Are you okay? What's wrong?" he asked me.

"One of y'all hit me in the back of the head, that's what's wrong," I replied, gently rubbing the throbbing spot.

"Damn, I am *so* sorry, baby," he said, his voice filled with remorse. He started to pull me into his arms but I eased back, glancing towards the dining room.

"They could come in here," I reminded him in a whisper.

He glanced back himself before sucking his teeth. "I don't care about them," he defied, putting his arms around me. "Right now, you're all I'm worried about."

I wanted to ask if that was because I was hurt or because he was still reeling from the news Harper just dropped on him, but I left it alone for the moment. My head was killing me and I was feeling the strong need to sit down. I sagged against Mario's chest and he looked down at me worriedly.

"I'm taking you to the hospital," he declared.

"No, no, I don't need to go to the hospital," I protested immediately. "I'm fine. If you could just get me some Tylenol..."

"Ava, don't try to argue with me. I played football too long and saw too much to be cavalier about it. You got whacked in the head, not to mention the fact that you're pregnant." He leaned closer. "And it's been confirmed that the baby you're carrying is mine. Unless of course, there's something *else* you need to tell me?"

My eyes flew to him. "There's nothing or nobody else. It was either you or Harper. I have an appointment to find out how far along I am and that was going to tell me whose it was. *Then* I was going to tell you. But that's moot now."

"I get it, but you should've told me immediately, regardless. We're supposed to be in this together."

"If it turned out to be Harper's, *and* because of what he did...I just wasn't sure that you..."

"Baby, you're gonna have to trust me when I tell you I'm *in* this," he said, sounding so sincere that it made my heart jump. He took my hand in both of his and looked me in my eyes. "I'm right here with you. I already know our situation isn't a usual one. But you can't keep major stuff from me. Dad *raping* you?? That's not something I should find out about during a family dinner."

"I know." I squeezed his hand. "I'm sorry. Please know that I trust you, though. Outside of Trish, you're the person I trust the most. You've been there for me more than anyone during some of my most difficult times recently. I don't know *what* I'd do if you weren't here."

"Well, you don't have to worry about that." He leaned in and planted a soft kiss on my lips. "I'm not going anywhere. I love you."

Damn, *again*, why didn't I meet this man first?? He had me all lovestruck and giddy and tingly, despite my throbbing head.

Smiling back, I gently grazed his jawline with my fingertips. "I love you, too."

He winked at me. "So let me take you to the hospital, please? I want to be absolutely sure that you're okay."

I didn't feel like I needed to go to the hospital, but he looked so worried that I wasn't about to refuse him. It probably would be the sensible thing to do, anyway.

"Okay."

Harper entered the room as Mario started helping me to the door. Everette and Vera were right behind him.

"Where y'all going?" Harper asked with a slight frown.

"I'm taking Ava to the hospital," Mario replied without turning around. The edge in his voice was unmistakable.

"Why? Are you hurt?" Vera asked, rushing over to us.

"One of y'all fools probably hit her when you were in there fightin'," Everette quipped.

"I'll go with y'all," Harper offered, starting towards us.

"No!" I shouted with a warning finger pointed at him, stopping everyone in their tracks. "I do *not* want you to come. Just stay here."

He had the nerve to look hurt. "Fine. I'll be waiting for y'all to come back. Maybe then you can tell me whose baby it is you're carrying."

Both Mario and I glared at him. Left up to me, I wouldn't even bother coming back to this damn house at all.

But as angry as I was at Harper, I still had to remember that I wasn't a total saint in all this. Regardless of any of Harper's actions, I still cheated on him. With his son.

"We'll be back when we get back," I muttered, holding onto Mario's arm as he led me out the door.

TURNS OUT I DIDN'T have a concussion, which was a relief, and the baby was okay. Mario was glad I was okay, but he still declared I wasn't about to lift a finger for a while.

"You still need to rest," he advised when we were back in the car. "Don't try to do a lot, at least for another day or so."

"I'll cancel the 5K run I had scheduled for tomorrow."

He looked over at me. "That's not funny."

I chuckled and shook my head. "Mario, sweetie, will you chill out? I'm totally fine."

"Yeah, but still. I don't want to take anything for granted."

"Is this how you're gonna be the whole pregnancy? 'Cause you will drive me crazy, just to let you know."

"Well, buckle up, then. You're carrying my baby. I'm gonna take care of you better than I do of my car."

"Lord. I mean, that's sweet and I love you for it, but...lord."

"Not to mention, I kinda feel responsible for this since I'm the one that started the fight."

"And I understand why you did. You just found out Harper had kept a pretty major piece of information from you you're entire life. Of course you're gonna be upset about that. And it could've been one of Harper's humongous elbows that did it."

Despite himself, Mario laughed. I couldn't help but join him, and we sat in the car laughing like that for a good five minutes. It felt good to laugh after such a disaster of an evening. And it wasn't even over yet, since we still had to go back to Harper's.

"Are you sure you wanna go back there?" he asked me after he calmed down. "We don't have to. Just say the word and we'll go to my place."

"We might as well get it on over with."

"Aight." He started the car, then paused a second before turning to look at me thoughtfully. "What you said he did...that really happened?"

I started to get upset that he was questioning me, but I quickly calmed myself. Mario might've been pissed at Harper and thrown for a loop by everything he heard tonight, but he was still Harper's son. I knew he still loved him. Of course he wouldn't want to believe his father would do such a thing. And I *did* blurt it out in anger without having told Mario anything about it first. I can understand him wanting to make sure.

"Yeah," I replied softly, placing my hand on his thigh. "It really happened."

Pursing his lips, he just nodded and looked out the window for a few moments. Then he put the car in gear and pulled out of the parking lot.

Harper was on the couch drinking a beer when we got there. He looked at us anxiously when we walked in. It was then that I noticed he had a couple of scratches and a budding bruise on his face, thanks to Mario.

"You okay?" he asked me.

"I'm fine." I glanced around. "Where are the stupidly betrothed?"

"Who? Oh. They left. But Vera did ask me to tell you she wants you to be her maid of honor."

I rolled my eyes. "Umph."

Harper's nervous eyes turned to Mario, but I could tell he didn't know what to say to him. Especially since Mario was giving him the evil eye right then.

Figuring it would be best for me to get this going, I took a seat in the armchair and turned to Harper. Mario opted to stand, hovering near my chair with his arms folded. A scowl was etched onto his face.

"Look, this has been an emotionally exhausting evening," I began, glancing at both of them. "A lot has been said tonight that has changed everything. I can't even say I know what to deal with first."

"I wanna deal with this first," Harper spoke up, then looked at Mario. "Son, I-"

"No," Mario barked, shaking his head. "We're not gonna do this now."

A little deflated, Harper reluctantly let it go.

"Okay, well, about that...*allegation* you made against me," Harper said to me. "I still wanna know why you would say something like that."

"Because that's what you did, Harper. There's no way I'd make something like that up. Rape is too serious a thing to play with."

"Exactly, which is why I don't know why you said it."

This was gonna give me another headache. "Harper...you came in my room in the middle of the night. I could smell the alcohol on your breath. After you had your way, you passed out. Maybe you were so out of it that you didn't realize what you were doing-"

Mario grunted, cutting his eyes at Harper.

"Or you just don't want to admit that you would do such a thing, but either way, you did it." I looked at him. "You *should* be behind bars right now. Maybe I'm stupid for not going through with reporting you like I started to. But right now, all I want is to just move on from it and from you."

Harper dropped his eyes. "And who are you gonna be moving on with? Whose baby are you pregnant with?"

I hadn't planned on having this conversation right then, but maybe it was best to just go ahead and tell Harper the truth about me and Mario. Things really couldn't get much worse.

But I'd be lying if I said I wasn't fearful about how Harper was going to react. Nervousness took over and I hesitated, suddenly forgetting all my words.

I glanced up at Mario, who thankfully sensed my apprehension and stepped forward, placing a hand on my shoulder.

"It's mine," he said strongly, looking right at Harper. "Ava is pregnant with *my* baby."

Harper's head snapped up, his eyes bugged. He looked back and forth between us, almost as if he was waiting on one of us to tell him it was a joke. But our faces were serious. I braced myself for anything, sure he was gonna explode at any second.

"Wha-what? How in the hell-*what*?!?"

"We're in love with each other," Mario continued, getting everything out. "Neither of us planned it. But the more time we spent together..."

"Wait a minute," Harper sat forward, his brow furrowed so hard it was turning red. "You mean to tell me that when I was trusting you with my wife, expecting you to just calm her down or keep an eye on her, you were sleeping together?"

Mario started to speak, but I held up a hand to stop him. He shouldn't be the only one having to explain this. "We didn't take it there until we were in Tennessee. But to be totally honest, we *did* kiss before that. It's not about sex, Harper; it's about compatibility. It's just the feelings we developed for each other. Like Mario said; we didn't plan it. I actually tried to fight it. But at the end of the day, you just can't help who you fall for."

"And let's not forget, it was *your* idea that we spend all this time together," Mario reminded him. "*You're* the one that kept begging me to go check on her and spend time with her, and go on your honeymoon with her. I tried to tell you-"

"Mario!" I looked up at him incredulously. I'm sure his anger at Harper was fueling a lot of this, but this was no time to point fingers. "Blaming isn't gonna get us anywhere.

When it comes right down to it, *all three of us* played a part in this. And at this point, I just hope we can all be mature about moving on without making things any worse."

"Move on? You just tell me that you've been having an affair *with my son* and I'm supposed to just *move on* from that??" Harper exclaimed angrily.

Trying to remain calm, I kept my composure when I replied, "Yes, Harper. Like I said, I'm not proud of everything I did. But I won't apologize for falling in love."

Harper's frown faltered a bit.

"Even before Mario became a factor, you know things weren't great between us," I continued. "We were having issues and I was beginning to wonder if we were gonna make it, anyway. We're just not compatible. So if anything, I'm sorry for agreeing to marry you before we really got to know each other. Because if we'd taken the time to do that, we could've saved ourselves a lot of pain now."

"But I love you," Harper protested, his anger vanishing for the moment. "I tried. Doesn't that count for anything?"

"I don't think you *did* try, Harper. You're *so* stubborn and refused to compromise; it was your way or nothing. And I'm not living like that."

"But-"

"Look," Mario cut in. "There's no need to go back and forth about this. Ava said she wants out."

"And it's not like this is a surprise, anyway. I gave you the divorce papers and you signed them, Harper," I reminded.

"I know, but...I guess I thought I could change your mind."

"Do you *really* think I would change my mind after everything that happened tonight? You not only dropped a huge bomb on Mario, you dropped one on me, too."

"I think the one y'all dropped on *me* was pretty damn huge, too," Harper rebutted grudgingly.

"The *point* is, how many more secrets do you have? It just makes me feel like I've been living with a stranger. I don't want to go through life with you wondering what surprise is gonna smack me in the face next, because you didn't think it was necessary to tell me about it up front. You share what you want to share when you want to share it, and not a second before. That's not a marriage. At least, not a marriage *I* want."

Harper looked away.

"I'm tired," I finally sighed after a few quiet moments. "I need to get some rest."

"Come on," Mario said immediately, taking my hand. "Let's go."

"Go where?" Harper shot off the couch. "You still live *here*."

"No, she doesn't," Mario stepped in front of me, glaring right into Harper's face. "Let it go, man. Maybe you and Everette can share Vera, since you like kissing on her so much."

"Mario!" I admonished, wedging myself between them. Both of them towered over me, but I did my best to push them a little ways apart. "That's not necessary. This situation is difficult enough as it is; let's not make it worse, okay? Please?"

Mario just continued to glare at Harper, his jaw twitching. I knew his emotions were too raw for him to think rationally right then. He hadn't had time to process anything. Hopefully after a few days, he'd calm down and start to deal with the drastic turn his life had just taken.

Gently pushing Mario towards the door while keeping an eye on Harper, I said, "I'll be back for my things tomorrow. And whether you choose to believe it or not, I *am* sorry for hurting you, Harper. I just hope one day you'll realize that you owe me an apology, too."

Harper just stood there staring after us as we walked out.

It was a quiet drive to Mario's place. He only said one thing during the entire ride:

"You know you're not going over there tomorrow to get your stuff, right? I'll handle that."

"Yes, I know," I droned, my head against the window and my eyes closed. I already knew he was gonna say that. "Everything is already packed."

By the time we got back to Mario's, all I wanted to do was crawl into bed and forget about the whole day. I was emotionally exhausted, physically exhausted, and my headache from earlier wasn't totally gone.

"Do you have any Tylenol?" I asked Mario softly, touching my fingertips to my head.

"Yeah, I'll get it," he replied immediately. "Go on in the room and get comfortable; I'll bring it in."

"Thanks, sweetie."

I got undressed and climbed under the heavy dark gray comforter on Mario's bed. He must have just had it laundered, because it had a soft, powdery scent to it. He'd admitted to me during one of our conversations that Clean Linen was his favorite scent for laundry.

I couldn't help but smile. It was those kinds of random facts that helped make me feel so close to Mario. Being in his place automatically made me feel better, more relaxed. When I was at Harper's, I was on edge. It had become a place I just didn't like to be in.

And I certainly didn't know what Harper's favorite laundry scent was.

Mario brought me the Tylenol, along with a bottle of water and a couple of peanut butter and jelly sandwiches, cut in half. I smiled at him appreciatively.

"You didn't eat that much at dinner, I noticed," he commented, gently placing the small tray on my lap before sitting on the edge of the bed next to me. "I'll go to the store tomorrow after I get your things from Dad – I mean, Harper's. Just tell me what you want. I already know chocolate milk is gonna be on the list."

My smile faded slightly. "Mario..."

"Let's not talk about it right now." He held up a hand, already knowing what I was gonna say. "I'm still trying to wrap my head around all this."

"Of course."

"And I don't wanna talk about him, anyway. I want to talk about us."

"Okay..."

"Do you wanna get married?"

I nearly spit out the water I'd just taken a sip of. Wiping my chin with the side of my hand, I looked at him incredulously.

"Mario, I'm not even *divorced* yet!"

"I know. I'm not talking about tomorrow. I just mean do you think you want to marry me at all."

"I mean, I've *thought* about it, sure..."

"But?"

"But I don't want us to get married just because I'm pregnant. If we marry, it's going to be because we're that much in love and want to spend our lives together."

"You don't want to spend your life with me?"

"Don't do that. Don't take my hesitancy as anything negative. Mario, come on, everything is happening so fast; I can't even think straight right now. We've both had a lot come down on us in one night. This isn't a decision we need to make when we're both this emotional."

He eyed me for a moment before finally nodding. "You're right. To be honest, my head is spinning a little bit right now, too."

"I'm sure it is." I reached over and rubbed his back. "I can't even imagine what you must be feeling right now."

He looked over at me. "I can't imagine what *you* must be feeling right now."

"I'm kind of a mess. But at the same time, a little relieved. At least everything is out in the open now."

"True."

"You would really marry me?" I asked after a few moments.

"Absolutely," he replied emphatically. "Regardless of everything that went down tonight, Ava, there's not a doubt in my mind that you're the woman I want to be with. And especially now that you're carrying my child...call me old-fashioned, but I just want us to be a regular family."

"I think that ship has sailed, sweetie."

"Not necessarily. How everything came about doesn't have to determine how it will end up. And if you're worried about Harper being a problem, we can just move. We can do our kind of work from anywhere."

"Whoa, move?"

"I'm just throwing stuff out there. I just don't want you worrying or stressing about anything. Now my focus is on taking care of you and our child, and I'd like for us to be in the same space. And *not* just shacking up."

Taking a huge bite out of my sandwich, I wondered if it was the right time to tell him what was on my mind. I didn't have the energy for an argument, but I also wanted us to be on the same page.

"Mario," I hedged after a few more stalling bites, "I might as well tell you this now. I'm not sure if us moving in together right away is the best idea. Moving too fast is what started all of this for me."

"I hope to hell you're not trying to compare me to *him*," Mario spat with a deep frown.

"No! You two are nothing alike and I know that. But even more importantly..."

He looked at me expectantly. "What?"

"I'm...not entirely sure I want to keep the baby."

Watching as Mario's face morphed into something I didn't recognize, I quickly slid my tray to the side and grabbed his arm.

"What did you just say??" he demanded.

"Mario, I've told you how I wasn't sure I wanted kids, and why. That doesn't just go away because I wound up pregnant."

He shot to his feet. "You want to kill our baby?"

I recoiled. "Why do you have to say it like that?"

"Because that's what it is!"

"I don't want to *kill* anything, but I also don't want to bring a child into this world without being sure it's what I want."

"And what about me? What I want doesn't mean anything?"

"Of course it does! Sweetie, please try to understand..."

"There's nothing to understand, Ava! We created a life together. That *means* something to me. I can't believe it doesn't matter to you."

"Wow. Are you really going to try to paint me as some kind of heartless, selfish person now?"

"Did I say that?"

"You might as well have! Look, Mario, I never said I *hated* kids. I've just never took the time to seriously think about whether I wanted to be a mother or not. And I never had to because I was never put in the position; the miscarriage I had back in the day happened before I even knew I was pregnant. But now I am in the position. And I will absolutely give it all the serious consideration and reverence this kind of decision deserves. But right now," I ran my hands wearily down my face, "I just want to turn my mind off for a while. Please, let's stop arguing. I can't handle it right now."

Stepping over to me, he wrapped me in his arms, kissing the top of my head. I closed my eyes and buried my face in his stomach, a handful of his shirt in my small fist.

"I'm sorry," he whispered, smoothing my hair. "For getting you riled up. We *do* need to talk about this, but it can wait. Right now, you just need to rest."

"We *both* do," I emphasized, looking up at him.

"I know." He planted a kiss on my lips. "Finish your food. I'm gonna go change clothes real quick."

"Okay."

I finished eating while Mario did his nightly ablutions. When I was done, he took my tray back to the kitchen before turning out the lights and getting into bed with me, pulling me to him. I gladly went into his arms. We just laid there quietly, neither of us having the energy to try to make any conversation. So much had happened in one night that I knew we'd both probably be up for a while, replaying all of it in our minds.

But at least we were there together.

Twenty-Five – Mario

I WASN'T ENTIRELY READY to face all of these new realizations.

Ava was right when she said everything was happening crazy fast. In the span of one evening, I found out my woman was having my baby and my father had been lying to me since I was born. Oh, and that my father had sexually assaulted my woman.

Dad - *Harper* - started trying to call me the morning after that drama-filled dinner, saying we needed to talk. Maybe we did, but it wasn't gonna happen until I was ready. So I called Everette and asked him to get Dad out of the house so I could go by there and get Ava's stuff. I didn't trust myself alone with him yet. The anger was too fresh.

For the time being, I just wanted to focus on Ava. It still blew my mind that we were going to have a baby together. At least, I hoped we were. Yeah, Ava had shared with me her lukewarm feelings about motherhood. I didn't necessarily fault her for that; not every woman wanted to be a mother. Hell, not every woman *needed* to be a mother. But things were different now that Ava was carrying *my* child. I definitely wanted to be a father. Abortion was never something I believed in, outside of extreme circumstances. And while I didn't want to tell her what to do with her body, this was *not* an extreme circumstance to me.

I could only hope that she developed a bond with her unborn child and put any thoughts of giving it up out of her mind.

In the meantime, I just tried to make her as comfortable and stress-free as possible. I moved the things she needed into the guest bedroom and put the rest in storage. We went to see the doctor, and were told she was around three months pregnant. Ava smiled when she heard that, but I didn't get my hopes up. That could've just been for the doctor's benefit.

"You good?" I asked her as we left the doctor's office hand-in-hand.

"Yeah," she sighed anxiously, running a hand across her belly. "A little tired."

"If you want to postpone meeting my boy Jayden, we can."

"No, it's okay. I'm gonna be tired for a while now, from what I've been reading."

My eyebrows shot up, surprised. "You've been reading up?"

"Yeah. Wanted to know what's going on in here." She put her hand on her stomach again. "I have to admit, it's all pretty amazing."

"Yeah, it is." I wanted to ask her where her mind was as far as keeping the baby, but I said I wasn't going to pressure her. She was talking positively about it so I chose to take that as a good sign. "You know, I had a dream about us last night."

She looked up at me curiously. "You did?"

"We were living in a cute fixer-upper outside of the city somewhere, and we had twin daughters that looked just like you."

Stopping in her tracks, she smirked at me. "You're not gonna make this easy for me, are you?"

"Of course not."

"Well, it just so happens that I had a dream, myself," she informed me, resuming our walk to the car. "You were coaching our son's football team. I was up in the stands wearing a custom-made jersey with his name on it. And whenever he scored, y'all would do your secret handshake and then he'd point up at me."

I grinned. "I *like* that dream."

"I liked it, too," she admitted wistfully. "Loved it, actually. I mean, how can you not?"

"Exactly."

"I just want to be careful not to idealize how real this all is. Yes, I'm sure there are a lot of great things about having children, but I'm sure it's a bunch of headaches, too. I just want to be sure I'm looking at this from both sides and staying rational."

"Sometimes, you just have to roll with it, baby." I stepped in front of her and put my hands on her hips. My eyes roamed over her adorably gorgeous face, amazed that I was the one blessed enough to be with her. "You'll never hear me say parenting is easy. No doubt there's plenty about it that makes you want to pull your hair out, but I'm willing to bet anything that the positives outweigh the negatives. More than anything, children are a blessing." I kissed the tip of her nose. "Just like you are."

She blushed and put a hand on my chest. "Oh, Mario..."

"But still, no pressure." I put my arm around her. "Come on, let's go meet Jayden."

I figured it was time for my woman and my best friend to meet, so I suggested we all link up. Jayden was already at the park, where he was hanging out with his son, Carson.

Carson usually lived out of town with his mother but was spending the week with Jayden.

"What's up, man?" I greeted Jayden as we approached him. We slapped hands then gave each other a half-hug.

"Hey, y'all." Jayden smiled at us. "How's everything?"

"Can't complain. Jayden, this is Ava. Ava, baby, this is my knuckleheaded homeboy, Jayden."

He waved me off and took Ava's hand as she giggled. "I ignore him. It's nice to meet you, Ava. I can see why my boy's nose is as open as Waffle House."

Ava laughed. "Well, it's definitely mutual. And it's great meeting you, too. Mario said you're like a brother to him."

"Yeah, I guess I'll claim him," Jayden quipped, playfully rolling his eyes.

I shoved him in the shoulder. "Shut up and get my nephew over here."

"If he tries to throw hints about needing money, don't fall for it. He's entering some kind of mini con artist phase."

Ava and I chuckled as Jayden turned and called Carson over from where he was tossing a baseball around with some other kids. Carson ran over to us, looking like a chocolate-dipped version of his dad.

"Hey Uncle Mario!" he greeted me, giving me a big hug.

"There's my man," I greeted, hugging him back. "It's good to see you, dude! You're getting about as tall as I am."

"Getting there!"

"How old are you now?"

"Eleven."

"Wow. Before you know it, your dad will be buying you your first car."

"He's already started teaching me how to drive," Carson announced proudly. "I've already started a fund so I can get the rims and window tint and stuff I want, when it's time. I'm pushing for a Charger. *So*, if you want to contribute-"

"Shut up, boy," Jayden interjected, lightly hitting him in the back of the head. "Meet Ava, Mario's girlfriend."

Carson took one good look at Ava and clammed up, his bravado from seconds before now gone. He was actually blushing. I tried to suppress my laugh.

"My goodness, you're so handsome!" Ava gushed, grinning. It only made Carson blush harder. "It's so nice to meet you, Carson."

"Nice to meet you, too," Carson mumbled, grabbing her offered hand for just a second before easing it back. He looked at Jayden, turning his back completely to Ava. "Can I go back over there with my friends now?"

"Go on."

Before he ran off, Carson subtly turned towards me, darted his eyes in Ava's direction, and gave a thumbs-up. I couldn't help but grin, winking at him.

"Something I said?" Ava asked, concerned, as we all watched Carson run back to his friends.

"Girl, no. He's probably gonna be drawing you in his notebook later," Jayden assured her.

"Yeah, you definitely don't have to worry about whether he likes you or not," I added. "He *does*."

Ava smiled, relieved. "Well, good."

The three of us went over to a picnic table and sat down, with Jayden facing where Carson was out running around.

"So what's going on with y'all?" he asked us.

"Man," I shook my head. "I don't even know if you're ready for all this."

"Try me."

I told him about the dinner at Harper's, everything that was revealed during it and everything that happened after it, up until the time we left his house. Just talking about all of that was exhausting. Jayden's mouth was agape when I finally finished, uncharacteristically at a loss for words.

"What the *hellllll*..." he marveled. He looked back and forth between Ava and me. "How are y'all dealing with all this? I'd still be at the shooting range, if it were me."

"I don't even know, honestly," I admitted. "Part of me doesn't want to deal with any of it right now, outside of me and Ava's baby. Ava and our seed have been the only things keeping me together these past couple of days."

Jayden turned to look at Ava. "And how are *you* holding up?"

"I'm a little all over the place. But I guess I'm doing as well as I can expect to, considering."

"Neither of y'all have talked to Mr. Downing since that night?"

"No," I quickly replied. "He's been blowing my phone up, though. I wish he'd take the damn hint and leave me alone."

"And Harper and I don't have anything else to say to each other," Ava chimed in. "Now that I know there's no way the baby could be his, I have no ties to him. Our divorce is in process and hopefully will be final sooner rather than later."

"Well, I hope it will be, too. He's not gonna contest anything?"

"He said he isn't."

"I'm still prepared for anything, though," I grunted. "It's not like his word means much of anything."

Ava and Jayden looked at me.

"You need to talk to your dad, man," Jayden finally advised.

"For what? So he can dance around it and make excuses for everything? I'm good."

"You don't know he's gonna do that. Maybe he realizes the magnitude of all of this and wants to finally get everything out on the table."

"It doesn't matter, man. There's really no justification he could offer to make me forgive that."

"So, what, you're just never gonna talk to him again, *ever*?"

I shrugged. "Haven't thought about it. Whenever."

"Mario. I get that you were blindsided, but did you ever stop to think that maybe Mr. Downing had a reason for not telling you that you're adopted?"

"Not really."

"You should, 'cause maybe he does. And anyway, he's the only father you've known for thirty-something years. What difference does it *really* make that you two aren't blood?"

"Even if I wanted to roll with that, it still doesn't excuse what he did to Ava."

"You're right, it doesn't," Jayden quickly concurred, glancing at Ava again. "And believe me, I'm not trying to dismiss that. I just don't think cutting him off completely is the move, either. If you're still pissed at him, hell, say that. But say *something*."

"Why should I?"

"Because it's not like you're blameless in all of this yourself, brother. Ava was *his* wife first. And you cheated with her. I get that you two fell for each other and it wasn't on some malicious shit, but the fact still remains..."

I cut my eyes at him. Ava was looking at her hands in her lap.

"No judgment, y'all," Jayden assured. "Just facts."

"You're right," Ava admitted softly.

I stubbornly remained silent. It *was* pretty easy to forget my part in all of this. Dad did a lot of stuff wrong, but my hands weren't completely clean, either. Not one part of me regretted getting with Ava, but I can't lie and say that it happened under ideal or honorable circumstances. When I started feeling things for Ava, I should've been straight up about it with Harper. But I kissed her, touched her, made love to her, and impregnated her, all while she was married to him. And knowing how much he loved her. Flawed as he was, Harper loved Ava.

If I was going to admonish him about not taking ownership for his actions, I couldn't be guilty of doing the same.

"Fine," I finally said. "I'll talk to him."

I DIDN'T LET HARPER know I was coming by; I just showed up. I'm sure part of me hoped he'd be out on a road trip or something so I'd have an excuse to put this discussion off. But his truck was in the driveway, so I had no excuses.

Everette was there, too, which I can't say I was thrilled about. I hadn't forgotten about him pushing up on Ava, and really hadn't had much to say to him since then. But at least he was a buffer between me and Harper.

"I'm glad you came by, son," Harper said to me as the three of us congregated in the living room. "I was wondering when we were gonna get a chance to talk."

"Yeah, well," I shrugged, avoiding looking at him. "I'm here. So what is it you want to say?"

"You want some cereal?"

"No, I don't want any cereal."

"A beer?"

I knew he was probably just nervous and told myself to be patient. "No, thank you."

"All right." He rubbed his hands on his jeans. "Well...okay. I guess you probably wanna know why I never told you that you were adopted."

"That would be nice."

"It's hard to explain because, really, I don't have a good excuse..."

"For the record, I told him he should've told you years ago," Everette told me, waving off Harper's hard glare. "It's not like it was a bad thing."

"Okay, so why didn't he?" I asked.

"Your guess is as good as mine on that."

"Y'all ain't gotta talk about me like I ain't sitting right here," Harper snapped. "I can speak for myself."

"Well, do it, then. You the one sittin' here like you don't know where your words are."

"Why don't *you* tell *us* why you went and got engaged to a woman you hardly know?"

"What does that have to do with anything?"

"You didn't tell anybody about *that*."

"So what?"

"I'm just saying. We all got secrets."

"You're stallin'."

"I'm not."

Yes, he was. Harper was clearly stalling. But I just sat there and listened to them go back and forth, remembering the promise that I made to Ava before coming that I would keep my cool and not turn this into a finger-pointing expedition.

But apparently, Harper and Everette beat me to that.

"Fine, whatever, if that's what it's gonna take to get you to put your big britches on," Everette sighed, adjusting his gold pinky ring. "I proposed to Vera because she makes me feel as good as I did back in my thirties. She's young but got one of those old-fashioned souls; she's all about taking care of her man. And since I started seein' her, I ain't been worried 'bout no other women. That's how I knew she was it."

"And you really think y'all are gonna work long term?"

Shrugging, Everette replied, "We'll work for whatever term we see fit. I'm just enjoying the days as I get 'em."

"Hmph," Harper grunted. "Well, it's gonna be a little hard for me to forget how she made those passes at me like she did."

"You're more hung up on that than I am. And it's not like you put up a big fight about it when she did it." Everette slapped his thighs and stood, returning his fedora to his head. "Now I'm gonna get on outta here so y'all can get down to business. Vera's waiting on me."

Harper rolled his eyes.

Everette stopped in front of me, looking at me earnestly. "And for the record, boy, I *am* sorry about what I did that night. After thinking about it, I'm actually glad you were there to stop me from doing something I can't take back."

He looked like he really meant it. And while I still thought the main person that he should apologize to was Ava, I could appreciate him saying what he said to me.

Nodding, I simply replied, "Thanks for that."

Tipping his fedora, Everette left.

"What is he talking about?" Harper asked. "What did he do?"

I shrugged. "It's a moot point now. So are we gonna talk about what I came here to talk about, or are you gonna keep beating around the bush?"

His nervousness returning, Harper rubbed the back of his neck. "I should've told you that you were adopted."

"Why didn't you? It's not like it's something terrible."

"I don't know. Your mama and I always planned on telling you when you got a little older but then she died, and I didn't have anybody to hold me to it. I got it in my head that if you knew you were adopted, you wouldn't want anything to do with me."

I frowned. "That doesn't even make any sense."

"I know it doesn't. But that's what I thought."

"This just leads to a lot more questions for me. Why wouldn't you ever tell me much about Mama? Do you know anything about my birth parents? Are they still alive? I just feel cheated out of so much information that I have a right to."

"I know," Harper sighed.

"You weren't ever gonna tell me about this, were you?"

"If I'm honest, probably not."

I shook my head. "It explains a lot, though. Maybe that's why I never felt a real connection to you. I mean, we look nothing alike. We have next to nothing in common. All this time I thought it was just because I took after Mama. But now I see that wasn't it."

"No. Truth be told, you don't look anything like her, either."

"Where are my birth parents?"

"It was a single mother. All I know is her name. I don't know where she lives now or anything."

"Why did she give me up?"

"She was barely a teenager and just wasn't ready to be a mother. She loved you, and cried when she had to give you up. But she knew me and your mama could do better for you than she could."

Hearing that made my eyes sting a little bit. I immediately wondered where my birth mother was and how she was doing for herself now. Would she even want to meet me after all this time?

"Did she...did she even try to keep up with how I was doing?" I asked, eying my fingers as they restlessly tapped the arm of the chair.

"A little bit. At first. But once you got a little older, I thought it would be best if she stayed away."

"What? You purposely kept my birth mother away from me? Even after Mama died?"

"I-I didn't want to confuse you..."

"Bullshit! You wanted to keep me all to yourself and never tell me a damn word about it! Even if I bought your excuse, that should've only lasted during my childhood. You should've told me everything when I became a grown man!"

"You're right; I should have," Harper admitted. "I know I was wrong for keeping so much from you. But after the years kept passing, it got harder to come out with it. Then I convinced myself that there was no real reason to tell you any of that. You got to be successful, we had a good relationship; figured there was no reason to rock the boat."

"Wow," I marveled, looking at him in disbelief. "You just figured I'd never find out and you'd be in the clear, huh?"

He looked away. "I guess in my own head, I was protecting you. But I see now I was wrong."

"Just now?"

"Okay, I see now *how* wrong I was; I knew it was wrong, but I didn't think about all the things you pointed out. And I never considered things from your perspective."

"Just from yours."

"Yeah." He shook his head. "I guess Ava was right. I *am* selfish."

My head was all over the place, but hearing Ava's name reminded me that there were some apologies of my own I needed to make. The stubborn part of me didn't want to, but I knew it was the right thing to do.

"Look..." I sat forward in my seat, rubbing my hands together. "Speaking of Ava...part of the reason I came over here was to acknowledge my part in this mess everything has turned into. I know I was wrong for ever doing anything with Ava while y'all were married."

Harper looked at me.

"It wasn't about stabbing you in the back. I tried like hell to ignore my attraction to her. But something just kept pulling me back to her, and I couldn't get her out of my head. Like I said the other night, the more time we spent together, the more we realized how right we are for each other. I fell for her and I fell for her hard. And after a while, I just gave in to it."

"I see."

"But regardless, I was wrong. At the very least, I should've been straight up with you when I realized I had feelings for her."

"Well, I can be honest and say that I don't even know what I would've said to that, son," Harper admitted. "I probably would've started seeing you as a threat or an enemy, like when I was the big fat kid in school and every girl I liked overlooked me and went right to the hunks. I wasn't anything but the baby-faced sidekick that stayed in the friend zone."

Him saying that made me realize how little I knew about his childhood. Harper had never been big on talking about his past. And us *not* talking about it was so normal that I never thought to ask. We each just always kind of did our own thing.

"I guess I knew in the back of my mind that Ava was out of my league," he continued. "I knew I loved her more than she loved me. And I was always worried about some younger man catching her eye, in the back of my mind. So I just turned my mind off and hoped for the best."

"You married Ava because you were desperate?"

"More like lonely. Got sick of being by myself. And like I said, I *did* fall for her. But I was too amazed that someone like her would even give me the time of day to let myself worry about whether she was actually the right woman for me or not."

"So you didn't really fall for *Ava*; just the *idea* of her."

He pondered my words. "I guess."

I was surprised he was admitting it. Some things made a lot more sense now. Harper and Ava getting married so quickly; him not trying to *really* get to know her after he did. He was so shocked that he was with her at all that it almost paralyzed him, which would also explain why he didn't really make any concessions for her. It was like getting a fancy promotion before you were qualified for it; you don't know how to handle the responsibility, think you can keep doing the stuff you did at your old job without adjusting to your new situation, and eventually you end up fired.

This conversation was making me feel closer to Harper than I'd felt in years, if not ever. There were still a ton of things I wanted to know, but he was opening up to me when I sincerely thought he wouldn't. I just hated what had to happen to get us here.

"I'm sorry, son," he finally said. His voice sounded pained. "I've just made one bad decision after another."

I sighed. "Well, it's not like I haven't made mistakes, either."

After a few moments, Harper asked, "Is Ava okay?"

"Yeah, she's fine."

"I bet *she's* never gonna forgive me for any of this."

"Over time, she will. But it *would* help if you took ownership of everything you did."

His eyes swung to me. "If you're talking about that rape stuff-"

"Rape *stuff*?"

"I still don't think I did that," Harper stated emphatically. "Why wouldn't I remember anything about it, if I did?"

"She said you were hammered. And why would she make something like that up?"

"To have an excuse to leave."

I frowned. "Please tell me you're not serious."

Sensing that he was getting me riled up again, he held up his hands. "Look, I'm not trying to call her a liar. I just can't imagine myself doing such a thing. Maybe she just had a bad dream or something."

"Bad dreams don't leave bruises."

"Maybe she was sleepwalking-"

I shot up from my seat. "I'm done."

"Where are you going?"

"I'm not gonna sit here and listen to this nonsense. I see you *still* haven't really learned much from all of this. You're still stubborn as hell."

"Son, you owe it to me to be patient," Harper declared, standing himself.

I stopped in reaching for my keys, looking at him as if he'd lost it. "I *owe* it to you??"

"Like you said, you messed up, too. You're really in no position to judge. And anyway, I don't see why you're just automatically taking Ava's word for everything over mine."

What this dude for real?

"So this is what you're gonna try now? Holding what I did over my head to try to absolve you of what you did?"

"I didn't ask to be absolved. I apologized. I said I messed up. But I'm not gonna cop to something like rape if I don't believe I did it."

"Fine, don't *cop* to it," I spat. "But don't tell me anything else about how sorry you are. And don't ask me about Ava again, either. Just keep her name out of your mouth."

Anger actually flashed in his eyes. "Don't forget, son; for the time being, she's still *my* wife. She technically still belongs to *me*."

Something in his voice didn't sit well with me. My eyes locked on his, I stalked over and got right in his face, giving him the most menacing glare I've ever given anyone.

"I don't give a flying fuck if she's walking around with one of your kidneys. You will *not* bother her again. Do not try me on this, *Harper*."

He glared at me with a slight shake of his head. "Is this where we are now, son?"

"Apparently so." I turned and headed for the door. "And from now on if you call me anything, call me Mario."

Twenty-Six – Ava

I FELT LIKE SHIT.

Not just because of the fun morning sickness that I was experiencing, but also because of the shambles that Mario and Harper's relationship was in.

And it was all because of me.

Okay, maybe not *all* because of me. Harper's secrets had a lot to do with it. But I kicked down the initial deteriorating domino when Mario and I shared our first kiss that day by the front door. Everything just kept steadily falling from there.

Mario tried to act like he was fine, but I knew the state his relationship with Harper was in bothered him. Ever since he got back from Harper's the night of their talk, he'd been in a sour mood. I could only assume that it didn't go well; he wouldn't go into the details of what was said.

"I'm *not* talking about this," he would growl whenever I dared to ask. "One day I will, but not now."

I had to respect that, but that didn't mean I wasn't worried about Mario. While he and Harper were never best buddies, they'd had a pretty good relationship. And I knew that even if they mended fences down the line, it wouldn't be the same. Too much had been said and done.

Thankfully, Mario's excitement about our baby and attentiveness towards me wasn't affected by what was going on between him and Harper. Our baby was doing great. I'd finally warmed to the idea of being a mother, to the point where the thought of a family with Mario brought one of those lovesick smiles to my face. Mario was going to make a great father, and I actually felt honored to the one that got to carry his first child.

"Hey, sweetie?"

I walked into the guest room where he was working. My plastic bins were still stacked against the walls because I hadn't had the energy to do anything with them yet. And my sweetheart Mario was being so great about it, more worried about my comfort than the temporary clutter. It just made me that much more excited about what I was about to tell him.

He was rubbing his chin and frowning, so I knew he was concentrating hard on something.

"What's up, baby?" he asked, glancing up at me.

"I don't wanna disturb you; just had a quick question."

"Yeah?"

"What do you think about Christine?"

"Who's Christine?"

"Maybe our daughter?"

His eyes snapped to me. "Are you serious?"

"Yep."

He grinned, which made me grin. Before I could blink, he had rushed over to me and was hoisting me up in the air like I was his championship trophy.

"Mario!" I squealed, laughing as he spun me around.

"You sure know how to make a brotha happy," he gushed as I slid down his body, my arms landing around his neck. He pulled me close to him, smiling down at me.

"I give because I receive." My hand caressed his face. He was *so* handsome.

"You know you are the best thing to ever happen to me?"

"Aww sweetie! I feel the same way. Even with everything that's happened to get us here, I couldn't be happier than I am right now. I love you *so* much."

"I love you, too. More than I can tell you."

He cupped my chin and brought my face to his. Our kiss made me melt on the inside. I loved the natural dance our tongues did together, with the familiarity of a couple that's been together for years. Kissing him was something I didn't ever see myself getting tired of.

When we finally pulled back, he grunted and bit his bottom lip, which always sent lightning bolts right to my lady parts.

"Stop that," I warned, pointing at the action as my eyes took on that lustful slant. "Or else you won't be getting back to work for a while."

"Good thing I work for myself, then, isn't it?" he growled as he picked me up and carried me to his bedroom.

Or as I had started to think of it, *our* bedroom.

A COUPLE OF DAYS LATER, I was looking all over the place for one of my flash drives. It had some important information I needed for one of the projects I was working on, and I was about to lose my mind, thinking I lost it.

"Still haven't found it yet?" Mario asked me, entering the room where I was going through my bins for the fourth time.

"No," I grunted, frustrated. *Where* had I put that damn thing?

"Well, I've looked all through the living room, our room, the kitchen..."

"Damn it!"

"I told you to start using Dropbox to save stuff instead of flash drives."

"Yes, I know you did, Mario, but if you could save the lecture for another time, I'd appreciate it."

"It's gotta be around here somewhere, baby. Try to stay calm; we'll find it."

"Mario, I have a deadline coming up. If I don't find that flash drive, I'm screwed."

"Are you *sure* you didn't take it anywhere else? Maybe one of those times you went to Starbucks to write?"

"Yeah, I'm sure. Pretty sure. Aww, hell..."

"I know it's important, but please try not to stress about it, okay? I'll go look in your car; maybe it fell between the seats or something."

I looked at him, brightening. I hadn't thought of that. "Good idea!"

While he headed outside, I racked my brain, trying to think of where else that damn flash drive might've been. I mindlessly popped a marshmallow into my mouth, satisfying one of my varied cravings. After a few more, though, I had to rush to the bathroom before I made a mess all over the carpet.

Mario came back in as I was exiting the bathroom, pressing a cold washcloth to my face.

"Had to throw up again, huh?" he surmised. It certainly wasn't anything new.

"Yeah. I'll be glad when this whole nausea part is over with."

"You need anything? Maybe some ginger ale?"

"Nah, I'm okay. I might just...oh!"

He looked at me, alarmed. "What? What's wrong?"

"I remember where I left my flash drive..."

"That's good, 'cause I wasn't looking forward to telling you I didn't find it in the car. Where did you leave it?"

I turned reluctant eyes to him. "At Harper's."

Mario's head fell back briefly in disbelief. "Are you kidding me, Ava?"

"Believe me, that's *not* something I would find funny."

"Fine. Tell me where it is in the house; I'll go get it."

"I wish I could, but I'm not quite sure. It'll be better if I just go get it myself."

"No. *Hell* no."

"Mario-"

"Nah, forget it, Ava. There's no way that's happening."

"Mario, I don't want to see Harper any more than you want me to, but it'll just be quicker if I go alone. If you're there, the two of you will probably just get to arguing or something and I think we've all had enough of that, don't you?"

"And what do you think will happen if you walk up in there by yourself? You don't think he'll try anything?"

I knew there would be no way I'd get out the door unless I could put Mario's mind at ease somehow. We'd be standing in that spot going back and forth forever.

"Tell you what," I offered, picking up my phone. "I'll call Vera and ask her to ask Everette if Harper is out on a trip or not. If he is, I'll run over there. If he isn't, you can come with me. Okay?"

"Why can't I go with you regardless?"

"Mario, I love you, but you don't need to babysit me. I can take care of myself."

"It's not *babysitting* you, Ava, it's having your back. And I just don't like the idea of you in that man's house, whether he's there or not."

I sighed, feeling my energy slide down a notch. "If he's out on the road, it won't matter, will it?"

"How 'bout I follow you but stay in the car while you're there?"

"Mario."

He threw his hands up. "Fine."

After calling Vera and having her verify with Everette that Harper in fact was out on the road, I started getting ready to go. Mario just stood in the doorway with his arms folded, clearly unhappy.

"I want it on the record that I'm *against* this," he proclaimed.

Glancing over at him as I put on my shoes, I shook my head. "I know, sweetie."

"I wish you would change your mind."

"And I wish you would stop worrying. I'll be fine."

"Hmph."

Flashing a reassuring smile at him, I grabbed my keys. "You just be here when I get back." I grabbed his chin and gave him a peck. "With your sexy self."

"Uh-huh. You call me as soon as you get there, all right? We'll stay on the phone while you're there and then I can hear for myself when you leave."

"Wow, I can just imagine how you'd be with our daughter," I quipped as I headed for the door, trying to lighten the mood a little bit. "Probably with our son, too."

Grabbing my hand right before I walked out, Mario looked right into my eyes. I could tell he was really worried.

"Be careful."

"I will. I'll be right back."

I headed over to Harper's, tapping my fingers on the steering wheel as I drove. If I was honest, going there *did* make me a little anxious, but I felt better knowing I wouldn't have to see Harper. My main concern was that he might've changed the locks since I moved out.

Thankfully, my key still worked. I slipped into the house, stopping to listen for any noise, just to be sure. Hearing none, I hurried up the steps to the guest room where I last remembered having the flash drive. Finding it in the nightstand, I breathed a huge sigh of relief. I was in such a hurry that I forgot all about calling Mario.

I headed back downstairs and took a second to make sure there wasn't anything else in that house I'd have to come back for later. Feeling satisfied that the flash drive was the last thing I'd need, I headed for the door.

"Ava?"

I was gonna kill Vera.

Hesitating, I turned around. "Um, hi, Harper," I said, suddenly nervous. "I'm sorry to just come in like this, but I forgot my flash drive." I held it up, as if I needed proof.

He looked a little disappointed, as if he'd hoped I was there for another reason. "Oh."

"I thought you were out of town..."

"I was supposed to be. There was some kind of issue with the shipment so it got postponed."

"Ahh. Well, umm...I got what I came for so I'll just...be on my way." I turned for the door.

"Ava, wait!"

I sighed, my back still to him. "Harper, let's not, okay?"

"I just wanna talk to you."

"We really don't have anything to talk about. Everything that needed to be said is already out."

"I'd like us to be friends, at least."

Incredulous, I looked over my shoulder at him. "Are you serious?"

"Yeah. I thought about it and I can understand how I drove you crazy. There's plenty of stuff I did wrong and I can't even blame you for losing your patience. I just don't want you to hate me."

I pursed my lips. "I don't hate you, Harper."

He brightened a little. "Really?"

"Yes, really. But I don't think us trying to be friends is a good idea, either."

He took a few steps towards me, stopping when I lifted a brow. "Why not?"

"I'd really rather not get into all that right now. I have to go."

"Back to Mario's?"

I looked at him, trying to weigh his question. And speaking of Mario, I knew he was probably freaking out that

I hadn't called him yet. I patted my pockets for my phone, then remembered that I'd left it in the car.

Great.

"I'm gonna go, Harper," I stated, choosing not to acknowledge the question. Where I was going wasn't any of his business, anyway. "Take care."

Moving faster than I'd ever seen him move, he darted over to me and blocked the doorway.

"What are you doing?" I asked, slightly alarmed. I took a couple of steps back.

"I want you to stay."

"Harper, please move."

"You owe me this, Ava. All I want is a little of your time. You can get back to screwing my son later."

Gasping, my face flamed with anger. All efforts to be cordial were out the window now.

"To hell with you," I spat. "I don't *owe* you a damn thing. I've already apologized for everything I did. What you need to do is get over it and leave me alone."

His eyes darkened. "Oh really? What if I don't *wanna* get over it?"

A thin streak of fear shot through me but I wasn't about to show it. "Too bad."

"Nope. This isn't going down like that." Harper moved towards me, and I simultaneously stepped back. "I want an hour of your time. The least you can do is give me that."

"An hour for what?"

He licked his lips. "For whatever."

Oh hell no.

I immediately regretted the stupid decision to not let Mario come with me. Harper had a hungry look in his eyes that sent my heartbeat into warp speed.

Without another word, I turned and ran towards the back door, but Harper caught up with me. He grabbed my arm, yanking me to him. I immediately started hitting him with my fists, not that it had any affect. The hits just bounced off his big stomach.

"Let me go, Harper!" I screamed as he picked me up, turning me away from the door.

"You owe me, Ava!" he repeated, dodging my attempts to hit his face. "I'm not gonna let you go back to another man without getting what's mine first!"

He dragged me back to the living room, with me kicking and screaming the whole time. Tossing me onto the couch, he dove on top of me, trying to kiss me. I can't believe this is the man I actually agreed to marry and spend my life with. What the hell had I been thinking?

When he saw I wasn't going to cooperate, Harper got angry. His face that I used to think was so adorable took on a look I didn't even think he was capable of.

"I'm tired of you playing with me, Ava," he growled through gritted teeth. "I was *good* to you! You're gonna learn you can't just toss people aside like they're nothing!"

His hands clamped around my throat, and I panicked. My eyes stretched a mile wide as I tried to scream and pry his fingers off, but it was doing no good. And there was no way I could throw him off me; he outweighed me by a couple hundred pounds. It was clear this wasn't going to be like the last time he attacked me, where he only choked me for a couple of seconds. No, he looked like he had every intention of finishing the job this time.

Oh my god, he's actually going to kill me...

My eyes started to drift closed. Mario's face flashed through my mind, and my heart began to ache that I'd never see him again. *At least I got to experience true love for a while.*

And my baby...I bet she would've been beautiful. Little Christine...

My hand that had been gripping Harper's wrist fell to my side. Harper's sneering image started to fade.

CRASH!

Suddenly, Harper's grasp on my neck released and there was a huge thud as he fell over onto the ground. Another set of hands caught me before I rolled off the couch myself, since my legs were caught in Harper's. I was coughing something terrible, and when my eyes opened, the last person I was expecting to see was Everette.

"Oh my god," I gasped, holding my throat. "Everette?"

He was standing there, looking down at his unconscious son. The shards of the vase he had hit Harper over the head with were littered around him. He turned his attention to me. "You all right?"

"What in the world...how did you..."

"When Vera told me you were coming over here to get something, I got a bad feeling," he explained. He sat next to me on the couch, nudging Harper's foot aside with his. "Vera didn't like the thought of it, either, and begged me to come over here to make sure you got in and out all right."

"Did you know his plans had changed?" I croaked.

"Nah. He told me he was going but didn't tell me it got canceled."

"Everette, I..." Tears sprang to my eyes, the realization of what had just happened starting to hit me. I started to hyperventilate, and Everette quickly put an arm around me.

"Calm down, darlin," he soothed. "It's okay now."

"Everette, I don't know how to even *begin* to thank you-"

The front door clanged open and Mario rushed in. He looked frantic.

"Ava!"

"Mario!"

I rushed over to him, throwing my arms around his neck. He held me tightly for a few moments before pulling back and looking me over.

"What the hell happened? You were supposed to call me! And what is Everette doing here? What's going on??"

My words came rushing out like a busted water pipe. "I was in such a hurry to come in here and get my flash drive that I forgot my phone in the car and then Harper came in 'cause his trip got canceled and he said he wanted to talk and when I tried to leave he said I owed him and he grabbed me and tried to kiss me but I wouldn't let him and he choked me-"

"*He choked you*??"

"Thank *God* that Everette came in or I'd be...I'd be..."

I started to lose it again, placing my hand on my rapidly heaving chest. Mario quickly grabbed me and held me close, placing his lips against my temple.

"Don't even say it, baby," he whispered, slightly rocking me side to side. "Don't even say it. I'm right here with you. Let's just thank God you're all right."

I clung to him, not believing any of this was happening. All I had wanted was my flash drive.

After several moments, I held onto Mario's waist as he walked me over to the couch, where Everette was muttering quietly into his cell phone. He hung up when we came over.

"Crazy stuff, huh?"

Mario was staring at Harper's huge body in a heap on the floor.

"I don't believe this," he muttered, shaking his head.

"And I always thought he was a good man," I droned. "But I never really knew Harper at all."

"Well," Everette sighed. "Cliff told me he would probably have some issues. I thought he'd grown out of all that by now, though."

Both Mario and I looked at him with curious frowns.

"Who is Cliff?" Mario asked.

Everette jerked his head towards Harper. "His real dad."

"What?!" Mario and I exclaimed in unison.

"Cliff was my old buddy from the service," Everette explained. "We got to be real close, and since he didn't have any siblings and both of his parents were dead, he asked me to take care of his son should anything ever happen to him. I only agreed because I thought nothing would ever happen, but unfortunately, Cliff died in combat. I had been discharged from the military by then, so I had to take him. Harper was about seven years old or so."

"Where was his mother?" I asked incredulously.

"Oh, she was all too glad to give him up. She cared more about getting high than being anybody's mama. She was using when she was pregnant with Harper, matter of fact."

"Oh my god..."

"I always kinda hated that I had to give up my freedom but Cliff was my main man, so I felt obligated." Everette shrugged. "But I grew to love the boy as my own."

"I'm surprised he never mentioned anything about this," Mario said. "But then again, I guess I shouldn't be."

"It's not something we really talk about. He probably doesn't remember much about Cliff, anyway, since Cliff was overseas back then more than he was at home. He wanted to be somebody that Harper was proud of. It's really too bad they didn't get more time with each other."

"Hmph."

This had to be another one of my vivid dreams, because it was all just too unbelievable.

"Listen y'all," Everette said, standing. "Go on outta here. Take care of each other, and that bun you got in the oven. Harper won't be bothering you again. I guarantee it."

I started to ask him what he meant by that, but decided I didn't care. Whatever became of Harper after that point was none of my business, as long as I never had to lay eyes on him again. I just needed to get the hell out of that house.

"Come on, baby," Mario said to me, standing and taking my hand. We started towards the door, then he stopped and looked back at Everette. He suddenly went over and hugged his grandfather, looking slightly choked up.

"Thank you for saving her. Both of them."

Everette smiled, patting Mario on the back. "My pleasure, boy." He pulled back, his hand clamped on his grandson's shoulder. "I'll always be here if you need me."

Nodding, Mario smiled at him before turning and walking back over to me, leading me outside. I couldn't help but look over my shoulder a couple of times, thinking Harper was going to come rushing out at any second.

"You need to go to the hospital?" Mario asked me. "It's probably a good idea, after all this."

"I feel okay, considering. I just wanna go home."

"Are you sure?"

"Yeah." I placed a hand on my tiny baby bump. "We'll be right behind you."

He eyed me warily. I know he wanted to insist that I go get checked out, but I really felt okay. All I wanted to go was go home, lay in my man's arms, and spend the night thanking God for sparing my life.

I did a little stretch to ease my slightly aching back before getting into my car. Mario's black Maxima pulled out of the driveway and I was right behind him, giving one last glance at Harper's house in the rearview mirror. Shaking my head, I felt a slight weight lift, since that brief part of my life was officially over.

We were halfway home when I felt a sharp cramp. I winced at the unexpected pain, then blew out a long breath, figuring it was nothing. But when I looked down, I screamed at the dark stain of blood that was slowly spreading on my jeans between my legs.

Tears streamed down my face as I pulled into the nearest parking lot. I saw Mario's car continuing down the street, apparently not yet noticing that I wasn't still behind him. But seconds later, my phone was ringing.

"Ava, where are you?" he asked me, panicked.

"Mario," I sobbed, looking out the window at nothing in particular. "Turns out I *do* need to go to the hospital. I'm pretty sure I just had a miscarriage."

THE END

I REALLY HOPE YOU ENJOYED this story! These messy, taboo-type love stories are always a trip to write.

I'd be super appreciative if you would consider leaving a review. And for *extra* love, share that you read it on social media! ☺

You can find me on Instagram, Facebook, and TikTok at @authorjessicaterry and on Twitter at @itsJessicaTerry. And don't forget to subscribe to my email list at jessicaterry.com. I give away stuff. 😊

Also by Jessica Terry

Some Like 'em *Thick*
It's All Right...Now
Not By a Long Shot
Get Right
Decisions and Consequences
Take One For the Team
When You Share Too Much
Backtalk
Emasculated
Restless
The Beginning of Again
Always and Nevers
She is Me
Split By the Bell
The Karma Call
Forehead Kiss

The Introvert Series

Discussion Questions (note: may contain spoilers, so don't read these first if you want to avoid that):

1. Ava and Mario's attraction to each other was instant. Did they make a mistake by not dealing with it head-on?

2. Ava and Harper married after knowing each other only a few months, and he was eighteen years her senior. Do you think they would have lasted if Mario wasn't a factor?

3. Harper was keeping a lot of secrets from both Ava and Mario. How big a part do you feel he played in the deterioration of his and Ava's marriage?

4. Mario constantly said that while he loved Harper, he didn't feel a strong father-son bond with him. Do you feel this is at least part of the reason why he didn't level with him about his growing feelings for Ava?

5. Ava kept saying she wanted to be sure she did everything she could to make her marriage work. Do you think she did that, or should she have kept trying?

6. Jealousy played a big role in this story. Desperation caused Vera to basically stab her best friend Ava in the back, and even rush into a relationship towards the end. Given everything Ava did, should she give Vera a pass?

7. Harper had a fear of flying. Does that justify what he did to Ava on their honeymoon? Did you feel any sympathy for him?

8. If Ava and Mario's story were to continue, do you think they would stay together or that they would eventually fall apart, given how they started?

9. Domestic/sexual abuse victims don't turn in their attackers for various reasons. What did you think about Ava's decision to leave the police station that night without turning Harper in?

10. Trish and Jayden were Ava and Mario's voices of reason, respectfully. Do you think they should have advised their friends to stay away from each other?

Did you love *All Because of Ava*? Then you should read *Forehead Kiss*[1] by Jessica Terry!

[2]

"How I met Cam - the love of my life, whether he knew it or not - could either be considered really cute or really embarassing."

Ever since Cam came to Nyla's rescue, they've been best buds. Only thing is, Nyla keeps having various fantasies about her buddy that are anything but platonic.

When Cam starts dating her new roommate, Nyla starts to wonder if she should even continue the friendship, since seeing (and hearing) him with someone else is just too hard.

---

1. https://books2read.com/u/38e7nd

2. https://books2read.com/u/38e7nd

She wants him to see her as a woman, not just the friend he feels obligated to protect.

But severing ties with Cam is way easier said than done. And there *is* a chance that she's wrong about how he sees her. Will Nyla keep chickening out, or will she finally go for what she wants?

Read more at https://www.jessicaterry.com/.

About the Author

Jessica Terry caught the writing bug at a young age and loves little more than holing up at home in Douglasville, GA, cranking out contemporary novels. And eating.

Another thing she loves is interacting with her readers. Sign up for her email list and keep up to date with new releases at www.jessicaterry.com.

Read more at https://www.jessicaterry.com/.

www.ingramcontent.com/pod-product-compliance
Lightning Source LLC
Chambersburg PA
CBHW021527250626
47154CB00006BA/2010